PRAISE FOR LAMB TO THE SLAUGHTER

"A well-crafted tale of murder begotten by the collision of two incompatible worlds." Kirkus reviews.

"*Lamb to the Slaughter* was an easy, enjoyable read that I completely enjoyed. I was over the moon excited to hear that there will be more books in this series. Serenity and Daniel will solve cases involving Amish communities throughout the Midwest!" Caffeinated Book Reviewer

"I would highly, highly recommend this one...From the mystery, the characters, and the writing this is a fantastic book! I cannot wait for book two!" Lose Time Reading

"From the prologue to the last chapters, Lamb to the Slaughter had me instantly hooked. Ms. Hopkins is a master at pacing and setting up her stories in a way that has readers connected to both the characters and the story line." Love-Life-Read

"This book had it all!! Murder, mystery, forbidden romance and left you needing to read the next book in the series ASAP!! Loved this book!" Curling Up With A Good Book

"Karen Ann Hopkins has delivered with Lamb to the Slaughter. I love the uniqueness Karen Ann Hopkins brings to the mystery genre, and I will DEFIANTLY be reading more from her in the future." Unabridged Bookshelf

"The characters are complex and dimensional, whether they have a large or smaller part to play in this story, and it really added such a richness that I enjoyed." Bewitched Bookworms Reviews

"Lamb to the Slaughter is a must read for fans of mystery novels. Karen Ann Hopkins made me a fan with her YA Temptation series, and she's made me an even bigger fan with this murder mystery." Actin Up With Books

Books by Karen Ann Hopkins

Serenity's Plain Secrets
in reading order
LAMB TO THE SLAUGHTER
WHISPERS FROM THE DEAD

Wings of War
in reading order
EMBERS
GAIA

The Temptation Novels
in reading order
TEMPTATION
BELONGING
FOREVER
RACHEL'S DECEPTION (Crossroads)

LAMB TO THE SLAUGHTER

Karen Ann Hopkins

ISBN: 1506157203
ISBN 13: 9781506157207
Library of Congress Control Number: 2015900901
CreateSpace Independent Publishing Platform
North Charleston, South Carolina

For my children, Luke, Cole, Lily, Owen and Cora.
And my best friend, Jay.

ACKNOWLEDGMENTS

Even though I published this one on my own, there were still a lot of people influential in bringing the project to life. Without help from the following, Lamb to the Slaughter wouldn't be available to the public.

A big thank you to Christina Hogrebe for asking me to write an Amish mystery.

Much appreciation to Carey Hardin Gleckler for helping with the social media. You're the best!

I was thrilled to have Grace Bradford, a former horse-back riding student of mine, babysitter to my children and close friend, bring her editing skills to the table. Many thanks for your detailed analysis and all the time you put into Lamb. Hang in there, your time will come.

A standing ovation goes out to Kendra Haynes, another one of my alumni riding students and 'adopted' little sister, for building my amazing Website. I can always count on you to be creative and clever!

Thank you, Jenny Zemanek and Seedlings Design Studio for the awesome cover! You got the combination of Amish and creepy just right.

Thanks to my mother, Marilyn Lanzalaco, for reading Lamb twice! You're my biggest fan and toughest critic all rolled into one and I love you for it.

A bone crushing hug for my teenage daughter, Lily, and her mad photo cropping and collaging skills! The posters you've painstakingly created are wonderful.

And a collective shout out to the following people for helping with the daily chores, providing shelter from the storm and for just plain being there: Luke, Cole, Owen, Cora, Dad, Anthony, Opal and Sue & Joe Detzel.

PROLOGUE

Hugging myself, I tried to stop shaking. I'd burned my last bridge. Forward was the only way to go.

The dim light was nearly gone when I finally forced my muscles into action and headed in the direction of the road again. The darkness caused my heart to race as I sped up. Usually, I loved when night arrived. It gave me the opportunity to hide from the others—but not tonight. The unexpected encounter had pumped adrenaline through my veins, making me ever more fearful.

I urged my legs faster, until my breaths came out in short, quick gasps. I alternated between jogging, walking and stumbling, all the while listening for sounds of another ambush. The countryside was quiet now. The wind that had been beating the corn stalks together only minutes before had died down to a soft breeze.

I reckoned that I wasn't too far from the road, but I wasn't sure. The last time I came this way was about four years ago when I was fourteen and turkey hunting with Dat and my brother, Samuel. It had been springtime and the corn had been only seeds in the ground then. The stalks were well past the top of my head now, turning the cornfield into an impossible maze.

The plants were the same as everybody else in my life. They were toying with me, purposely making my escape from Blood Rock even more difficult. I was glad to leave them behind—along with the people.

I paused in my tracks to listen again. With the toe of my shoe still pressed into the mud, I was ready to lurch forward in an instant if need be. Taking a calming breath, I focused on the dark shapes of the treetops jutting above the corn. The hedgerow wasn't that far off. The best thing to do was to leave the cover of the cornfield and follow the edge of the wood, I decided.

A sort of excited panic ran through me at the realization that I was almost free. With renewed energy, I swatted the razor sharp leaves aside, ignoring the bloody little scratches they were tearing into my arms and hands. With chin raised, I fixed my sight high on the shadowy tree line and sprinted, closing the distance quickly. With only a few more rows to go and the glorious tangle of bushes and trees in view through the gaps in the corn, I murmured, "Thank you, Jesus."

The sound hit my ears less than a second before an invisible force slammed into my belly, knocking me backwards. When I opened my eyes, I was lying on the ground. Pieces of stalks jabbed into my back painfully. I tried to rise, but the tightness in my stomach wouldn't let me. Dragging my hand from my side, I felt around until I touched warm wetness.

Blood.

A reddish-gold harvest moon was rising above the tree line and I stared at its blazing colors, wondering at my ill luck.

Maybe I was being punished for running away and for all my other sins. The possibility filled me with fear and I tried to ask the Lord for forgiveness, but the only sound that came out from between my chapped lips was a ragged breath.

I lay motionless in the whispering chill. There was the smell of damp leaves and moss in the air, and the night breeze scratched the dry corn stalks against each other noisily. And then there was a more sinister, unidentifiable sound from further away—the sound of something large moving.

I turned my head slowly, peering into the darkness when a shadow appeared. It leaned over me, framed by the light of the fiery moon. I blinked, confused. Was it an angel?

I strained to see, but blackness was peppering my vision quickly. My head felt heavy and sleepiness pressed my eyes closed. I was so tired.

The soft, warm breath on my face reminded me that I wasn't alone and for an instant I was afraid. But then my mind drifted and I thought of Will.

How long would he wait for me?

...and then there was only darkness.

1

SERENITY

November 6th

I couldn't stop myself from glancing back at the green combine. The swath of mowed corn in its wake ended abruptly where the body had been found. I shivered, imagining what the crime scene would have looked like if the farmer hadn't seen the girl before he crossed over these rows.

The warm air of the Indian summer would have been a treat if I wasn't standing in the blazing sun, sweat beading on the back of my neck, and smelling the rank odor of decaying flesh. Swallowing hard, I took shallow breaths and turned to look at the balding and arthritic Bobby Humphrey, as he bent down over the girl.

The words, *are you fucking kidding me*, kept repeating in my head. I'd left my Indianapolis job for my home territory to get away from this kind of senseless violence. And here I was, just a month on the job, with a suspicious death on my hands.

The bright sunlight through the corn leaves disappeared for a moment to be replaced with a dull illumination from the street light. I didn't want to remember the scene, but I had no choice. The memory had been my constant companion for the past two years, coming several times a day like clockwork. The overpaid therapist had been dead wrong. The shock of some things couldn't be softened with time.

I thought back to another time, even though I didn't want to, and I was suddenly far away, standing in the center of the vacant city street.

Dim light from the lamp overhead sprayed down on the scene and the smell of the wet pavement filled my nostrils. My heart pounded furiously in my chest as I watched the gloved hand slip into the opening of the oversized coat with the Colt's logo in the upper left hand corner.

"Raise your hands! Raise your fucking hands!" I shouted.

My voice pounded in my ears, matching the beating of my heart. The gun was steady in my hand when my body suddenly became deadly calm. Refusing to obey me, the person's hands went deeper into the coat, pulling something shiny out. The body tilted toward my partner, Ryan, just before I pulled the trigger.

The blast of the gunshot blurred with Bobby's awkward cough, pulling me back to the present.

I hoped the coroner didn't notice my shiver when I said, "Can you tell me what she was hit with, Bobby?" I knelt beside him, gazing at the girl's face, which was still beautiful, even with its ghostly grey shade. I knew the side of her face touching the ground was a different story though.

"Can't say for sure until I get her into the examination room," Bobby swiveled to look at me, removing his glasses, "but from the quarter inch hole I can see in her coat, I'd place a bet right now that it was a slug from a twelve gauge shot gun that did her in."

Before I had a chance to say a thing, my first deputy, Todd Roftin, who was peering over my shoulder at the body, said, "There's a deer stand in a tree about thirty yards that way. I reckon a slug shot could have gone the distance." While I was digesting Todd's words and gazing at the crude, weathered boards jutting out from the trunk of the oak tree, Bobby covered the girl with the paper thin sheet. He took his time rising into a standing position.

Once the old man was up, he said, "The bullet entered the stomach, but there's no exit out the back, suggesting to me that it's probably lodged in her spinal cord." His eyes moved between the body and the tree stand before he added, "Don't hold me to my words until I've given you a report, Ms. Adams, but after examining the body in these crude conditions, I would say that the trajectory from the stand appears to be the most likely shot."

I narrowed my eyes, staring at Bobby, a man I'd known since I was a kid. We'd attended the same church when I was still in pig tails. In those days, his wife, Mary, used to pass a steady supply of peppermints down the row to me, keeping me occupied during the long, boring sermons.

Now, the man was addressing me as if I was a stranger—and after I'd already corrected him twice that morning. Was he purposely giving me a hard time or was he going senile? I didn't want to be completely paranoid. I gave him the benefit of the doubt, deciding that old age was probably the culprit.

"Bobby, you can call me Serenity…remember, like you've done my entire life. My new job as the sheriff in Blood Rock hasn't changed how I want to be addressed by my friends."

Bobby cleared his throat in acknowledgment while Todd shifted nervously on his feet. I wished everyone would get over the weirdness of me being the boss and get back to business.

Ignoring the men's discomfort, I turned to Todd and asked, "So you think it might be a hunting accident?"

"The stand hasn't been used much in years, but there were enough disturbances in the brush at the base that I'd say the most probable scenario is that a redneck had been sitting in that rotted stand all day. He was probably poaching for deer, when he heard the rustling of the girl coming out of the corn," Here Todd brought his arm up as if he were shooting off an invisible, long-barreled gun and aimed at the girl on the ground, "...and bam, shot her midsection. With a shotgun, she hit the ground instantly. The fellow clamored down to see the deer he thought he'd nabbed. Discovering that it was a little Amish girl, he high-tailed it out of here in a hurry."

Even with his disgusting theatrics, I had to admit, it was a good hypotheses. Still, there were so many questions to be answered, like what the hell was an Amish girl doing at the edge of a remote cornfield anyway?

"Bobby, you said earlier that you believed she'd been lying here for several days. Do you still maintain that time period?"

Bobby scratched his head and frowned at the body. "I'm thinking more like two weeks. We had that colder weather back the third week of October, you know. This body hasn't undergone as much decay as it would have if it'd been this warm straight through. The way the girl was bundled up leads me to believe that she was out here during that cold snap."

"It's surprising that she isn't more chewed on than she is, with all the critters that must surely prowl around here at night," Todd said, scratching his chin and looking around.

Bobby had a pensive frown fixed on his face again when I said, "Maybe with the abundance of corn available, the smaller scavengers weren't interested. With turkey season in full swing, there are a lot of hunters wandering about. Most of the larger predators are probably being cautious..."

The roar of the department's SUV as it approached and parked behind the combine brought all our heads up. The black hats and beards emerging from the passenger seats of the vehicle caused my heart to skip.

This was the part I dreaded the most. Again, my thoughts strayed to another place.

The bright lighting in the mortuary hurt my eyes as I watched the pale faces of the man and woman while the body was rolled out of the cooler, stopping in front of them. The woman's dark brown hair was in a ponytail and as she crumpled onto the body. Her hair bounced with her sobs.

I stood in the corner beside my partner, fixated on the thick length of locks rocking on the side of her head. She was younger than I thought she'd be...

Shaking the image from my mind, I left Bobby and Todd, walking over to Officer Jeremy Dickens and the three Amish men. I was silently relieved that Jeremy kept the men close to the vehicle and out of sight of the body. I'd have to commend young Jeremy on his forethought and consideration. This was, after all, the first human shooting incident he'd dealt with as an officer in the sleepy little agricultural community of Blood Rock, Indiana. Hell, if my memory served right, it was the first death under unusual circumstances since John Hinton shot his wife and then did himself in. That incident had occurred almost a decade ago when I was entering the police academy in Indianapolis.

One of the Amish men had a near white beard and the direct look of the leader of the group. I'd been meaning to read up on Amish authority since a large community of Plain people resided in the northern region of my territory. Unfortunately, I hadn't had time.

Taking a gamble, I focused my introduction at the oldest man. "Hello, I'm Sheriff Serenity Adams." I extended my hand. Sure enough, the snow-bearded gentleman stepped forward and grasped it warmly.

"It's a shame that we have to meet under such trying circumstances, Ms. Adams. I'm Aaron Esch, the bishop of the community. This is James Hooley and Joseph Bender, both ministers in our church."

I shook James' hand first. He was probably in his fifties with a fair share of gray speckling his black beard and the bit of hair flaring out from under the brim of his hat. His handshake was weak compared to the bishop's, but his huge size was intimidating at a glance. Joseph didn't reach out to take my hand, instead tipping his hat and nodding.

Knowing how close knit Amish communities were, I realized that the girl lying dead in the dirt behind us could be related to any of these men. I sobered at the thought before I spoke again.

"Mr. Esch, has there been a young woman missing from your community recently?"

The warm air quieted, only a few chirping birds at the hedgerow breaking the silence. My skin tingled at the stoic looks the men exchanged. After several uncomfortable seconds, Bishop Esch finally spoke.

"Could we please see the body, Ms. Adams? We are all busy men, needing to get back to our day's activities."

I held the bishop's gaze. His eyes were steady, almost arrogant. They didn't look away in embarrassment at what he'd just said. They should have though. He was treating the body of a girl like a dead cat in the road that nobody cared to claim.

I needed to know who the girl was—that was my first priority. The bishop's cold demeanor could be put aside until later.

"It might be better for you all to come down to the morgue in town to view the body after we've processed it fully," I suggested.

The crime scene wasn't the best place for the body to be identified, even though there wasn't any indication at this point in the investigation that a crime had been committed.

The bishop spoke for his buddies, saying, "We'd like to see her now, if it's possible." His voice indicated that he was not taking no for an answer.

We'd already spent several hours combing the area for evidence, finding few clues to what happened to the young woman, other than her being shot dead in the corn. Allowing the men to view the body now might give me the victim's name that I so desperately wanted and possibly shed a little light on this tragedy.

Making up my mind, I said, "Right this way gentleman." I turned, not glancing back. I didn't need to. I could hear their steps behind me, crunching on the cropped corn stalks.

Bobby and Todd stepped aside. They were joined by Jeremy, who didn't look at the body. The young man stared into the tree line instead. After I folded the sheet down to reveal the girl's face, I moved to stand with them. Even with their uncomfortable behavior toward me, I still felt drawn to their little group and away from the black coated, bearded men.

I watched intently as the three men leaned over the body for only a moment. After simultaneously bowing their heads and closing their eyes for a silent prayer, they looked up at me with no emotion at all. Their hard eyes stilled my heart.

The bishop spoke, his voice level and calm. "This is Naomi Beiler. She is the daughter of Timothy and Patricia Beiler."

I pulled the little notepad and pen from my back pocket and began writing.

"Do you know how old she is?" I asked the Amish men.

The bishop glanced at James, who finally spoke. "I do believe she's the same age as my Roseanna—eighteen."

James Hooley's nonchalance startled me, but I was careful not to let it show. "Has Naomi been missing?"

The two ministers looked in opposite directions, and neither at me. Bishop Esch took a few seconds to gather his words. "You will need to speak with the Beiler's about that, Miss. I ask that you give them a few days to deal with the loss of their child."

I couldn't help but glance at Bobby who slightly shrugged his shoulders when he met my gaze. Jeremy looked at the Amish men with wide eyes and mouth slightly gaping. Todd held the small smirk of a very amused man.

I exhaled and said, "Yes, of course. We'll give the family time to mourn...but, we'll need to have a few questions answered for the report today. I promise you, Mr. Esch, I'll be very discrete when I notify them of the death."

Too quickly, the bishop said, "Oh, there will be no need for you to talk to them today. I'll bring the news to their home." He must have recognized my incredulity at his dismissal of my authority. He added with a somber frown, "It will be much easier for Timothy and Patricia to hear the news from me, rather than a stranger. Your presence will upset them needlessly."

I was a newly elected sheriff and I already had a young woman dying under strange circumstances in my jurisdiction. As if that wasn't trying enough, I now had a clash of cultures on my plate too. The worst part was that I got what the bishop was saying. Still, I hated to deviate from protocol on my first investigation in Blood Rock.

I looked to Bobby for the answer. He seemed to be expecting me to do just that and was ready. He nodded his head subtly.

"Jeremy, please escort these men back to their homes." I focused on the bishop, "Mr. Esch, I'll honor your wishes on this matter, but I'll be visiting the Beiler's in a few days to get some questions cleared up. We need to know what happened to Naomi."

"Yes, of course." He tipped his hat to me and walked briskly back to the patrol car with the ministers.

Jeremy raised his eyebrows as he passed by. He was obviously as disturbed by the Amish men's behavior as I was. Bobby made a soft huffing noise and began to motion to the emergency medical personnel to come over to help him with the body bag when I stopped him.

"Don't you think those men were acting awfully blasé about seeing a young woman from their community dead in a cornfield?" My voice rose a little higher than I intended. I turned my back to the paramedics who were patiently leaning up against the ambulance, waiting for someone to give them the sign to approach.

Bobby said, "Ms....ah, Serenity, you had better get used to the fact that the Amish will not be any help to you in your investigation. They don't like outsiders, and they don't want them knowing their business."

As my mouth opened, Todd cut me off, "Hell, they're practically their own nation—not having to pay social security tax or serve in the armed forces. Did you know that they're done with school in the eighth grade?"

"Actually, it's my understanding that the Amish can be drafted, but they only serve in non-combat roles, such as medical and food service," Bobby told Todd.

Listening to the men shoot off their knowledge of the Amish made me realize how little I knew about the simple, yet flourishing culture. I'd grown up in town, only a few miles away from the field that I now stood in. I'd spent my time playing soccer, going to movies and hanging out with friends—that did not include any Plain people. The only interaction I'd had with the Amish back then was when I'd worked part-time at Nancy's Diner in high school. Occasionally, one of the families had come in for lunch. When I'd left Blood Rock for college, I was even more separated from the rural living of the place I'd grown up in—a county that had a relatively small population, but a very large land area.

Before the two men could get into a long, drawn out conversation about the Amish lifestyle, I interrupted, "Bobby, are you telling me that there are different rules involved when we're dealing with the Amish?"

Bobby smiled as if he was a grandpa humoring his grandchild. "No, that's not it at all. I'm simply telling you in advance to expect them not to be forthcoming with you. I've been dealing with their nonsense for thirty years. I know what

I'm talking about. The quicker you wrap this case up, the better."

It didn't take long for Naomi Beiler's body to be bagged and loaded into the ambulance. I remained in the field for some time after the van had driven away and Bobby had left in Todd's patrol car.

I walked out into the corn stalks, searching the ground and trying to figure out which way the girl had come from. Any tracks she might have left had been washed away by several days of rain. The plants themselves left no traceable clues, with so many of them sporadically broken from the wind or deer crossing through.

I stopped and looked around. The stalks lightly brushed against each other in the warm breeze and there was the scurrying sound of a small animal in the leaves on the ground. It was just a cornfield, and yet, I had to admit to myself that standing there alone felt pretty damn creepy.

Why the hell would Naomi Beiler have been out here?

I'd remember Bobby's advice, but I hoped he was wrong. There were too many questions running through my brain to let them go easily. Maybe the pretty young woman was killed in a random hunting accident, but if that hadn't been her fate, I was determined to bring the truth to light.

And dammit, I wouldn't be handling the Amish any differently than any other citizens.

2

NAOMI

August 2nd, three months earlier

Naomi kept her eyes locked on Eli Bender's, daring him to turn first. The handsome Amish boy wouldn't glance away, even when he called out the hymn number and the singing began again. Butterflies danced in her belly when Eli finally tore his eyes from hers, the one side of his mouth tilted mischievously.

Naomi wasn't surprised at the attention Eli was showing her. She'd always known he was sweet on her, but his sudden openness about it was perplexing. Maybe he was ready to begin courting and he'd chosen me, Naomi thought. She wouldn't know for sure until later, when the ball games were going on. If Eli had any inkling of wanting her, he'd surely show his attentions then. At least that was her wish.

Three songs later, her back sore from sitting on the hard bench for over an hour, Naomi smacked the hymnal closed and handed it down the line. In a flurry of movement, everyone else was doing the same. The popping noises of so many books shutting filled the air—a sound that was sweeter music to her ears than all the songs before it.

"I saw the way you were so brazenly staring at Eli. You should be ashamed of yourself!" Sandra whispered loudly in Naomi's ear, her hot breath tickling her friend's lobe.

"Hush, now. That's none of your concern." Naomi giggled, bumping softly into Sandra's side.

"We're best friends, aren't we? That makes it my concern." Sandra snorted, hands on her hips.

The room had emptied quickly. The only inhabitants other than Naomi and Sandra were a few of the mothers packing the hymnals away and chatting non-stop as they worked.

Naomi clasped Sandra's arm, tugging her toward the barn door opening and the blazing maroon sunset. The rush of warm air caressed Naomi, pressing her sky blue dress against the front of her body. She exhaled in excitement, relishing the way the hot breeze made the blood bubble inside of her. She was feeling pretty tonight and she had the inkling that Eli thought so too.

She leaned in closer to Sandra, not wanting anyone to hear, not even the other girls. "Did you catch the way Eli was staring at me during the singing?" she practically hummed the words.

"Yes, I did. I reckon you two will be courting in no time. Then you won't have need for me any longer." Sandra said it in a joking way, but Naomi could see that her friend's smile was pinched. Poor thing was jealous, Naomi realized.

"Silly bean, I'll always need you and you know that. Besides, I'd wager that if Eli asks me to court, Matthew Yoder won't be far behind in asking you."

The girls flopped down in the grass near the volleyball nets the same as they'd done every Sunday for the past few years. Naomi didn't enjoy playing volleyball. Instead, she liked sitting on the sidelines and watching the other girls look foolish as they tried to hit the ball over the net. Of course, a few of the girls were really good, like Melinda or Susie. But they were built similar to boys, with no curves at all to get sore after a whack from a hard ball.

The other girls who weren't playing the game didn't approach Naomi and Sandra. They took their seats on the far side of the net. Naomi was glad that she didn't have to be bothered by the company of the snooty, goody-two-shoes girls anyhow. They were all so boring. Still, Naomi followed the girls with her eyes, watching them whisper back and forth to each other, and wondering what they were saying.

"Did you see the look that Lydia gave you when she spied Eli making eyes in your direction?" Sandra spoke softly into Naomi's ear after she'd taken a good look around first to make sure no one was close enough to hear.

Naomi tore her gaze away from the gossipy girls at the same moment that Lydia looked up, staring straight at her. Naomi felt the hair on the back of her neck tingle. It was almost as if the horrible girl had heard Sandra's whispered words from across the net and over the voices of the players. Of course, Naomi knew that was impossible, but she couldn't help the wariness that swept over her. The threat of spies was always present.

"Course I did. Like she thinks she'd have a chance with a guy like him anyway. Is she nuts or just stupid?"

"Maybe both!" Sandra giggled.

When Sandra calmed herself, she added, "You were probably too busy to notice that David was watching how you and Eli were acting too. He wasn't pleased either."

"Oh, who cares about him anyway? David is so moody—I don't know how any girl could put up with him. He always looks as if he just swallowed a lime."

Naomi did her best impression of the sour look that usually resided on David's face, sticking her tongue out limply for good measure. Sandra shook her head and scolded, "You're awful!" Her outburst drew the eyes of the girls standing nearby.

Naomi felt his presence before he even sat down in the grass beside her. When she looked over, she wasn't disappointed. Eli held the same amused expression on his face that he had earlier. A handful of dark brown locks nearly covered his left eye. She was surprised that his mother hadn't gotten onto him about his hair needing cutting yet. But then, knowing that she had eight children, and four of them under the age of five, she probably hardly even noticed her oldest son's head. Naomi really wanted to reach out and brush the stubborn hair away from his eye, but of course she couldn't do that. Instead, she let her fingers play with the soft blades of grass, plucking them in frustration.

"How's it going?" Eli asked. His voice was deep and husky, making Naomi's heart speed up. She was well aware of the closeness of his body to hers. She could even smell the cologne on his skin.

"I'm wonderful. What about you, Eli? Are you enjoying this lovely night?" She tried to keep her face straight, but the tug of a smile was too great. She glanced down, shielding her mouth from his gaze for a second.

When Naomi looked up, he was grinning at her confidently. "Do you want to help me get the marshmallows? Mother talked Father into starting a bonfire. We're going to roast them."

It was way more information than she needed or cared about. She would have gone with him to clean the toilets if he'd asked.

"Sure!" She bounced up and he was right behind her. Seeing the grumpy look on Sandra's face, Naomi winked at her, "I'll come back soon, Sandy. Maybe, you should go over there and talk to that person that I mentioned earlier." She pointed her chin in Matthew's direction. He was leaning up against the side of the barn with a few of the other guys clustered around him.

Sandy rolled her eyes, shooing Naomi away with her hands. Naomi hated abandoning her friend that way, but she reasoned that maybe sitting alone for a few minutes would give Sandra the incentive to flirt with the boys a little bit. At this point, she'd hardly even look at any of them. She certainly wasn't going to have Matthew asking after her unless she loosened up and took Naomi's advice. After all, Sandra was always dispensing advice to Naomi about men. Even though the girl had no experience at all, Naomi still listened.

Eli and Naomi walked as slowly as was humanly possible, a full foot of space separating them, to the two story, white sided house. Eli's home was as plain as the rest of the homes in the Amish community, but the display of flowers in the beds leading to the porch was a brilliant burst of color even in the low light of dusk. Naomi focused on the purple blooms creeping over the trellis, ignoring the eyes of the other teens, and even the few adults present. She felt the heat of their stares as she walked by. Naomi knew that their minds were speculating already.

Just before they entered the house, she caught David's angry gaze. He stopped talking to the other boys and snapped his blond head in her direction as she passed by. His face was red and scowling, and the sight of it caused a prickling sensation to run along her arms. She looked away quickly, determined not to allow his jealousy to dampen her good mood.

The busy kitchen was hot from everyone gathered there. Even though the women were spread out in small groups around the room, all dressed similar with navy, hunter green or maroon dresses and pristine white caps adorning their heads, it took only a second for Naomi to spot who she was searching for. Eli's Mother, Katherine, was in the corner seated comfortably on a plush sofa and nursing her littlest one. Eli walked past her without glancing in his mother's direction, but Naomi purposely slowed to acknowledge her.

Careful not to stare at the pale flesh of the breast surrounding the babe's face, Naomi said, "Good evening, Mrs. Bender. Are you doing well today?"

Katherine's light blue eyes looked up and she smiled warmly. Even though the woman was well into her thirties, she looked younger. She was still attractive, her features fragile and soft. Unlike most of the Amish women, she'd maintained her youthful weight and hadn't blossomed into a pear even after eight pregnancies.

"Why, I'm very well, Naomi. How may you be doing?"

"I'm enjoying this lovely weather and your beautiful farm. If it's all right with you, I'll be helping Eli gather up the marshmallows now." When Naomi's eyes drifted a fraction, she noticed Esther Lapp's frown. The middle-aged woman sitting close beside Katherine looked as if she'd bit into a lime from the same bucket as her son. When Naomi's eyes drifted

Esther's way again, she saw the same dark expression that David often held. The woman didn't shy away when the girl's eye's locked on hers for a second either—forcing Naomi to drop her gaze in submission.

Naomi looked back at Katherine who was distracted for a second while she repositioned the babe to the other breast fluidly. Seeing the tiny boy latch onto the new nipple with vigor, Naomi wondered what it would feel like to have a baby sucking on her own breast. Katherine tilted her head, and said, "Oh, I'm so pleased you're having a good time." She added with a knowing smile, "Yes, it be would fine with me if you helped Eli with the dessert."

"Thank you." Naomi turned from the ladies and met Eli at the top of the steps that led down to the basement. She quickly brushed off the chill she'd felt when her eyes passed over Esther as she'd left. That woman didn't like her one bit, Naomi knew. Maybe it was the fact that Naomi had ignored the attentions from Esther's son or maybe it was because Esther was a dried up old prune that couldn't appreciate any spirit in a girl.

"You're a very clever girl, Naomi," Eli whispered over his shoulder to her as she followed him into the basement. The room was only dimly lit from the traces of evening light shooting through the little windows.

Naomi smiled. At least Eli was smart enough to recognize and from the sound of it, appreciate her wit.

"Well, I certainly didn't want anyone accusing us of sneaking off together to…"

"*To what?*" Eli paused at the last step, his voice velvety smooth with feigned curiosity.

Naomi appraised him openly for a few seconds before she licked her lips and said, "Don't be coy. You know perfectly well what we might do alone together."

Her words were enough. Eli grasped Naomi's hand and pulled her around the corner into a storage room. Winter coats pressed against her back as Eli lowered his head. When his lips touched hers, the hot jolt that streaked through her groin made Naomi gasp. The feeling caused her mouth to widen, giving his tongue access to lace with hers.

Naomi had always been a flirty girl. She'd been disciplined on many occasions by her mother about her friendly ways with the boys. But until that moment, she'd never felt the press of a man's body against hers or the soft searching of a tongue inside her mouth. Suddenly, the entire world came into focus. She knew that she'd been born to be hugged and cuddled in that way.

Eli groaned, pulling back a few inches. Still holding Naomi's head tightly with his hand at the base of her cap, he said, "Maybe this question is silly now...but will you be my girl?"

Eli's blue eyes pierced deeply to Naomi's soul and she knew that she was a goner. She could never say anything except yes to this young man.

And, that's exactly what she said.

3

SERENITY

November 10th

I was exhausted from four hours of watching the steady traffic going up and down the Beiler's driveway. As the minutes continued to tick by and the sun dropped lower in the western sky, my hopes of talking to Timothy and Patricia Beiler in private dwindled. The thought of waiting another day had my stomach in knots and I exhaled softly, glancing at the clock on the dashboard. I'd wait another hour before I gave up.

Although I was surprised at the high volume of visitors, the mixture of buggies and giant white vans was truly the amazing part. The steady rain and tires had turned the sides of the gravel drive to a thick mud that gave the vans increasingly more trouble as the day wore on. I cringed as one of the vehicles lost traction on the hillside and began slipping sideways in front of a horse. The driver of the buggy was quick to react and just missed being run over by the van. The juxtaposition of buggies, vans, slick conditions and the steep hill was a disaster just waiting to happen.

I stared at the scene beyond the raindrop streaked window of my unmarked patrol car with quiet concentration. The entire day had seemed fog-like, from the early morning hour that Bobby had handed me Naomi Beiler's coroner's report, to the arrival at the girl's showing. Bobby had encouraged me to release the body to the family, which I did, but the revelations of his report further convinced me that I really needed to speak with the girl's parents as soon as possible.

Bobby had warned me that Amish funerals were big events, but I'd never dreamed that so many Amish people would be here to show their respect. For the past several hours, the only thing that kept my mind from wandering too far was the sound of Todd's fingers pressing onto his phone as he texted his girlfriend constantly.

"Doesn't Heather have anything better to do than message you all day?" I growled, wondering for the hundredth time how Todd even got his job.

Todd rolled his eyes, ignoring me until he finished typing. He made a display of turning off the phone for my sole benefit and then turned to face me.

"Why, are you lonely, Serenity?" Todd said, wearing the same smirk that had been cemented on his face since high school. The fact that the jerk had been irritating me for almost twenty years showed how twisted the forces of the universe truly were. Who would have thought that the obnoxious boy who used to hit on me in tenth grade would be doing the same thing now? Being Todd's boss made no difference. I would forever be stuck-up Serenity to him, and he'd always be a redneck jock to me.

"Take a look around, would you. Could a person be lonely here?"

As if Todd just noticed the traffic jam, he whistled and said, "Damn, looks like a wreck waiting to happen." He glanced back at me and added, "Aw, maybe the Sheriff should intervene and direct traffic."

I breathed deeply before speaking, trying desperately to control my infamous temper. I would not let Todd push my buttons.

"If you bothered to take a good look, you'd see that everybody is being as orderly as possible under the circumstances. I get the feeling they've all had a lot of practice with this sort of thing."

"Yeah, sure they have. The Amish are prone to accidental deaths. Did I ever tell about that old geezer, Jonathon Yoder, and how he fell from the barn loft into a stud's stall...?"

I raised my hand to shut him up.

"What are you, a walking encyclopedia—how do you come up with all this crap?" I asked in a tired voice.

"Actually, I do a lot of reading. Last night I was up 'til after midnight immersed in a book about the history of Blood Rock."

I laughed and said, "I'd think that would put you to sleep quickly."

"No, no, our town has quite an intriguing past. Like the name—do you know why it's called Blood Rock?"

I couldn't help rolling my eyes and thudding my head back against the headrest. Was I really having this conversation right now?

"Let me enlighten you then." Todd took a deep breath before, he continued, "The late seventeen hundreds were pretty rough in these parts. The settlers were having regular run-ins with the Indians, and neither the law nor the military was able to get a hold of the situation. When some criminal-cowboy types decided to take matters into their own hands, shooting up an Indian family that was down by the river, the Indians were stirred into a blood lust. It all came to a head one Sunday morning. A group of settlers were having their Sunday service up on that hill above town. Their preacher was calling out the word of God while standing on a giant boulder when the arrow pierced his heart. It's said, the Indians killed twenty-six men, women and children on that day...and took scalps from them all."

I couldn't help interrupting him. "There's no giant boulder on that hill, and no documented proof about this massacre you're talking about. It's just an old wives-tale."

"Would you let me finish the story?" Todd said.

I shrugged, relenting. It would be impossible to shut him up about it anyway.

"The Indians piled the bodies on the rock as a warning to anyone else aiming to settle the area. Of course, more people came and they couldn't keep up with the flow of humanity and it was the Indians themselves that left, moving further west."

"What about the rock?"

"Hold your horses, I'm getting to that part," Todd said with annoyance. "By the time the bodies displayed on the rock were discovered, several days of July heat had put them in a pretty gruesome way. Even after the dead were taken away for burial, the heavy blood stains remained. The locals were mighty spooked by the constant reminder of the massacre. It was the incentive they needed to light dynamite around the rock and blow it into a good number of chunks. They pulled the remnants away with horses and pushed them into the river."

I looked back at the bright expression on Todd's face. How could such an awful story make him look so damned pleased?

"Yeah, I've heard that one and several more. But there's no proof that a giant rock even existed, let alone got blown up."

"That's the fascinating part. No one knows for sure where our little town got its morbid name."

"Myself, I think it should have been changed a long time ago. Something like Meadowview or Sunnyvale would be nice."

Todd was just about to open his mouth when I saw the shiny Buick coming down the driveway.

"Is that who I think it is?" I said.

"Well, shoot. I reckon it is." Todd looked at me and shrugged. "You do know that he has relations with some of the Amish families, right?"

The sight of Tony Manning's car made my palms sweat, and I hated him all the more for it. The codger had run the most unprofessional campaign imaginable in his attempt to be reelected as sheriff of Blood Rock. I still hadn't replaced my mail box, which I'm sure he had a hand in destroying. And, then there was all the crap that he accused me of. From having a fling with my high school soccer coach, who turned out to be gay, thankfully, to insinuating that I was a witch, because I had my fortune read at the local spring street festival when I was sixteen. Lucky for me, so did half the town that year.

Hell, he probably would have won, if the whole incident with the prostitutes in Indianapolis hadn't come to light. The people of Blood Rock might forgive one dalliance, but they were too country to forgive multiple hookers at the same time. They'd decided that they would rather take a chance on a young and inexperienced female sheriff with some morals, than stick with the good old boy whose exploits were making them more and more uncomfortable on Sunday mornings. I was the first woman to hold the position in the entire tri-county area and I counted myself damn lucky to have gotten the job.

Todd and I both straightened and gave each other the, *oh, great, here we go* look, when Tony had the balls to pull up beside the unmarked patrol car we sat in. I reluctantly lowered the window at the same time he did.

"I would think that you had better things to do Sheriff, than hang around an Amish funeral freaking everybody out," Tony said.

If Tony was thirty pounds skinnier, he'd be Clint Eastwood's twin. That made everybody respectful of him—even those that didn't like him much. But, everybody wasn't me.

I used my sweetest voice. "I'm a bit confused, Tony. The Amish don't vote, so why your interest in them?" Tony's pinched laugh was overpowered by Todd's louder one. I shot Todd a warning look. Amazingly he obeyed, covering his mouth and quieting.

It was hard to tell from the tinted windows, but as usual, Tony was traveling with several big guys. Most folks assumed that people only drove around with body guards in the movies, but nope, it was reality here in Blood Rock.

Tony smiled sadistically at me. "I see you haven't learned much from your month on the job. Maybe you should take the time to get to know the people that you've promised to protect." His smile disappeared and his face tightened, causing the hair to rise on my neck. "I'll give you one little bit of advice since I'm feeling generous today. Leave well enough alone. If they aren't too concerned about this thing with the girl, then we shouldn't be either. Trust me, the Amish take care of their own."

The dark window went up and Tony and his cronies disappeared up the road. I grabbed my ponytail in frustration and pulled it tight into my skull before I rounded on Todd. His eyes were wide with thought for a change.

"What the hell was that all about? You worked under him for two years. Surely, you have a guess what he was talking about."

Todd shook his head. "Honestly, I don't know. I mean, I knew he was in tight with some of the Amish, but that's about it. Nothing ever came up with the Plain community while he was my boss."

"Didn't that sound like a threat to you? Telling me to forget the investigation, and just let the Amish handle their own problems. *Is he serious?*" I tried to keep my voice level, but didn't succeed.

"Maybe he has a point. He was sheriff for twelve years after all. He might know things about the way the Amish authority works that we don't," Todd suggested with a shrug.

"Are you kidding? The last I knew, the Amish are citizens of the United States of America. Even though the first amendment allows them to get away with not doing a lot of things that the rest of us have to, they're still under our jurisdiction."

"In theory, you're absolutely right, but, as far as practical application goes, maybe not. I don't know. It's really none of my business."

"This absolutely is your business—and mine. Naomi Beiler might have been murdered," I nearly shouted.

Todd's eyes popped open wide. He said, "Do you really think that? What evidence suggests that it was anything but a hunting accident?"

I was so frustrated that I felt as if I was going to pop. "Don't you think that it's awfully strange for a young Amish woman to be alone in a cornfield in the first place?"

"She might have been going for a walk, escaping some chores at the house for an hour or two," Todd suggested.

"Or, running away." I was happy that Todd was actually thinking, but he wasn't going near deep enough.

Todd scratched his chin. After several long seconds, he said, "Maybe…but she didn't have anything with her that would point in that direction. Wouldn't a girl running away have a bag of some sort?"

I stared at the driveway, noticing that the traffic had quieted considerably. Only a few of the black buggies were making their way back onto the road, and no others were heading toward the house. There were a couple of them beside the barn and only one van was parked on the hill now. It was as good of a time as any to talk to Timothy and Patricia Beiler about their daughter. Especially, after what Bobby had discovered. They should know.

I looked back at Todd, who was waiting for me to answer him.

I finally said, "Not if she was in a hurry."

From where I stood, I could see the plain, wooden casket in the corner. The top was up, and an elderly Amish woman was standing in front of it, clasping Naomi's hand. Todd and I waited a minute more until the woman moved off to join a small crowd of black clad women standing at the far end of the room. There were rows of benches filling the concrete floored basement that had been set up as a temporary funeral home. The room was overly gloomy, even for a funeral, with no flower displays and only the dim light from the rainy afternoon coming in through the small basement windows. The emotion level was off, considering that a teenager had been taken violently from her community. Other than the old woman's hand holding, no one else in the room appeared in any way distraught.

I tried to wrap my mind around the strangeness of it all as Todd and I approached the casket. It seemed only right that we should pay our respects before we talked with the Beilers, but I wasn't looking forward to it. I'd never like showings. When I was ten, I'd become inconsolable at my grandma's wake. But, at least my Grandma had been well on in years. Naomi was almost a child.

Seeing bodies on the job didn't really bother me much, but the intimacy of the casket, and the loved ones around, was another story altogether. For once, I was thankful for Todd's company.

Bobby had done a good job, but the lack of any makeup showed Naomi clearly for what she was—a very dead girl. Her dress was a deep hunter green that contrasted sharply with the white cap on her head and the ashen color of her skin. I also noticed that her face was placed in the same position as I'd seen her in the field, to the side. Bobby, being both the coroner and the only mortician in town, could only do so much.

As I looked at the dead girl with morbid curiosity, my eyes travelled to the girl's cap. Her head had been bare when we'd found her in the corn. It was another question to file away in my head, and hopefully get the answer to someday soon.

Todd and I spent less than a minute beside the body, long enough for each of us to say a silent prayer for the girl, before we moved on to the row of family members seated in the plastic chairs to the side of the casket. At least, I assumed that these people were Naomi's family.

After a fast appraisal, I approached the middle aged couple sitting closest to the casket. The little bit of hair that I could see poking out in front of the woman's cap was the same blondish color of Naomi's locks. Her eyes were brown, and completely free of tears or redness. I fumbled mentally for a second wondering if this woman was indeed Naomi's mother, when Bishop Esch appeared beside me.

"Sheriff Adams, this is Timothy Beiler and his wife, Patricia." The bishop motioned to the couple who I'd guessed were the parents. James Hooley and Joseph Bender were suddenly there, flanking the bishop. I wondered how they'd managed to sneak up without me noticing.

I extended my hand in greeting to Timothy. Patricia remained seated with her hands tightly clasped on her lap. I didn't offer my hand to her.

"I'm sorry about your daughter's death. I certainly don't want to burden you during such a difficult time, but there are a few things we need to discuss. If you aren't comfortable speaking with me now, I'd be happy to schedule an appointment to meet at my office in a day or two."

When no one spoke, I added, "Or, I could come back."

Timothy had a shaggy, brown beard, and dull, blue eyes. Patricia was being the quiet one at the moment, but a glance at her face told me she was the keener of the two.

After Timothy received an approving nod from the bishop, he said, "I'd rather get it over with now."

The room had mysteriously emptied in the time it took me to approach the Beilers. Besides myself and Todd, only the couple, the bishop, and the two ministers remained. Todd's eyebrow lift told me he was feeling as weird as I was.

"Would you like to speak somewhere more private?" I asked Timothy, hoping to get him away from the church authorities.

"No, this is fine." Timothy seemed almost bored, while Patricia nervously tapped her fingers together. I wondered again, where was the anguish over losing a child?

Pulling the note pad out of my back pocket, I took a breath and began. "When did you last see Naomi?"

There was silence while Timothy looked to his wife for the answer. Patricia finally spoke, "I saw her on the morning of October twentieth. Timothy hadn't seen her since the night before."

The woman's voice was matter of fact, but the words she said confirmed my suspicions. "Mr. Dolson, the farmer working the cornfield where Naomi was found, discovered the body on November sixth…that's seventeen days. You mean, neither of you saw her after the twentieth?"

They both shook their heads meeting my eyes with sureness.

Bishop Esch, said, "No one else in the community did either, Ms. Adams."

"Why didn't you report her missing?" I asked Timothy and Patricia, but my eyes were focused on Patricia, wondering what kind of mother ignores her daughter's disappearance.

Timothy sighed, stretching his beard tight between his fingers.

"We believed that our daughter had run away," Timothy said, averting his eyes.

"And why would she do that?" I asked.

Timothy met my stare defiantly and said, "Naomi was always a strong willed girl, even as a child she caused mischief. We had every reason to think that she'd left the community in search of another way of life."

"Was she having difficulties that you knew about?"

Both Timothy and Patricia shook their heads, but said nothing. I was about to open my mouth when Bishop Esch spoke. "It's uncommon, but occasionally, a young person decides that the Plain ways aren't for them. You see, we don't practice rumspringa in our community. If a teenager has wild oats to sow, they typically leave."

The rain was coming down harder again, streaking the basement windows to the point of obscuring any sign of the outdoors. The room had turned darker with nature's onslaught. After watching the drops travel down the window for a few seconds, I turned to the bishop and asked, "What's rumspringa?"

I had just about forgotten that Todd was even present until he piped up. "It's when the Amish kids get to run wild for a couple of years before they decide to settle down and join the church."

The bishop forced a smile and said, "You've simplified the definition, but achieved the main idea."

Todd grinned, satisfied with his show of knowledge. Even though my mind acknowledged that Todd knew a hell of a lot more about the Amish than I did, I dismissed him, turning back to the parents.

"Let me make sure I understand you both correctly. You believe that Naomi ran away from her home because she didn't want to be Amish?" I spoke to Timothy, but turned my gaze to his wife again.

Timothy said, "Yes."

"But, where did you think she'd gone?" I knew the Amish thought differently than the rest of us, but still, their indifference to their daughter's disappearance was inexcusable.

Timothy shrugged, and Patricia ignored me. I looked to Bishop Esch, who replied, "Once one of the young members of our flock chooses to leave us, we do not give it much thought, besides praying for their safe return and well-being. Our hope is always that they will find their way back to us and the Lord in time."

"If Naomi had run away as you believe, where would she have been heading to in the cornfield?" I was overflowing with questions, but I paced myself, knowing that at any moment the Amish might stop talking altogether. I had to pick my questions carefully.

The bishop answered me. "Only our heavenly Father knows for sure, but possibly she was making her way towards one of the county roads."

After studying a topographical map, I'd already decided that Naomi was aiming for Burkey Road. It was interesting that the bishop had guessed the same thing.

I breathed deeply and glanced at Todd, who urged me on with the lift of his chin. I was dreading the next question.

"Did Naomi have a boyfriend?" I asked softly.

The only sound was the pattering of the raindrops against the house. I saw the exchange of looks between the Amish, and was beginning to think that they were done with me, when Timothy said, "No. She didn't."

Why did it take so long to answer? And, why was Timothy Beiler lying?

"Are you saying that she didn't have the attention of any of the Amish boys that you know of?"

"That's right," Timothy confirmed as he stared out the window, avoiding my eyes.

I wrestled inwardly whether I should tell them now or wait until after the girl was in the ground. Either way, it wouldn't make it any easier on them. Then again, maybe they wouldn't be as surprised as I hoped they'd be, judging by their nonchalant manner toward the situation.

"Mr. and Mrs. Beiler, I really do need to have a moment alone with you. There was a discovery during the autopsy that I'd like to talk to you about in private," I said, hoping they'd agree.

Timothy said with conviction, his gaze suddenly sharp, "You may speak freely here. Aaron, James and Joseph are close friends."

I stopped my eyes from rolling at his words. Damn. I expected him to say that.

"Your daughter was six weeks pregnant when she died," I blurted out, wanting to get the revelation out of the way as quickly as possible.

Patricia sucked in a breath, bringing her hands to her face. Timothy put his arm tightly around her shoulder. Finally, I had a show of emotion, but for a potential grandchild, not their daughter.

The bishop and ministers remained silent, their faces expressionless. If these men ever played poker, they'd be good at it.

Patricia rose abruptly, turning her suddenly pale face away from me. I didn't understand her customs, but I saw the angst just the same. Timothy talked to her and then to the bishop before he left with Patricia. His hand still gripped her shoulder as the two made their way to the stairway that led up to the house.

I would have given up the contents of my savings account to know what they'd said before they'd exited. The fact that they spoke a language that only their own people were privy to could be a real disadvantage in this investigation.

I turned to Bishop Esch. "I'm sorry that the news upset them."

"It is what it is." The bishop shrugged, keeping his gaze locked on me.

"I need to talk to the father, Mr. Esch. Do you have any ideas who it is?"

It might have been my imagination, or a continuation of the heebie-jeebies that I was feeling, but I could have sworn that my words had caused Joseph Bender to suddenly shift his weight and take a soft intake of breath.

I narrowed my eyes on Joseph and asked him, "Do you have any information pertinent to this discussion, Mr. Bender?"

"No, I do not," Mr. Bender said, and then he turned and followed the Beiler's tracks up the stairs. James Hooley wasn't far behind, leaving me and Todd alone with the bishop.

"It's been a long day. I'll be going to get the horse and buggy ready now. Before I depart, I must ask you a question, Ms. Adams. Why is it so important for you to know who the child's father is?" Bishop Esch asked quietly.

There was no need for the man to know that the discovery of Naomi's pregnancy could turn the accidental homicide into a murder investigation. I searched my mind for the best words to use. After all, I was sure I'd be seeing quite a bit of the bishop in the days to come.

"It's just protocol, Mr. Esch. I want to make sure all the paper work is filled out completely before I close the case."

"And, I assume that there are ways in your world of science to determine exactly who the father is?" The bishop asked.

"Yes, there are."

"I see…well, I must be going." He tipped his hat, and said, "Have a blessed day."

When Todd and I were back in the car, I finally relaxed.

"What do you make of all this?" I glanced over to see Todd staring out the window at the saturated landscape.

"It's fucked up if you ask me."

I translated his words to mean that he agreed with me. There was more going on in the Blood Rock Amish Community than anyone was willing to tell us.

"With these people being so damned tight lipped, how am I going to get any straight answers? No one's going to talk to me because I'm not Amish," I said to myself as much as to Todd.

"Maybe that's your solution." Todd shrugged with a lopsided smile appearing on his face. A face that I guess, some women would find attractive.

"What?"

"You need an Amish person to help you get in with the Amish people." Todd's voice was smug with concealed knowledge.

I pulled off the road, careful not to get into the soft ground too far before I turned the engine off.

"Will you just spit it out!" I demanded.

"Has anyone ever told you that you're cute when you get all riled up?" Todd joked, but seeing the look on my face that told him plainly that he was about to get hit, he went on quickly, "Go talk to Daniel Bachman. He might be able to help you."

The picture of the gorgeous building contractor sprang to mind. The man was unusually tall with bulging muscles in all the right places. His dark wavy hair and midnight black eyes had triggered romantic images of pirates and sailing ships when I'd first seen him.

I was more confused than before. "Do you mean the Daniel Bachman who put a new roof on my house last spring? Why ever would I want to talk to him about this mess?"

"You've already met him? Well, forget it then. He's probably scared of you now." Todd actually looked deflated. I had to fight my pride to ignore the comment.

"Be serious, Todd. *Why, Mr. Bachman?*"

Todd looked at me sideways, saying, "Because, he used to be Amish."

"What! You must be mistaken…Heather told me about all the women that the guy's been through. Not to mention, the two DUIs on his record."

I settled back in the seat, trying to think of any clue that the man had given when I'd dealt with him during the roofing job, but came up empty.

"You ran his name?" Todd sounded appalled.

"Hey, I don't know anything about roofs. I wanted to make sure the guy was reputable. Just forget about that anyway. When did he leave the Amish?"

"I ran into him over at Charlie's Pub one night," He eyed me and went on to promise, "I wasn't on duty, don't worry. Daniel joined me and Daryl at the table. He was a little wasted, but not too bad. Anyway, he basically gave us his entire life story."

"*And…?*" I could have kicked myself for being so curious, but damn, the guy was unusually hot.

"Told us he left the Amish when he was nineteen. Didn't say exactly why, but I gathered it wasn't exactly on good terms."

"The Blood Rock community?"

"Yep."

"Oh," was all I could sputter out. Todd was turning out to be a lot more useful than I ever thought he'd be. If nothing else, I could talk to Daniel about the Amish ways.

I frowned remembering clearly how his alpha male personality hadn't meshed well with me when he did my roof. Maybe Todd was right—the guy may not even be interested in talking to me. But, it was worth a try. I could put on the charm, when it was really needed.

"So what are we going to do for the next hour until quitting time?" Todd asked.

"We're going to pay Mr. Bachman a visit. In this weather, I'm sure he's not busy."

"Yeah, I figured you were going to say that." Todd sighed, and then he added, "You might want to let your hair down and change into street clothes. You don't want to freak him out, or anything."

The look I sent Todd was so fierce that his smirk disappeared and he mumbled, "—just saying."

4

NAOMI

August 16th

Naomi yawned as she gathered the dirty dishes from the table. She wondered how she was going to stay awake the rest of the day at the same time that she turned to frown at her mother. Instead of Mamma getting up to take care of three year old Emma, who'd woken in the night sick, it had been Naomi who'd sat with her little sister for hours, patting her hot forehead with a cool, wet cloth until the fever broke. The children were Mamma's responsibility, not hers, but she was always taking up the slack since Mamma was too tired or depressed to do anything.

"Don't forget, Naomi, you need to pick up those groceries before you come home this evening," Mamma said over her shoulder from the sink.

"Jah, I won't," Naomi said in a defeated voice, not allowing the bitterness to show for fear of what Mamma might do to her. She didn't have the energy for a fight this morning.

Maybe, another time she'd be able to speak up for herself, but not today.

Besides being up all night caring for her baby sister, Naomi had risen at five o'clock to do four loads of laundry by hand. Now, as she scraped the remnants of breakfast from the plates into the bucket, she was already exhausted. She rubbed her eyes vigorously to clear the haze from them. To top it all off, she had the shopping to look forward to after a full day of working at the butcher shop.

The beeping horn pulled Naomi from her resentful thoughts. She grabbed her bag and headed to the door without a goodbye from Mamma. If her mother had wished her well that day, she would have been shocked. The silence didn't darken her mood any more than it already was.

Emma and Nathan did smile at her though, and she patted each of their small heads when she walked by. At the door, she turned and winked at Emma before stepping out into the misty morning air. The chilly breeze lifted the hairs on her arms, but she wouldn't return to the kitchen for her jacket now that she was finally free. Knowing that the afternoon sun would have her sweating later on, she confidently stepped off the porch, heading toward the maroon Suburban that would be her chauffeur for the five miles or so to the butcher shop. Thankfully, the distance was too great for her to have to take a horse and buggy. Seeing the other girls' white caps blazing through the windows lightened Naomi's mood a little and she quickened her pace. Sandra would cheer her up. She always did.

Naomi glanced at the wall clock and rolled her eyes in disgust. The last ten minutes always went on forever, she thought, as she took the sharp blade and quartered the loin meat neatly. This particular piece was awfully bloody and she used the paper towels to pat the meat several times, soaking up the extra juice before she placed the pieces on the foam trays.

The bellow of the steer in the adjoining room sent a shudder through her. Naomi had been working at the butcher shop for a year, but she still had issues dealing with the killing part. She knew that if she lifted her head even a fraction, she'd see the steer go down through the open doorway. The sound of the shot was bad enough, but watching it happen was far worse. She prayed inwardly that she got picked up before this particular cow was done in.

"So, did you enjoy spending time with Eli after the singing on Sunday?" Sandra's voice startled Naomi. The girls had been too busy to talk much, especially when Mr. Zook was so serious about them paying close attention to what they were doing with the knives. It seemed to Naomi that almost every month, one of the girls was rushed to the doctor for stitches.

Naomi stalled her hands above the chunk of meat and raised her eyes to Sandra, thinking how lucky her friend was that she only worked two days a week at the shop. She, on the other hand, worked all five. Her Father's crops hadn't done as well the previous year and her family desperately needed the money. The responsibility fell onto Naomi's shoulders, being that she was the oldest child.

Naomi held the knife in the air and said, "You know I did. Eli and I have such great chemistry that it always feels right being with him. I just wish Mamma wasn't so uptight about it." She frowned at the meat, remembering how Mamma had barged onto the porch a whole hour before Eli was expecting to head home the night before, ordering her to bed. Dat wasn't nearly as bad. He actually seemed embarrassed by his wife's tirade.

Sandra lowered her voice to a whisper and Naomi had to strain to hear her words over the bellowing of the cow. "Is she giving you a difficult time about you courting Eli?"

"Of course, she gives me grief about everything in my life. And all I do is slave for her. You'd think she'd be at least a little grateful, but nooo." She pouted for effect, causing Sandra to shake her head in sympathy.

The young English man standing in the doorway caught Naomi's eye. He had dusty blond hair and wide set brown eyes. His nose was straight and his frame strong and muscled. It registered in her mind that he was close to as good looking as Eli was. Then he said Naomi's name and she froze, nearly fainting.

"I'm Naomi," she squawked out, hating the sound of her voice.

As the young man approached her, she noticed his comfortable, athletic stride and the way he flung the hair from his face before he spoke to her. He held out his hand for a second, but quickly dropped it to his side after seeing that one of hers was holding a knife and the other was encased in a bloody glove.

"I'm Will Johnson. Jerry is my uncle—his wife, Teresa, got real sick today. He asked me to come get you after he talked to your mother on the phone this afternoon. I'm supposed to take you to the grocery store and then home."

The information swirled around in Naomi's mind, leaving her light headed, and giddy at the same time. She set the knife into the bucket to be washed later and stripped the gloves off quickly.

"I'll go get my purse," she chirped.

"Okay." Will smiled and went back out the doorway.

Sandra whined, "You are always so lucky, Naomi! Why can't I have a driver that looks like that?"

Naomi smiled brightly and shrugged, "See ya later."

While Naomi walked across the gravel, she listened to the cheerful chorus of chirping coming from the tree that the black club cab truck was parked beneath. The birds' singing, along with the warmth of the bright sunshine, filled Naomi's heart with happiness as she stretched her legs, climbing into the passenger side. When she saw the blond girl sitting in the cramped, back seat, her good mood suddenly dampened, until Will introduced them.

"This is my little sister, Taylor."

With another glance, Naomi saw the resemblance and guessed the girl to be a few years younger than she herself was. Taylor had the same layered locks her brother did, and a mischievous smile curled up on her lips.

"You're the first Amish person I've ever met," Taylor said with no shyness at all.

"*Really?* That's kind of amazing around here," Naomi said, not sure how else to respond.

The truck pulled onto the roadway to the soft beat of a country western song. Naomi peeked over at Will, surprised by his choice of music.

"Well, 'course I've seen your people all over the place, but I never actually talked to one—until now." She took a breath and rattled on, "How can you stand wearing a dress all the time? I can hardly put up with it when my mom insists that I wear one for a wedding. Do those little caps hurt your head?"

Taylor's wide eyes and open curiosity kept Naomi from becoming angry. Instead, she laughed, the sound filling the truck. Naomi couldn't recall ever having laughed in the company of strangers before. She was amazed at how comfortable she felt with these particular Englishers, to do such a thing.

"Sorry about my sis. She's mental," Will said in a solemn voice. He softly shook his head.

"I am not! I'm just trying to get to know Naomi, that's all. By the way, your name is so pretty."

Naomi was overwhelmed. Never before in her life had she been around such a forth right person—and a girl besides. She stared down at her hands as she laced her fingers together in her lap, suddenly feeling shy.

"Thanks," Naomi mumbled.

The trip into town was anything but quiet with the constant chatter from Taylor. By the time the truck reached the store, Naomi was worn out from answering Taylor's questions, but not in a bad way. When Taylor insisted that she help Naomi, the Amish girl let her. Since Will had remained in the truck, Naomi finally got some of her own questions answered.

As the girls strolled through the cereal aisle and Naomi tried to read her Mamma's messy handwritten list, she asked Taylor, "So, how old is your brother?"

Taylor eyed Naomi, suddenly calmer, as if her mind had finally quieted. "He's nineteen. Why?"

Naomi didn't face Taylor, instead giving her attention to the boxes of flakes. "Just wondering, that's all. Has he ever driven Amish before?"

"Yeah, he's been driving some to and from work lately. He likes making the extra money. He's planning to move to Montana to ride in rodeos."

Naomi stopped and stared at Taylor in disbelief. "Really?"

"Yep, he almost has enough money saved right now, but he wants to be fully prepared for the trip. I'll miss him. He's the only brother I got. But if he does go, then I'll be able to visit him sometimes and that would be cool," Taylor said with a misty, faraway look.

The rest of the time in the store, Naomi fell into a moody silence, thinking about Will leaving Indiana and traveling all the way to Montana. Even though she wasn't exactly sure where the state was, she knew it was a great distance away. She was confused about the angry feelings that were bubbling up within her. She'd just met Will and had no reason to care at all about where he went. But as Naomi paid the cashier, and Taylor was busy loading the bags into the cart, Naomi thought about what she would give to leave Blood Rock and go somewhere as exciting as Montana.

When they reached the truck, Taylor complained that she was hungry and Will insisted on treating the girls to supper at McDonalds. Naomi worried inwardly that Mamma would have her hide if she arrived home a minute later than her mother thought she ought to. But the pull of spending time with the Englishers was too strong for Naomi. She remained silent, happily watching the stores and businesses pass by as she tapped her foot to the beat of the music playing from the radio.

Once they were seated in the booth, Naomi tried to ignore the stares from the other patrons as she ate her food and listened to Will and Taylor discuss Taylor's teachers and how unhappy she currently was with them. Naomi was used to being rudely ogled by Englishers, but today was different since she was actually sitting with two of them. She didn't think that the brother and sister were even aware of the stir that the three of them were causing in the restaurant. They didn't seem to notice that the little girl in the neighboring booth was pointing at Naomi and asking her mother questions about the funny looking hat and dress she wore.

As Naomi took a sip of her cola, she quickly glanced from Will to Taylor and back again. It suddenly dawned on her that the young Englishers weren't concerned about the other people around them. They weren't paying any attention because they didn't care what the others thought. Naomi, wanting to emulate their indifference, took a breath and turned away from the strangers' faces, ignoring them too.

When Taylor went to the restroom, leaving Will and Naomi alone at the table, Naomi's heart sped up nervously. She quickly scanned the restaurant to make sure that no Amish people had entered the building without her notice. Being alone with a man was completely forbidden for Naomi, especially since she was courting Eli. Although she knew she was doing wrong, she didn't care as much as she should have.

Swallowing the butterflies, Naomi said, "Do you go to school, Will?"

He leaned back in a comfortable way and replied, "No, I graduated last year. I've been working all kinds of odd jobs to save up money for a trip out west."

"Taylor told me you're going to Montana," Naomi said, realizing that her feet had stilled, along with her heart.

"That's the plan," Will said. His gaze settled on Naomi's face as if he was seeing her for the first time.

"That's so neat. Is it going to be very expensive?"

"The cost to drive out there isn't the problem, it's having the money to rent a place until I find permanent work and start making money riding." He continued to stare at Naomi way longer than he should have.

"Isn't riding the bulls dangerous?"

He laughed heartily, drawing the attention of several of the people in the neighboring booths away from Naomi and onto him. "Yeah, that is dangerous, but that's not what I do. I ride in the team roping competition. I'm a heeler. I figure I can hook up with a partner better out there than I can here in the middle of Indiana. There are a lot more rodeos in that part of the country, too."

"Oh, that sounds so exciting," Naomi breathed, envious to the bone.

"You're welcome to join me, but I can't guarantee the accommodations being comfortable." He laughed again, and Naomi loved the sound of it. She knew he was just chiding her, but she wished deep in her soul that he wasn't.

When Will quieted, he said, "Do you have a boyfriend?"

Naomi didn't know if it were the words or the smooth way he said it that caused her skin to tingle. Why would he ask such an inappropriate question, she wondered? Was he sweet on her? Naomi didn't want to lie to him about Eli, but she didn't want to tell the truth either. Lucky for her, that's when Taylor showed up and distracted both of them.

"Where to now?" Taylor bubbled, and Naomi envied her energy. She was plum worn out, the long night and day finally catching up to her.

"Home, I do believe." She turned to Will who held an amused expression on his face. "If that's all right with you?"

"Of, course, you're the boss."

By the time they reached the farm, Naomi felt she'd known Taylor, and even Will, for her entire life. The atmosphere was easy going and fun in the cab talking with the two of them. She hated when she had to say goodbye.

"Thanks again for helping carry the groceries in, and for dinner too." Naomi eyed Will who'd stepped back into the cab. He was leaning out the window staring at her with interest again. When he grinned and told her, "You're welcome," she shivered and turned to Taylor who was standing beside her.

"Hope I see you again, Taylor."

"Oh, I'm sure you'll be seeing a whole lot of me with Will driving for Uncle Jerry all week." Taylor smiled brightly.

Naomi turned back to Will, her heart skipping a beat, "Are you really picking me up in the morning?"

"Yeah, you and the other Amish girls, but since we've become good friends and all, I'll make sure to drop you off last."

Will looked serious and Naomi hastily said in a whisper, moving closer to the window, "Please don't take this the wrong way, but don't talk to me in front of the other girls, or else I'll get into trouble."

Understanding flickered in Will's warm brown eyes. He said, "Sure thing. You can count on me being discreet."

Taylor's voice jumped into the air, tearing Naomi's gaze away from Will's handsome face. "It's almost Fair time. Maybe you could come with us when we go?"

Naomi had never been to a Fair. It wasn't allowed. But she wasn't going to tell Taylor that right now. Who knew, maybe she could work it out somehow.

"Sounds like fun. I'll see you all tomorrow," Naomi said.

Naomi smiled to herself as she slowly made her way to the house. After the horrible start, what an amazing day it had turned out to be. And, no matter how ill-tempered Mamma might be, Naomi wasn't going to be brought down tonight.

As she reached the porch steps, Naomi wondered which guy she'd be dreaming about that night, Eli...or Will?

5

DANIEL

November 10th

Looking out the window, I thanked God that the sheriff had called first. I would've been extremely rattled if she'd shown up at the front door unannounced. Holding the curtain open just an inch, I watched Serenity Adams walk through the soggy grass with Todd Roftin by her side.

There was no denying that the woman was beautiful, even in the manly officer clothes she wore. But, her fiery and independent nature was disconcerting. Maybe that's why she wasn't settled down with a few kids by now. It would take a man of strong constitution to win her heart. Letting my rampant thoughts go, I crossed the floor to open the door when the knocks sounded.

"Hello, Sheriff Adams and Todd, it's good to see you both." I motioned for them to enter.

"Oh, please call me Serenity," she said as she removed her hat.

"Would either of you like a cup of coffee or tea?" I asked, growing more uncomfortable by the second now that the officers were standing in my foyer. Serenity's face was anxious, as if she wanted to get down to business immediately, but her partner was more relaxed, looking around at the interior of my home.

"No, thank you," Serenity said hurriedly, then she glanced at Todd and added, "unless you're thirsty?"

The tone of voice she used with Todd made me smile. I quickly rubbed the expression away with my hand.

"Actually, I could do with a cup of coffee, Daniel, if it's not much trouble." Todd shot Serenity an annoyed look.

"No problem at all. I have a pot just brewed."

When the three of us were seated at the table, Serenity began to open her mouth to speak, but Todd got to the air space first.

"Did you build this house yourself?"

"Yes, I did, about three years ago," I said, noticing the way Serenity rolled her eyes and slouched back into the chair, waiting for her turn to speak.

"I've always liked a log house. Are they much maintenance?" Todd asked, staring at one of the wood beams above his head.

I was about to answer when Serenity burst out, "Really, guys, maybe you should get together some other time to talk shop. We have an investigation to launch and I believe that we need to focus on it at the moment."

Did the woman ever relax? I could almost picture her with the honey blond hair loose on her shoulders and wearing a snug fitting pair of jeans and t-shirt—almost.

My eyes met Serenity's blue ones. I said, "You mentioned an investigation over the phone, but you didn't say much else. If I could be as forth right as you, why exactly do you want to talk to me? I'm not in any trouble?"

"No, not at all, Mr. Bachman," Serenity said.

"If I can call you Serenity, then it's fair for you to call me Daniel," I said quickly.

Serenity glanced down in embarrassment, her upturned lips lighting her face. "Right, the reason we wanted to talk to you is that there was a shooting incident in the Amish community. It involved an eighteen year old girl named Naomi Beiler. There are some oddities surrounding the case that we're trying to figure out."

"The newspaper said that it was a hunting accident. Has the person come forward yet?" I asked without thinking. I remembered Timothy and Patricia Beiler. They were close to my age, and people that once upon a time, I had called friends.

"Yes, well, it appears to be a hunting accident, but no one has come to us with information. I've discovered that dealing with the Amish is not as straight forward as I had hoped it would be," Serenity said with a frown and a glance at Todd. Her partner was still observing my interior walls and not paying much attention to the conversation at all.

I laughed at Serenity's words, not able to stop myself. When her eyes rounded wide, and even Todd turned to me, I said, "I'm sorry, but you obviously haven't spent very much time around the Amish have you?"

"No, I haven't. That's the problem. And why I wanted to talk to you. I was hoping that maybe you could give us some insight into the Amish community here, and perhaps its people too." Serenity tried to smile sweetly, but it didn't work. The woman was too honest a person. The little show of friendliness was hollow.

"Why me?"

She glanced at Todd in confusion, "Ah, I heard that you used to be one of them and had left the community. Is that correct?"

Todd interjected, "Sorry, man, you got a little loose with your lips one night at Charlie's."

"What could I possibly help you with?" I looked at Serenity. I could have sworn that she blushed for a second before she spoke. Maybe there was a soft woman underneath all the bravado that actually liked men.

"I think that would be pretty obvious, Daniel. I need to understand why these people are acting strangely and being so secretive. It seems to me that they'd want to know what happened to their daughter as much as the rest of us do."

"How do you mean strange?" I had to admit, as much as I hated to, that I was becoming intrigued.

"For one thing, Mr. and Mrs. Beiler aren't acting at all like the usually grieving parents of a dead child," Serenity said, straightening her back to make her case.

"The Amish believe in God's divining hand in everything and they have extremely strong faith that the Lord takes care of his followers in life…and death. Maybe, the lack of hysteria is because of their strong Christian beliefs," I suggested.

She shook her head, "No, sorry. Even an Amish mother would shed tears on the day of her daughter's funeral."

I remembered back to the Amish funerals that I'd attended as a child and young adult, and there'd been a slew of them. There were always tears—especially from the mothers. Maybe Serenity was on to something.

"I know the Beilers—they're good people. But, I do remember Patricia was cold and unemotional as a teen. She might not have out grown it."

Serenity latched on to just a few of the words and dove in, "So you grew up with Timothy and Patricia? What about James Hooley and Joseph Bender—and Bishop Esch?"

"Whoa, slow down." I patted the air, grinning at Serenity's enthusiasm. She certainly wasn't subtle. "I know all of them. 'Course they're fifteen years older now. Bishop Esch had just gotten the job right before I'd left the community. James was quite a bit older than me, so I wasn't close to him. But Joseph was a good buddy of my older brother's and I spent quite a bit of time around him."

Serenity took a deep breath and leveled her pretty eyes on me. "Would you be willing to assist me with the case by telling me what you know about these people, and their roles in the community?"

She seemed to be holding her breath, waiting for my answer. A little warning bell in my head told me to say no and run away. But another voice was encouraging me to take the opportunity to get to know the sheriff better. After all, my life had been rather dull lately. I'd dated a lot of women over the years and each relationship had ended before it even got started. The wall around my heart was too high to allow anyone in. I'd accepted a while ago that I was probably destined to be alone. There was just too much emotional baggage attached to me for a woman to stick around for very long. To say that I was damaged goods was putting it mildly.

But the tingle of anticipation I felt in my gut made me wonder about Serenity. Maybe she was different. It had been close to seventeen years since I'd experienced the uncomfortable sensation before—and that time had not ended well. Still, it was a revelation that I wasn't completely numb. I could almost touch the pulsating energy between Serenity and I. I'd felt it the first time I'd met her. The day we'd talked on the porch of her bungalow-style house was still vivid in my mind. As she'd shielded her eyes from the bright sunlight, I'd become mesmerized by their pale blue color. I even remember stuttering a couple of times when I answered her questions about her roof. I left that day happy that she'd signed me on, but frustrated that she hadn't given me any sign that she was interested in anything other than the roofing job. Nothing changed in her demeanor during the work week either. The job ended with not even a flirtatious look from the little sheriff, though I had to admit, she'd materialized in my daydreams on many occasions since.

But, damn, to get mixed up in all the backward thinking, back stabbing and drama of the Amish people again was the real issue here. Was a woman worth it? Normally, I would have said, hell no, but glancing at Serenity's anxious face, I wavered. Maybe, just maybe, she was worth it.

As scary as it would be to see everybody again, it would be nice to check in with my brothers and sisters and their children. Father and Mother would probably still not welcome me to their table, but they were getting on in age. Perhaps their anger had cooled some in all these years. I wouldn't be alone either. I'd have tough little Serenity at my side. I pondered, weighing the pros and cons in my head, quickly.

When I looked up, Serenity must have read my mind before I spoke. She suddenly had a very pleased look on her face.

"Sure. But, on two conditions," I said, not able to keep from smiling as Serenity's happy expression changed to one of dread.

"What conditions?" she nearly growled.

"That you let me do the talking...and you accompany me to the Amish School House dinner tomorrow evening. It would be the perfect place for you to immerse yourself in the Amish world and get a good dinner to boot."

Serenity was thinking it over as if it was a trick. She looked at Todd for encouragement. I felt the prick of jealousy as her eyes sought the other man's, but I was fairly certain that there wasn't anything going on between them. Todd was definitely not Serenity's type.

Todd said, "They have a benefit dinner twice a year, in the spring and fall. I saw the banner advertising it this weekend on the corner of the road that the school's on. The entire community will probably be there."

Serenity turned back to me and narrowed her eyes a fraction when she said, "I'll go with you tomorrow to the dinner. And, I'll let you do most of the talking. But I'm not guaranteeing that I won't say something if it needs to be said."

That was probably the best I was going to get out of her.

The shiver of anticipation crawled up my back as I said, "Then we have a deal."

6

NAOMI

August 28th

Naomi knew she'd stayed in the truck too long already when she gripped the door handle, but she was still reluctant to leave Will behind.

"Will you come with us, Naomi? If you're worried about getting away from your house, just tell your folks that you're staying with that one friend of yours that you trust."

Will's voice held a hint of pleading that sent a shiver of delight through her. Spending just a few minutes alone with him each afternoon was not near enough for her. Naomi's lips wanted nothing more than to feel the press of the English boy's mouth on hers. That would never happen though if she didn't do something to make it possible. But, the thought of lying to Mother and Father about spending the evening with Sandra, and attempting to sneak away with Will and his sister to go to the Fair was beyond frightening. If she got caught, Mamma would have the belt on her bare butt for sure. And that wouldn't even be the worst of it.

LAMB TO THE SLAUGHTER

"I'll see what I can do, but I'm not making any promises. You just don't understand all that I'm risking if I do what you ask." Seeing his look of disappointment, she added quickly, "But, I really do want to go. We'll see what I can work out."

Naomi put on her most pouty, sad face. Will couldn't help but smile warmly at her. "Don't worry. If it doesn't happen, there'll be another time."

"Promise?" she said softly.

"Yeah, I promise." Will didn't take his eyes off of her, causing the heat to spread onto her cheeks. She slid from the truck and without looking back she hurried up the walkway to the house.

Naomi could still hear the rumble of the diesel engine when she went through the doorway. She was immediately struck with the broom across the back of her legs.

"Owww! What was that for?" she shrieked at Mamma who had the broom ready for a second blow.

"What are you up to, staying in the truck all that time? Have you been batting your big eyes at the English driver? Have you?" Mamma's voice was ragged and crazed, so different from the relatively good mood that she'd been in that morning when Naomi left for work. Of course, Mamma's moods could swing wildly in a few minutes, let alone a long day, Naomi knew.

"Mamma, I promise I wasn't doing a bad thing. Mr. Johnson was just asking about our goat kids and if any of them are for sale. He wants to buy one for his little sister for her birthday." Naomi didn't know where the words came from, but they flowed from her mouth as if someone was whispering them into her ear.

Mamma's wrathful face calmed a bit. She lowered the broom to the floor. Naomi was still ready to bolt, her weight on the balls of her feet.

"I see," she said. Her eyes narrowed and she pointed a chubby finger at her daughter. "You best be watching what you do, Naomi Mae Beiler. I will not have you flirting with any outsiders. You have a fine young man interested in you. Better be careful not to do anything to mess it up."

"Jah, Mamma, I know how fine Eli is. I love him more than anything. I wouldn't be making eyes at a stupid English boy. I wouldn't." Naomi hoped Mamma believed her.

Mamma's face hardened and her emotions swung angry again. "I've been meaning to have a talk with you about Eli anyhow. Now is as good a time as any. Especially, since he's fixing to come over for dinner tonight."

Her words shocked Naomi. She'd completely forgotten that Eli was visiting that evening. She was immediately torn from feeling excitement to see him, to major guilt at the way she'd been acting with Will.

Naomi wanted to get the conversation over with. She needed to wash the sweat and grime from the butcher's shop off of her before Eli arrived. Carefully, she said, "What about?"

Mamma breathed out uncomfortably before pulling a chair away from the table and sitting her plump backside onto it.

"I'm giving you a warning young Naomi that you would heed if you had any sense in that stubborn brain of yours. Don't be sneaking off with Eli to be touching each other, and worse. You already know that our community has the rule of hands-off courting, but I'm not a dolt. I know what goes on behind the barns and in the sheds. I was young and pretty like you once and I remember those days. And how I didn't heed my mamma's advice and ended up pregnant by your father when I was a year younger than you are now. Don't get me wrong, I'm not saying that I don't love your father, but back in those days I was trapped, with only one thing to do. What little choices I had in life were taken from me in a flash. You don't want to end up like that. Trust me, you don't."

With that, Mamma rose and crossed the kitchen floor to descend into the basement without another word or glance at Naomi. It was probably the most that Mamma had ever said to her oldest child at one time. Naomi was at a loss about what to think. *Mamma had been pregnant when she'd married Dat?* That was news to Naomi. She could hardly even imagine the uptight, crazy woman ever being a teenager, let alone playing with Dat and getting her belly full of a child. Naomi reasoned that she and Eli were more careful than that.

The disgusting thoughts made her feel even more unclean, and she pushed them from her mind. She didn't have much time if she was going to bathe before Eli arrived. As Naomi jogged up the steps, her thoughts wandered back to Will. She began thinking again about what it would be like to kiss him.

7

SERENITY

November 11th

As I approached the barn-like school house that was surrounded by a mix of Amish people and non-Amish ones, I felt a sudden wave of nervousness. I'd already been dealing with a fit of embarrassing shyness ever since Daniel had picked me up in his hard bodied Jeep and told me how nice I looked. What did he mean? Normally, such a compliment could be taken at face value, but with the former Amish man things weren't so clear. I could admit that I probably did look pretty good. I was wearing hipster denim jeans with a wide belt and a fitted, black leather jacket. I'd taken Todd's advice and left my hair down, although I'd never tell him that. My long, blond layers were now billowing around my face in the cool wind. With annoyance, I brushed the hair back so I could see where I was going. I wished that I'd worn a pony-tail, but there was no way that I was pulling it up now. The way Daniel's eyes kept straying to my locks said he approved. Having the gorgeous guy at my side finding something other than my clothing attractive was a definite goal, even though I could have slapped myself for thinking so. Daniel's side brushed against me and he bent down to whisper loudly, "Remember what we talked about in the Jeep. You're my girlfriend. We've just started dating, and if anyone brings up the investigation, tell them it's closed for all intents and purposes." He grasped my hand and pulled me to a stop. I couldn't help but look up in annoyance. "Don't go asking any questions tonight. Let me do the talking for the most part... okay?"

All kinds of doubts swirled in my head. The whole thing seemed so damned unprofessional. Is this really what a woman in small town rural America needed to do to get information for a possible murder investigation? What would happen to my reputation if it ever leaked out that I'd masqueraded as Daniel's girlfriend to infiltrate the Amish community? I had a bad feeling about it. Unfortunately having my hand held snuggly in Daniel's large, warm one felt nice enough to allow me to push the rational thoughts away. Still, as good as it felt, I looked down at our hands and back up at him questioningly.

"It's all part of the act, Serenity. Englishers hold hands when they're dating—no way around it." Daniel smiled, and it nearly took my breath away. Was he that good of an actor, or was he enjoying the charade as much as I secretly was?

We walked toward the crowd in the buttery light of the evening, hand in hand. I tried to remember when the last time was that I'd held a guy's hand. It had been a long while, that's for sure.

Feeling comfortable enough with Daniel to confide my biggest fear of the night, I slowed his forward momentum with a tug, and said, "I don't believe the bishop will buy any of this. He's way too sharp."

"You'd be surprised what they'll believe, including Bishop Esch. We're an attractive couple, just a man and a woman tonight. That's what they'll see and it will make perfect sense to them."

He sounded awfully sure of himself. I let go of the doubts and shifted my focus to the Amish people around me. Immediately upon entering the throng of people, all eyes were on us. Most of those eyes widened first with recognition of Daniel. Then they settled on me. So far, I hadn't seen any of the Amish I recognized. I relaxed even further, allowing Daniel to be my guide through the mass of caps and beards.

"Why, Daniel Bachman, it's been a long time since I saw you last. How are you doing?" An Amish man stopped in front of us, grinning broadly. He had friendly blue eyes and a golden brown beard. His hand shot forward enthusiastically as he squeezed Daniel's shoulder with his other hand at the same time.

I could feel Daniel almost pull back in surprise before he let go of me and reached for the other man's grasp. Daniel's face beamed. I could almost touch the joy that emitted from him. Suddenly, I realized that Daniel must have been a nervous wreck himself about this encounter with his people. He hadn't known what to expect after all these years away. Obviously from his huge smile, he was quite satisfied with his reception from this man.

I tried to step back and let him have his moment. Before I could, he reached over and grabbed my hand, pulling me tightly into his side.

"This is Serenity, my girlfriend. Serenity, this is one of my oldest friends, Lester Lapp. Lester and I used to spend whatever time we weren't doing farm work in each other's company, getting into all sorts of trouble."

Daniel continued to hold me close to his side. I was amazed that it didn't feel as weird as it should have. I continued to play the loving girlfriend, leaning into him and slipping my hand around his waist. I enjoyed the quick glance he gave me, accompanied by a slight smile and eye brow lift. I would show him that I could act just as well as he could.

Lester laughed heartily at Daniel's words, saying, "That is so, my friend." His eyes fixed on me and he asked Daniel, "How long have the two of you been courting?"

Daniel said smoothly, "We just recently found each other, but we've been inseparable since." He punctuated his statement with a tighter hold on me.

Then Lester became distracted, calling over to a group of teenage boys who were leaning up against the side of the building. Lester was speaking in Pennsylvania Dutch, so I didn't know what he was saying, but when a boy limped over, I guessed that this was one of his children. The boy was probably fifteen or sixteen and he wore a short sleeved blue dress shirt with black suspenders. The black felt hat on his head added to the picture of a boy plucked from the nineteenth century. I couldn't help but think how odd it was to see a teenager who should have been in jeans and a t-shirt dressed so.

Lester said, "Daniel, this is my second oldest son, Mervin. He reminds me a bit of you in his personality."

Daniel shook the boy's hand heartily and said, "Surely he's not that much trouble. Or, is it that he likes to be out in the woods turkey hunting whenever the chance arises?"

Lester's demeanor changed, becoming more reserved as he looked at Mervin. He patted his son's shoulder. "I reckon that may be it, but he also enjoys singing the hymns on Sunday mornings, same as you did."

Mervin spoke to his father in the foreign language and his father nodded his head. As he walked away, I noticed the limp again. Without thinking, I asked, "Did he have an accident?"

Just as Lester was opening his mouth, an Amish woman with a stern face and sharp green eyes stepped up beside Lester, and said, "Why, yes he did. Just the other day a horse threw him off. The poor boy is still sore from it."

Without touching the woman, Lester introduced her to us as his wife, Ester. Although Daniel must have known the woman, he was careful not to offer a handshake. I made a mental note of how much more reserved Daniel was toward his friend's wife than he'd been with Lester.

Ester forced a smile that I could read immediately as fake. She tilted her head at me and said, "You look familiar. Have we met before?"

I was at a loss for a second. Daniel's fingers pressing into my side told me that he was about to say something when Bishop Esch appeared out of nowhere. My heart thumped madly at the sight of the man. Did he have a Serenity homing device built into his old body?

"You probably saw Serenity at Naomi's funeral, Ester. She's our county Sheriff. Although I must admit, without her uniform, she looks much different," the bishop said. He immediately dismissed me and turned to Daniel, offering his hand to my fake boyfriend.

Daniel let go of me again to grasp the bishop's hand for a shorter time than he had Lester's. He greeted the man with less enthusiasm, but still with a feel of genuine friendliness.

"Why, it's a surprise to see you here, Daniel, and with the sheriff on your arm. But a welcome one at that," Bishop Esch said.

"Didn't you know that we were dating?" Daniel asked innocently.

"No. That information did not come up in our previous discussions. How did the two of you meet?" the bishop glanced between us.

Maybe the nerves of having the bishop show up out of nowhere had gotten to me. After a pause, I began to open my mouth to answer him with some made up nonsense when Daniel beat me to the punch.

"We met in church, Aaron. Although, I must admit that I'm still searching for the spiritual experience that feels right to me. I never thought I'd say this, but I do miss a Plain church service."

Bishop Esch's eyebrows raised and he leaned in closer to Daniel. "Do you miss our ways as well?" he asked with quiet directness that made me look up at Daniel. I waited for his answer with the same intensity that the bishop held.

What Daniel said made me suck in a breath and my own words of denial. Was Daniel still playing the game, or was there some truth in his crazy words?

"Actually, Aaron, I've been thinking strongly about the possibility of coming back to the Plain people."

This had not been discussed in the Jeep. I clenched my teeth together at how out of hand the fiasco had become. But then a flicker of dread slowed my heart. Maybe Daniel was thinking about converting back.

While I was staring at Daniel's face, trying to read his words as a lie or the desires of his heart, I felt the bishop's gaze on me.

"Oh, my, from my impression of how seriously Ms. Adams takes her very important job, I can't see her fitting into your plans," Aaron Esch said smoothly.

He knew I was an imposter.

I didn't want to mess up whatever the hell Daniel was up to. I played along, telling myself in the far recesses of my brain, that it would all be okay in the end—and maybe I'd find out what really happened to Naomi Beiler.

"The job is pretty stressful, Mr. Esch. If I do get married someday and have children, I can't foresee myself being able to keep up with it," I lied.

The bishop rubbed his beard thoughtfully. Lester clasped Daniel's shoulder again and said, "Daniel, it would be good to have you back, my friend."

After the insane encounter with the Lapps and the bishop, Daniel and I spent nearly an hour reaching the food line for all the people that came up and greeted Daniel with smiles and handshakes. The Amish people were treating Daniel with genuine warmth, as if he was already one of them again. It was obvious that before whatever happened to run him off from the Amish way of life, he was quite popular with both people from his own age group all the way up to ancient ones remembering him. Many of the non-Amish people knew Daniel too. I was beginning to feel that I was on the arm of a celebrity.

It was almost humorous how few people recognized me dressed in street clothes. I didn't go out much. When I did,

I kept my hair pulled back tightly and half my face hidden behind supersized shades. I didn't want to be noticed when I was off the job.

When we finally sat down on the bench at the long line of tables positioned under the canopy tent, I was famished. The smell of the food on my plate made my mouth water. The Amish girls at the counter had heaped the servings high with shy eyes and mumbled words. I'd imagined Naomi standing there among them, all prim and proper and quiet. The thoughts had sobered my mind, reminding me what my purpose here was.

As I began to eat the chicken and mashed potatoes, I listened to Daniel talk with animation to his sister and brother-in-law. After Daniel had hugged his sister, whose eyes had glistened with moisture at the unexpected encounter, the couple had followed us to the table.

Daniel had told me on the drive over that he had three brothers and the same number of sisters. Only one of those, a sister, had remained here in Blood Rock. The others had made homesteads in newer communities in southern Ohio and Kentucky.

I couldn't understand a word they were saying, but frequently, Daniel's sister, Rebecca, would glance my way and smile. When I wasn't trying to get the gist of Daniel's conversation with his family, my gaze wandered to the gray haired couple sitting a few rows away. Daniel had subtly pointed his parents out to me before we'd sat down. Even though both of them had seen their son, they'd made no move to speak to him. He'd returned the favor by turning away quickly and ignoring them.

My head shot up with my name.

"Serenity, what is it like being a police officer? Is it very scary?" Rebecca asked, sliding down the bench and stopping directly across from me. Her white cap and navy blue dress were very neat and her face was still tight with youth. Rebecca's eye's sparked with curiosity, telling me she was an intelligent woman.

I usually didn't hang out with women, finding their company to be both uncomfortable and confusing at times, but Rebecca immediately made me feel at ease. Maybe it was the fact that she looked very much like Daniel, only a feminine version. She would have been striking with normal clothes, her hair down and a touch of make-up.

"There were times when I first got my badge and I was working in Indianapolis that I was intimidated by the job. Maybe even a little frightened. But the fear isn't the difficult part—dealing with the aftermath of violence is."

Rebecca looked confused, glancing between me and Daniel. I suddenly felt extremely self-conscious. I stared at the white, plastic table cloth, gathering my thoughts before she even asked the question.

"If you don't mind me asking, what do you mean? I'd always assumed that police officers are in danger much of the time," Rebecca said.

I sighed. "Yes, that's true, especially in the larger populated areas. Unfortunately, that's only a part of being a cop. I've seen all kinds of awful things over the years; domestic violence, child abuse, and murder. But for me, witnessing first-hand the effect on the children…and sometimes their parents, is worse than being shot yourself."

I almost said more, but the penetrating look from Daniel closed my mouth. He didn't need to know my demons. None of them did.

Covering up my awkward pause quickly, I said, "I moved back here to Blood Rock almost two years ago to leave the violence of the city behind…or so I thought."

Daniel and his brother-n-law became stone silent. I could tell from the corner of my eye that Daniel was still staring at me. His steady gaze made me want to squirm on the bench. I struggled not to fidget in front of him.

Rebecca said, "Yes, it is a sad thing about Naomi Beiler. It must be hard for you to see a person after the Lord has taken them away. I know I couldn't do it."

It was interesting how Rebecca had understood exactly what I'd meant. I admitted that the Amish people I'd met today weren't as creepy as the bishop, ministers, and Beilers were. Maybe, Tony Manning had been right about getting to know the Plain people better. Even with a softening of my attitude, I couldn't keep the paranoia completely from my mind. I wondered if I would have been received in such a friendly manner if I hadn't been on Daniel's arm.

Rebecca reached over and placed her soft, small hand on mine and said, "Please come by and visit sometime. We can get to know each other over a cup of tea."

"That would be nice. Thank you," I murmured, feeling overwhelmed by the woman's invitation. I also felt like shit that at some point it would come out that my relationship with Daniel was a ruse. When she learned the truth, Rebecca would never want to talk to me again.

After we deposited our plastic plates into the trash can, Daniel led me by the hand into the school house and the site of the auction. Another bearded Amish man was rattling off numbers too fast for me to catch when we entered the building. Daniel shuffled me to a bench near the front, continuing to greet almost everyone we passed. I would've bet that he'd already met up with every bearded man on the property, except for his own father, when a new one would pop up out of nowhere. It was difficult to keep them all straight. Their beards, matching dress code and tight genetic pool made them all look the same at a glance.

Daniel's hand had somehow settled on my knee and remained there for the rest of the time we spent watching the quilts, furniture and pies sell. I tried to ignore the warm, heavy feel of it and focus on the auction, but it was difficult. I was shocked to see several high dollar items, such as a hand stitched quilt and a rocking chair get bought by local banks and then be donated back to the Amish people to be auctioned off once again. I certainly hadn't known about the close business ties these people had to the outside community. By the show of non-Amish people spending their money at the event, it became clear that many of them were ready to support the Amish not only with smiles and handshakes, but with their wallets as well.

When a beautiful blue and burgundy quilt reached eight hundred and seventy five dollars and then was offered back to the Amish, I swiveled in my seat to look for the person who'd spent so much money, just to give it all back.

My face heated when my stare met Tony Manning's. He smiled crookedly and left his petite, blond wife, to stride purposely towards me. I turned back around and sighed loudly. Just what I needed, I thought.

"What?" Daniel whispered near my ear at the same time he squeezed my hand, sending a pleasant tingle coursing through me.

"Nothing you need to worry about," I said.

Tony's voice came close to my other ear, along with the strong smell of peppermint. "So, I see you've taken my advice, Serenity, and come to mingle with the people."

I ignored him. Nobody needed a shout fest between me and the former sheriff, especially not Daniel.

"You're even quieter with your tongue. Let's just hope that you take the rest of the advice I gave you."

I didn't even bother to turn when Tony left. I couldn't deal with his nonsense right now. But I'd be lying if I said that his appearance hadn't set my nerves on edge. I ignored Daniel's raised eyebrow and questioning look to silently watch the auctioneer begin selling buckets of the leftover chicken from the dinner. My mind wondered as the drone of the sale went on, again wondering why Tony Manning was pestering me to leave the Amish alone. I rolled the conversations with the man around in my mind, but I couldn't fathom what Tony's connection to the investigation was. The more I thought about it, the deeper the throbs in my head were. I decided to let it go for the time being before it gave me a migraine.

A couple of hours later, I found myself tiredly walking in the dark to Daniel's Jeep. He'd finally let go of my hand, needing both of his to carry the two new garden shovels that he'd purchased. Personally, I thought he paid way too much for them, but he bought them for a good cause so I didn't say anything about it. My butt was sore from the hard benches and I was imagining the hot bubble bath I planned to climb into as soon as I got home, when a hand snaked out of the darkness and grabbed my arm.

"Ma'am, I'm sorry to bother you and all, but I need to talk to you. Not here though. We can't talk now." The girl's voice was quietly whispering and talking so fast that I had to strain to hear her. I didn't have to work hard to feel her trembling body next to mine though. Whether she shook from the cold or fear, I had no idea.

"What's your name?" I asked, aware that Daniel had stopped beside me. He was waiting for the girl to speak too.

"Sandra. I won't tell you my last name. You don't need to know that. But I do know something that I think you'd be interested in. It's about Naomi. She was my best friend, and she didn't deserve what happened to her." Sandra paused to look behind her and then she came even closer. From instinct, I leaned in to meet her. "You being the sheriff and all, you'll want to know this. It might help you."

"Where do you want to meet?" I asked the short, plain faced girl.

"We can talk at the butcher's shop. Be there at eleven on Monday morning. That's when I take my break to get fresh air and eat my lunch. That's the only time, so please be there."

Before I could say anything, Sandra was gone, disappearing into the night as quickly as she had appeared.

I was going to speak, but Daniel pulled me the last few feet to the Jeep. He motioned me to get in when he opened the door.

Neither of us spoke until we were well away from the school house. Then both of us began speaking at once.

"You go first," Daniel said.

"What the hell was that all about? Are the Amish always so damn cryptic?"

Daniel laughed nervously, and said, "Yeah. That's the way we're trained from childhood. Everything is a secret.

"Do you think that girl really has information that will help solve the case?" My heart still thumped with adrenaline from the unexpected encounter.

"She very well might. The young people are the ones who'll talk to you."

"Why them?" I turned in the seat and faced the handsome guy beside me, wishing that we had been on a real date and not some fake investigation set-up. The soft glow of the dashboard lights illuminated his strong facial features. I couldn't help but stare at the black stubble on his jaw line when he spoke.

"Because most of them are disgruntled with their lives, and they still have enough spirit to go against the governing body. Once they join the church and hook up with their significant others, their will to stand up to authority evaporates right along with their independence. Their spirits are broken with the desire to fit in and not be frowned upon by their peers. At that point, it's next to impossible to get them to deviate from the set of rules and customs. They are terrified to be put in bad graces within their society—it motivates them completely as adults."

"What about you? You left. Why didn't you get dragged in like the rest of them?" I chanced the question.

Daniel sighed and gripped the steering wheel. Staring straight ahead, he said, "I got out in time. They didn't succeed in breaking my spirit or intimidating me into submission, because I fought like a demon. I guess for a while, the demon had a hold of me. But it's gone now."

Daniel had some deep issues. I almost asked him if he meant figuratively or literally about the demon, but I pressed my lips together tightly and kept quiet. I was afraid what his answer would be.

"Do you know what this means?" Daniel asked me, his voice upbeat once again.

"Hmmm?" I mumbled, thinking about how difficult growing up Amish would be.

"That we'll be together again on Monday," Daniel smiled brilliantly.

"Why?"

"You can't show up at the butcher's shop in your police cruiser. You'd give the girl away for sure. If I pick you up and you dress normally and I order some steaks, you'll be able to talk to the girl while she's on her break unnoticed. Trust me. You don't want to get the poor kid into trouble for talking to you about this. You don't want that on your conscience."

"What would they do to her?" I was envisioning torture devises and dungeon cells.

Daniel turned into my drive and I blinked, not believing that the trip was already over. A twinge of depression squeezed my insides. I shook the feeling off, hating myself for even giving a damn.

"She might get sent off to live in another state with family members or to an Amish home for problem children. Or, she could be whipped with a belt. The worst thing would be sitting on the splintery bench in front of the entire congregation while the bishop tells the community what sin she'd committed."

Daniel's voice was angry, as if he were talking from experience. Just when I was going to invite him in and try to find out exactly what made him leave his family, friends and the only life he'd ever known, he said, "Good night, Serenity. I'll pick you up on Monday at ten."

His dismissal brought a fan of warmth across my face. It was clear that Daniel was in need of some time alone to deal with his stirred up emotions at seeing his people again. We all had our inner demons—maybe the demon he thought he'd rid himself of was still lurking about.

"Thanks for helping me out with the investigation. I appreciate it. And I had a good time tonight," I said, holding his gaze for a long second before I shut the jeep's door.

By the time I'd walked into the kitchen, my mood had lifted a couple of notches. There was the real possibility that Sandra would have information that would crack the case wide open, and that was enough to take the sting out of being blown off by the only real crush I'd ever had.

8

NAOMI

September 5th

The stars twinkled brightly in the sky. Naomi tried to imagine what it would be like to be up there among them. She'd heard talk that people had actually flown there on special air planes, but she hardly believed it. It seemed impossible.

Naomi sighed. She knew that this was the only place in the world where she was truly safe. No one would ever guess to look for her in the cornfield. The stalks were tall, and she was thankful for the leafy walls that hid her.

A pocket of cooler air settled over Naomi and she cuddled against Eli's body for warmth. His fingers played with her hair softly and she closed her eyes thinking how nice it felt.

"You know, Naomi, we ought to be setting a date for the wedding, at least in our minds. We don't need to tell no one else about it until later in the summer. That would give your folks time to prepare."

Eli's words caused Naomi to shiver. He hugged her closer, probably believing that she was cold, but that wasn't the problem. The thought of becoming a married woman was the last thing on her mind.

"Oh, I don't know if Dat will allow us to marry so soon. My income from the butcher shop is all that's keeping the family above water right now."

"We can't postpone all our plans because of your parents' financial problems. Your mother works you too hard at the house. And the butcher shop is no place for a woman to be spending her days. Don't you want to be away from all that?"

Eli had lifted up onto his elbow and looked seriously down at Naomi. His worried frown made her feel wanted, but still she hesitated.

"It'll be up to them, won't it?" Naomi said, staring up at the stars again and wishing that she were up there with them.

"No. When we decide to marry, my parents will support us. That'll be enough for yours to go along with it. We just need to get them mentally prepared. That's all."

Naomi sighed, wondering what his big hurry was. They were meeting in the fields at least one night a week and he was getting his need taken care of. True, being away from Mamma's glares and the endless work would be a blessing, but it almost seemed to Naomi that marrying Eli was just trading one prison for another. She'd still be held to the church's Ordnung, and all the rules that went along with it. Was it so wrong to want to be free?

Naomi couldn't bear the thought of Eli being angry with her though. She tried to think of a way to make him realize that marriage wasn't the best thing for them right now.

"Do you have any money saved up, Eli? We've only been courting a month after all." Naomi said as she began buttoning up his shirt for him.

"Father allowed me to start saving more of my money back when we began planting. So together with the money I'll be able to keep once I've told him of the wedding, I reckon we'll have enough to get by on in the beginning."

"Won't you miss being single? You know, hanging out with your buddies and all. Once we're married, you'll have to work all the more to take care of a family," Naomi rushed the words out. She knew that she'd been too hasty when Eli narrowed his eyes and sat up.

"Don't you want to marry me? Is that why you're acting like a skittish colt about it?"

"That isn't it at all. I just don't like change much."

Eli clasped her hands and said, "It will be a good change for you. Just think how nice it will be to take care of your own home, instead of slaving away under your Mother's orders. And you won't have to work at the butcher's shop no more, neither."

Things were moving way too fast. Naomi just wanted it to stop. She knew that if she kept blowing Eli off, he'd quit her for sure and she didn't want that. Her belly tightened as her confused mind tried to straighten her thoughts outs. She didn't know what she wanted. That was the problem. Eli was the perfect Amish guy and all, but her mind kept sliding back to Will and his smoldering dark eyes. A part of her wanted to see what it would be like to be Will's girl and experience life with him. But she wasn't stupid either. He might not be interested in her at all that way. English guys didn't commit to a woman and take care of her until they were older. Should

Naomi risk losing the best guy in the community to chase after an English one, not knowing if it would even work out? Her head ached with it all. She squeezed at the hurt with her hands, wanting to tear it from her brain.

Eli looked at Naomi with frustration. After a moment, he seemed decided and reached down, pulling her up. She melted into his chest, loving how safe she felt in his arms.

"It will be all right, Naomi. I promise." He leaned back a little and lifted her chin with his hand, "Can we tell our folks that we plan to wed in the spring?"

Seeing Eli's eager eyes and knowing deep in her heart that she didn't really have a choice, Naomi said, "Yes, we can tell them."

Eli gave Naomi a bone crushing hug before his mouth slammed into hers. When his lips opened, hers did too and their tongues played together in perfect rhythm. When the two of them were kissing, all doubts and fears slipped away. Maybe things would be okay after all, she thought, just before Eli brought her to the ground again, and she forgot about everything.

Naomi tiptoed across the wooden floor, feeling pretty certain that Mamma and Dat were sound asleep in this deepest part of the night. When the lamp suddenly lit, she swallowed her heart and braced herself for their wrath. Dat held the look of complete shock, while Mamma's round face was more knowing, and more frightening.

"What are you doing, Naomi, with your coat and your shoes on in the dark kitchen?" Dat asked, frozen in place.

"I needed some fresh air. I was feeling a bit ill in the stuffy room." Naomi ignored Mamma and searched Dat's face to see that he relaxed, believing her.

Mamma crossed the room at a speed that was not expected from a woman so round, her hand coming up as if to slap her daughter. Naomi kept her arms at her sides and tightened her face, waiting for the sting. But, instead, Mamma's hand landed with no force on her cheek.

"She's lying—her face is too cold with night air for just a step out. And there," She pointed at Naomi's shoes. "...her shoes are muddied."

Dat approached cautiously, looking at Naomi's feet, but not bothering to touch her. "What mischief have you been up to?" His voice hardened, "Tell me now, for the Lord will know your lies and uncover them to us, if it be His will."

Naomi didn't think that the Lord cared much about what she was doing. At least, He hadn't up until that moment. She knew she couldn't tell them about Eli—that would get them both in trouble. She decided to stick with what usually worked for her; deny, deny, deny.

"I only went for a walk out behind the barn for some air. That's all I done." Naomi said, continuing to look at Dat, instead of Mamma.

"She's lying," Mamma said in a hiss.

"Be quiet, woman. I'll take care of this. You best go back to bed," Dat said in a firm voice that held no room for an argument.

Mamma left the kitchen slowly, her face turned and looking back over her shoulder with each step she took. Naomi lost her breath for a moment when she met that stare. When Mamma disappeared into the darkness of the hallway, Dat

84

went to the cupboard and pulled out the smooth switch. Naomi cringed, remembering the many times the branch had touched the skin of her backside. But even so, she was relieved that it wasn't Mamma rendering the punishment.

"I don't know if you're telling the truth or not, but you know you are not to leave the house during the night for any reason. You will receive two strikes for your disobedience."

Later, when Naomi was lying in the bed and staring at the ceiling, she wished that she was back in the cornfield, the night sky above her. There was only a mild tingle where the switch had wacked her bottom, but the pain of it wasn't the part she hated. It was the demeaning act in itself that made her blood boil. Naomi was no child. She knew that if she were English, she was at an age where she could come and go as she pleased.

The anger inside Naomi continued to grow through the hours of tossing and turning under the sheets, her mind becoming steely and stubborn.

Tomorrow was the night that Will and Taylor wanted to take her to the Fair. The plan was for Naomi to sneak out and meet them a quarter mile up the road where Will's truck would be waiting. They'd stay for a few hours, and then she'd be dropped off at the same place to make her way secretly back to her bedroom.

Up until the moment that she was discovered, her mind was set on telling Will that she couldn't risk doing it, and that she wouldn't be flirting around with him anymore either. Naomi had chosen Eli and married life, the same path of least resistance that all the Amish followed.

But not now—Naomi didn't care if they beat her half to death for it. She would live her life as she saw fit.

9

DANIEL

November 14th

O f course I'd driven through the Amish settlement many times in the years since I'd left, but this day was different. Today, I felt that I could wave at the people I saw, and they might actually raise a hand back to me. The possibility put me in a damn good mood. And that wasn't the only reason I was smiling. Even though I worked hard to give the impression of admiring the beauty of the passing homesteads, my eyes kept drifting to the even prettier picture beside me, raising my spirits even more.

Serenity's hair was down again, framing a face that had little make-up on. Her large, sky blue eyes darted around, studying the Amish homes and watching every buggy that we passed with intensity. Her cheeks were naturally rose hued and they complimented the pink sweater that hugged her shapely breasts.

I turned back to the roadway, not wanting to get all worked up right before we talked to the girl. I'd finally accepted the fact that after years of messing around with all kinds of women, the one beside me was the most enchanting of all. I could imagine making a commitment to a woman like her and maybe, finally settling down, and starting a family. The irony was that settling down was probably the furthest thing from this particular woman's mind.

Pulling up to the metal building with the sign that read Yoder's Butcher Shop in bold, black letters, I cut the engine off and chanced another look at Serenity.

"It's hard to believe that young women work all day cutting up meat in a place like this." Serenity said, craning her neck to see as far around the building as possible.

There was a corral and cattle chute to the one side of the shop and a small loading dock where a meat packing truck was parked on the other. Surveying the scene, I didn't think it looked that bad, but she had a point about the girls.

"There aren't many jobs available for the teenage girls in the community. The butcher shop pays better than the rest, I'd imagine," I said, content that Serenity was keeping her gaze glued to me a little longer.

"What other jobs are the girls allowed to do?" Serenity asked, bringing her leg up under her butt as she turned toward me.

"Rebecca worked at the bird house factory for a while until she got the job babysitting the English kids that lived up the road from us. Some of the other girls I knew stocked shelves at the Amish general store or worked at the bakery. A very few gifted girls assisted the teacher at the school house," I said, enjoying Serenity's full attention. If I breathed deeply, I could smell a warm vanilla scent in the cab. I couldn't help but imagine how intoxicating it would be to have her skin beneath my mouth.

Serenity was thoughtful for a moment. When she finally spoke, it was with some hesitation. Her words cleared my randy thoughts. "Was the reception you received from your family and friends at the school house what you expected it would be?"

Normally, I didn't like talking about my past, especially with women. But strangely, I felt comfortable with the little sheriff. My heart told me that she would not judge me unkindly if I opened up a bit.

"You know, I wasn't sure what to expect. I've known other Amish who left their churches and still remained friendly with their immediate family. But my situation was different. My shunning was from an extremely stubborn and prideful father who wouldn't bend in the slightest to keep up a relationship with his own son."

"You were shunned?" Serenity exclaimed. She leaned in closer with a concerned face.

I had to laugh. My reaction caused her to sit back and frown. "I'm sorry. I forget that you don't know much of anything about the Amish, do you?" When she shook her head, I continued, "Once a person joins the Church, he's committed himself to being a member of the community and following the Church's Ordnung. If someone breaks from the Church and leaves the Amish, the others in the Church have no option but to openly shun that person." Seeing the appalled look on Serenity's face, I controlled a smile, and added, "Don't you see? If people could leave freely, without being shunned, there wouldn't be much incentive to remain Amish, would there?"

"But, that's like, blackmail," Serenity breathed.

"Yeah, but it works. Very few people leave the Amish once they've joined the Church in their community. Sometimes, families will pick up and move to another Amish community, but they are still Amish, so they are not shunned. Leaving all together is a very serious matter."

Serenity paused, her lips pursed. She looked back at me and asked, "If you don't want to tell me, I understand...but why exactly did you leave?"

I glanced at my watch, a luxury I didn't have when I'd been a member of the Plain people. We'd arrived early, having just enough time for me to give Serenity a basic telling of the story. But, did I really want to?

"It's okay. Really, I shouldn't have pried into your personal life," Serenity said, becoming all business-like again. I didn't enjoy seeing the hardening of her features or the way that she now looked out the window at nothing in particular.

"I was like all the other Amish boys, occasionally getting into trouble, but nothing serious." I had her gaze back on me and seeing her face open up again, I was happy to tell her the story. "When I was nineteen, I felt I'd sowed my wild oats. Even though there were many things about the lifestyle I didn't agree with, like not driving cars or listening to music, I was lured in by a pretty Amish girl named Rosetta. The idea of having my own wife and family became very intriguing to me. In a rather short period of time, I was seriously courting Rosetta and planning a wedding."

I paused, looking out the window at the cloud covered sky that hinted of snow in the near future. I remembered that the weather had been similar when all hell broke loose in my life years before. The day that I'd walked away from my Amish life and my family.

"The November that I turned nineteen, just a few months before I was to wed Rosetta, I began a job on a porch on a house in town. I was working on my own while Father and Paul, one of my brothers, worked at another site. The driver would drop me off each day and then leave to taxi my father and Paul to their job. It was the first time that I'd been left entirely alone, and I remember distinctly the joy I'd felt from the solitude of not being constantly watched. Thinking back, if I hadn't been alone, none of it probably would have even happened. But then, I would never have escaped either.

"There was a young woman named Abby who rented the house with several of her girlfriends. She would sit and chat with me the entire day on that porch, bringing me sandwiches and lemonade. I was immediately smitten with her carefree and out going manner. I found myself working extra fast so that I could quit early and spend time walking with the English girl in the park or grabbing a bite to eat at the Diner."

I stopped and saw that Serenity was hanging on my every word. For a brief second, I wanted to end the story, worried about what she'd think of me once she knew. But the expression on her face told me there was no backing out now.

"Within days of meeting the young woman, I was being intimate with her—the first time for me. Maybe it was that she was my first or maybe deep down I didn't want to be Amish. I don't know, but the day I finished the porch, I went home to tell my parents that I'd fallen in love with an English girl and that I wasn't going to marry Rosetta. I was leaving the Amish to be with her."

I glanced at Serenity. She was pressed back into the seat with a thoughtful look on her face. When she spoke, her voice was soft and sweet. "What did your parents say?"

"Father went into a rage and Mother wouldn't speak to me at all. As a matter of fact, she never spoke to me again after that day. Father continued to shout at me the entire time I was packing a few personal belongings and walking out to Abby's waiting car. I was immediately shunned by my family and the other members of the church."

"What exactly does it mean to be shunned?" she asked with eyes wide.

"Different communities handle shunning in their own way, but for ours, it means that you aren't welcome to have a meal with church members any longer, even family. Although parents will sometimes help a child out financially after they've been shunned, they will not receive aid in return. In most cases, as with mine, the parents don't want to corrupt their other children with the rebellious one, so they'll have little or no contact with the shunned child."

"But your sister ate with you at the school house." Serenity said.

"That was different. It was a community event to raise money. The rules are looser in such a situation. She wouldn't invite me to her home for the holidays or her children's birthdays." I probably said it harsher than I should have, but those first few years on my own had been rough, especially for a young man who was used to the close company of a large family.

Serenity asked quietly, "What did Rosetta do?"

My chest tightened. Thinking about Rosetta was always difficult, but talking about her was even worse.

"From the gossip I'd received from Lester afterwards, she was torn up about it for a few months and then she began courting another Amish boy. She married a year later than our intended wedding date." Seeing her lips begin to form words, I guessed what her question would be. "She moved to

Ohio with her husband a few years following their marriage. I haven't seen her since."

Timidly, Serenity asked, "What happened to Abby?"

I wasn't expecting that question. It was the most difficult part to remember. But I'd told Serenity too much already not to finish the story.

"I'd say it was just a month after I'd moved into the house with her that I began pestering her to marry me. Marriage and a family wasn't a goal for her. She had wild oats to sow and I'd become a hindrance to her freedom. One stormy night after I'd begged her not to go out with her friends, she told me she didn't love me—that she'd never loved me." I couldn't keep the bitterness from my tone. "She said she was sorry for fucking up my life, but she wasn't going to do the same to hers. Last I heard she was living in Indianapolis, working as a nurse in a big hospital. That was some ten years ago. I reckon she's finally settled down herself by now."

I stared at Serenity waiting for her to chastise me for being so stupid and impulsive. Instead, she asked, "Do you miss being Amish?"

"Some things I miss, like the sense of community and having people always there to pick you up when you fall. I miss my family. I wish I'd had the chance to know all my nephews and nieces. Now that my parents are getting older, I fear that they'll pass away without us mending fences. But no, I don't miss being Amish. I love my freedom too much now to ever give it up. It's better to have a choice and make a mistake than to have no choice at all."

"But you told the bishop that you were considering joining back up—"

I chuckled at her gullibility. The annoyed frown she shot my way amused me even more. "I knew that if I mentioned that I might be interested in going back, word would spread quickly. People would be more comfortable talking with us. It's not as if I signed a contract in blood saying that I was growing a beard right away."

Serenity was beginning to speak again when I spotted the Amish girl coming out of the building. I shushed her and nodded my head in the girl's direction. Sandra made eye contact for only an instant before she made her way to the side where the corral was set up. It was then that I noticed the picnic table. What a shitty place to eat lunch, I thought.

Without a word, we slipped out of the Jeep and headed toward the table. I stepped up to the corral and leaned against it pretending to look at the two young cows within while Serenity sat down across from Sandra.

"I'm so glad you came. We have to talk quickly. I don't want anyone getting suspicious. If they ask you inside why you stopped to talk me, tell them you wanted directions to Mr. Manley's. He sells venison jerky."

"Okay," Serenity said slowly and I grinned, imagining how her brain was handling the cover up story. "You were a friend of Naomi's?"

"Her best, that's why I'm talking to you like this." Sandra looked around and lowered her voice even further. "Naomi was messing around with an English boy and I think you ought to go talk to him about what happened to her. Maybe he knows something."

Serenity leaned over the table, close to Sandra and said, "What's his name?"

"Will Johnson. He drives a big black pick-up truck. And, he has a sister named Taylor. That's all I got to tell you. You better go now. Please don't say a thing about what I told you. Please?" she begged.

"No, of course not, it'll be our secret." Serenity rose promptly as she was asked to do. I couldn't help but feel sympathy for the Amish girl. Her face was tense as she chewed a bite from her sandwich and stared down at the rough wood of the table.

"Thank you," Serenity told the girl as she passed by, only to be ignored in return.

I was considering asking Serenity to join me for supper that night to dine on the steaks that we were purchasing, but there was clearly something else on her mind. She looked up at me and said, "You better hurry up with the meat, Daniel."

"Why the rush?" I asked, pausing before I reached for the door knob of the shop.

"Because we have to pay Will a visit—now," Serenity said. Her face was masked of all emotion.

"Do you know where to find him?" I figured it would take some time to track the guy down.

"Oh, yeah," Serenity's eyes met mine.

My heart sped up when she said, "He's my nephew."

10

NAOMI

September 6th

The bright colorful lights decorating the amusement rides and the blaring music were overwhelming to Naomi's senses. She took a deep breath, smelling the grilling hamburgers, cotton candy and fried food. Without thinking she smiled up at Will. He returned the smile and reached for her hand, which she gave to him without hesitation. She giggled and bumped her side into his as the warmth of happiness spread through her. With a belly full of funnel cake and fries and a purple stuffed bear clenched tightly under her arm, she could honestly say that she was having the best time of her life.

Glancing down at the jeans and t-shirt she wore, Naomi could hardly believe she was in borrowed clothes from Taylor. Luckily, the girls were about the same size. Naomi had to admit, she felt more self-conscious in the clingy shirt and tight pants than she thought she would. She savored the moment though, knowing that she'd probably never get the chance to dress like an Englisher again.

Flinging her long hair over her shoulder was the strangest part of all. To be out in public with her blond hair bouncing against her back was a real treat.

As if Will was reading her mind, he said, "It must feel awesome to let your hair down."

"You have no idea. But people keep looking at me—maybe it's too long," Naomi said, noticing a middle aged guy eyeing her as they passed in opposite directions.

"Are you kidding me? Any girl would kill for hair like yours. The guys—well, let's just say that men dig long hair." He winked at Naomi, causing another round of butterflies to flutter in her stomach. She glanced away, blushing. Will laughed and squeezed her hand. She tried to keep her mouth still, but she couldn't fight the sensation. She grinned back at him.

"Can we go on that one?" Naomi asked, staring up at the giant wheel in the sky.

"Of, course! You can't go to a Fair without riding the Ferris wheel. I bet we'll be able to see half the county from up there."

Just before it was their turn in line, Will noticed a young girl about to be turned away from a ride because she didn't have enough tickets. Naomi watched as he reached into his pocket and handed the girl how many she needed. The girl thanked him shyly before she sprinted up the ramp to join her friends.

Naomi's cheeks reddened with emotion. She turned away quickly so that Will wouldn't see. His act of kindness had touched her in a way she wasn't expecting. The English boy surprised her at every turn.

Once they were loaded up, they moved a little ways and then stopped while other people got on or off. Naomi was impatient to get moving. She leaned over the edge, marveling at how high they were already.

"Are you afraid of heights?" Will asked.

"I don't know. I've never been up this high before. But so far I just feel really excited."

Will took up her hand again and said, "If you get nervous, just squeeze my hand. You'll be fine."

"Is that all I have to do?" Naomi smiled wickedly at him.

Will laughed, "Well, you're more than welcome to do anything you like."

Naomi felt the heat burn her face just as the wheel began moving with more speed. The quick jolt caused her to press in against Will.

Will's hot breath tickled her ear when he asked, "Are you enjoying yourself?"

"Oh, yes. It's wonderful."

With the light from the nearly full moon illuminating the country side in all directions, Naomi turned her head and searched. Squinting, she could just make out the top of Raymond Schwartz's silo. The sight of its copper tiled roof shining in the distance sent a ripple of tension through her. A mile or so from that silo was her family's farm. She imagined her brothers and sisters fast asleep in their quilt covered beds and hoped that Dat and mother were doing the same. After all, it had been a busy day for everyone, what with Mother baking extra loaves of bread for the mother-to-be Beatrice Miller and Dat and her brothers spending the evening digging a hole to bury the old plow horse who had unexpectedly gone down that morning.

Naomi said a silent prayer that no one woke and went looking for her and then she did her best to erase the worried thoughts. There wasn't anything she could do about it now anyway. She'd already committed sin and she only hoped that God would forgive her.

They went around too many times to count, the warm wind whipping Naomi's hair out behind her until she became dizzy. About the time she wished that the machine would slow, it did.

Naomi breathed out and exclaimed, "Can we ride it again?"

Will was a good sport. He rode all the rides with her twice, to the point that he said if he rode one more he might not be able to drive home. By that time Naomi was hungry again, so Will bought two ice cream cones. They licked them while they wandered through the livestock barns.

The rides were amazing, but seeing all the prize animals was a treat for Naomi too. Will enjoyed petting the wide foreheads of the cows and looking through the wire mesh at the fancy chickens as much as she did. Naomi even had to argue with him not to buy her a fluffy white bunny that she petted. She explained to him that if there was a new critter in the barn in the morning, Father would become suspicious.

"You're eighteen, right?" Will asked as they left the pig barn and headed back toward the midway.

Naomi nodded.

"How do you put up with being treated as if you're a small child all the time? Taylor is fifteen and she has way more freedom than you do. All this sneaking around is insane," he said with an annoyed tone.

Naomi was used to her lack of freedom. Although it did upset her, it was just part of life to her. Seeing Will so bothered by her circumstances made her giggle.

"Are you stressed, Will?"

"Yeah, I am a little. I feel as if I've kidnapped you, instead of taking you on a proper date. I'm worried that you're going to get into deep trouble for this, and it's been on my mind all evening."

Their walking had slowed with the conversation. His words ran through Naomi's mind several times causing her heart to beat rapidly. She grabbed his arm, stopping him.

"Did you say, proper date?" Naomi stammered.

Will eyed her with a slight smile, as if he knew a secret that she didn't. "Uh, that's what you usually call an evening like this...a date."

Naomi was both elated and horrified. She pictured Eli's face and guilt crashed over her. He was the guy she was going to marry come springtime, not Will. But the entire night with Will had been so magical. She couldn't deny that she had strong feelings for the young English man. And not just lust either. She really liked everything about Will. He had a joyful, fun loving spirit that was contagious. And he'd proved that he was kind too.

"Will, this has been the most wonderful night of my life. But I already have a boyfriend, you know that," she said, staring at the ground, unable to face him.

He lifted her chin and said, "That doesn't matter. It's not as if you're married yet. You can still change your mind. I'm going to do everything in my power to make you do just that."

KAREN ANN HOPKINS

Naomi's mouth dropped open in wonder. Just as Will's lips brushed hers, Taylor's voice shrieked through the air. Naomi pulled back abruptly. Will just smiled, as if to say, I told you so.

"There you two are! I've been looking everywhere for you guys." Taylor skidded to a stop and then looked back and forth between Naomi and Will.

"You've got great timing, sis," Will joked, tugging a handful of Taylor's hair playfully.

"Hmmm, well, I don't know about that. I wanted to tell you that I'm going home with Meghan tonight. Her mom says that it's okay," Taylor paused, and as if a light bulb had just blinked on in her head, she stared at Naomi with wide eyed curiosity.

"Did you talk to mom about it?" Will asked in a stern voice that Naomi hadn't heard him use before.

"Course I did. She says its fine with her. You two be good and don't do anything I wouldn't do," Taylor winked at Naomi and then jogged away.

"She's an irritating little creature, but the only sibling I've got, unlike you. Did you say that you have eight brothers and sisters all together?"

"Yes. And, since most of them are boys, except for the littlest ones, I have to do all their laundry." Naomi pushed the thought quickly away, wanting laundry as far from her mind as possible.

"You have to use one of those old fashioned hand ringers, don't you?" Will asked. His face wrinkled in disgust. They were slowly approaching his truck in the parking area and Naomi dragged her feet, not wanting to go home yet.

"Yes, it's awful."

"Why do you do it then?" Will asked as he held the truck door open for her.

Naomi climbed in and turned to him. "Because I don't have a choice," she said.

The ride through town was silent. Naomi filled with depression at the thought that she wouldn't see Will again until the following week. Making her heart even heavier, she knew that there wouldn't be any more nights like this to look forward to either. She had to stop her feelings for Will from growing any stronger. She was marrying Eli and she had better start acting like it. Naomi inwardly scolded herself.

Will parked in the pull-off that sat conveniently in a copse of trees at the side of the road. They were still a couple of miles from the farm. Naomi hastily changed back into her dress in the back seat while Will stood outside, facing the trees. Her heart was pounding by the time she shoved Taylor's clothes into the plastic bag and climbed into the front seat again.

"I'm done," Naomi spoke through the small opening at the top of the window. She immediately began coiling her hair up. The droning calls of the frogs in the ditch made her feel isolated from the rest of the world. She wasn't afraid though or even uncomfortable to be completely alone with Will. Somehow it just felt right.

When Will was settled in the driver's seat, he watched Naomi work with her hair. He said with a sigh, "It's a shame that you have to hide your beautiful hair."

Naomi paused with a bobby pin in her mouth. "You think my hair is beautiful?" she said.

"Of course I do."

She had just got her cap in place and was about to tell Will that he could start the engine, when he said in a distant voice, "I bet you'd like Montana. I went out there on vacation when I was thirteen with my family. It was the most amazing place

I'd ever been to. The land is so wild looking, yet inviting. And the mountains are incredible. After spending my entire life in the flatlands, I can really appreciate seeing mountain tops with snow on them."

"Are your parents unhappy that you're going way out there?" Naomi hadn't been thinking about Will's trip lately. Somehow, she'd hoped he wouldn't be going now that he was her friend. She inwardly chastised herself. What a silly thing to think.

"No. They'll miss me, and Taylor's been giving me fits about it, but Mom and Dad want me to be happy. They know how important roping is to me. They'll support me fully in going out west and trying to make a name for myself." He looked at Naomi and grinned. "I have big plans. I'm going to become a successful team roper. With my earnings, I'm going to buy me a small ranch out there where I'll train horses and sell them."

"You are so lucky that you can do whatever you want to do and that your parents will still love you." Naomi slumped down into the seat, imagining what her parents would do if she told them that she was moving away to follow her dreams. It wouldn't be pretty.

Will's face was tight with concern when he leaned over and said softly, "I'm sure they'd still love you, even if you didn't do exactly what they wished of you."

Naomi couldn't help the tears that suddenly appeared in her eyes. She tried to wipe them away, but it was too late. Will had seen. He pulled her into his arms and held her as they sat parked alongside the quiet country road.

Her tears were making Will's shirt wet. She sucked in the sob, saying, "You don't understand. You can't understand.

Your life is completely different than mine. I have no choices about anything. If I don't do as they say, I'll be shunned. And, then I'll be completely alone."

"You'll never be alone, Naomi. I'll be with you," Will said, just before his mouth finally found hers.

Their kiss was frantic and tender at the same time. It would be the only time Naomi would be in Will's arms and she didn't want it to ever end. Will wiped away the tears from Naomi's wet cheeks with his own face, and the pricks of his tiny stubble sharpened Naomi's senses even further.

She would live in the moment. That's all she could do.

"I believe you," Naomi murmured into his mouth.

11

SERENITY

November 14th

I was glad that Daniel was driving. My heart raced as fast as my toes tapped the floor board. What the hell had Will gotten himself into this time? I knew that my nineteen year old nephew wasn't a murderer, but I worried about the implications that his possible relationship with the dead girl could do to him. I thought about the baby. Was it Will's?

"Are you close to your nephew?" Daniel's voice startled me. For once, I was so distracted, I'd completely forgotten about him.

I looked over to see his interested face going back and forth from the road to me. "Yeah, real close. Will and his sister, Taylor, used to spend almost every weekend with me when they were younger. Then they hit their teen years and became too busy to hang out with their aunt as much."

"You didn't know anything about him dating an Amish girl?" Daniel asked with hesitation.

"Hell no! The last girl he brought around me was a couple of years ago. I didn't like her much—too many facial piercings. I've been so busy lately with the election and settling into the new position that I've hardly seen any of my family. I'm sure my sister is pissed at me that I haven't been over for the usual Sunday dinners, and now I'm kicking myself about it."

"Why?"

"If I'd been around more, I probably would have picked up that something was going on with Will. He's a gentle spirited person and his emotions show through clearly when you're paying attention. Of course, since my brother-in-law owns his own automotive center and my sister being the receptionist, secretary, and accountant for the business, they're both as busy as I am. I should have known something was up though, when I heard that Will postponed his trip to Montana."

"He was going to Montana?"

I motioned for Daniel to turn into my sister's driveway. The two story brick colonial blasted suburban success, but I knew that Ryan and Laura didn't get to enjoy the fruits of their labor much with their hectic schedules.

"It's been his dream for a while. He has a couple of Quarter Horses that he boards at Whispering Pines' Stables. He was taking his horses out west to compete in roping events at the rodeos."

Daniel's face lit up. "Really? I have three horses myself, but I don't have as much time to ride as I'd like. What a spectacular opportunity for him."

Clutching the door, I said, "Yeah, let's hope he hasn't screwed it all up for himself."

I didn't knock. Instead, I let myself in the side doorway of the garage that wasn't locked and then went into the house.

"Gee, I guess you and sister are pretty tight? Or, is that you're the sheriff and can go anywhere you like?" Daniel asked with his eyebrow raised.

"Yep, Laura and I are super close. I lived here for a few months when I first moved back to Blood Rock. It was so comfortable that I hated to leave, but I needed my own space."

When I glanced back at Daniel, he was looking at me thoughtfully and my pulse rushed. I turned away quickly and set my purse down on the kitchen counter. Going to the fridge, I pulled out two colas and handed Daniel one before I sat down at the kitchen table.

Daniel followed suit, taking the chair beside me, saying, "Do you know when he'll be home?"

"Oh, he's here now, asleep upstairs. Will's not a morning person. He's taking a few college classes in the evening and spends the rest of his time riding and working afternoon odd jobs."

"How on earth would he have met up with Naomi?" Daniel asked before he took a swig from his bottle.

"I don't know. Like I said, I haven't spent much time with the family lately. I'm out of the loop," I said, pulling my phone out of my pocket and pressing a number.

"Who are you calling?"

"Will." I put the phone to my ear. When my nephew answered groggily, I said, "I'm in the kitchen. You have two minutes to get your butt down here or I'm coming up." I smiled at Daniel's surprised face.

"It works every time," I said, taking a drink myself.

It was probably a little under a minute when we heard the thumps of footsteps coming down the stairs. When Will turned the corner, his hair was messy and he was wearing sweat pants and an AC/DC vintage t-shirt that probably had belonged to my brother-in-law.

"What's up, Aunt Rennie?" Will said, flopping down at the table and running a hand through his tussled hair. His eyes were red rimmed and swollen. If I didn't have the suspicion that my nephew had been crying, I'd have chewed him out for partying the night before.

"Did you know Naomi Beiler?" I didn't mean for my words to be harsh, but the way he reacted, they must have hit the poor kid as if I'd thrown a ton of bricks at him.

Will's eyes bulged, and then his face was in his hands trying to hide the flow of tears. I got up like a bullet out of a barrel and wrapped my arms around him. He let go of his face and held onto me for dear life. I used to hug him the same way when he was a kid, but now, his body was quite a bit bigger than mine, and it was a little awkward. Especially with Daniel sitting there watching us. I met his eyes and I saw sympathy there, and something else that I couldn't quite identify.

After a few minutes, Will quieted and I pulled back, leaving him for a second to grab a clean dish towel. I handed it to him and situated my chair close to his. The thought occurred to me that Will's show of grief was what I expected to see from Naomi's family, but had been completely absent. Even with all the sorrow in the room, my heart lifted a fraction thinking that at least someone was mourning the girl's death—I just wished it wasn't my nephew. His outburst wiped away any doubt I'd had that he knew the Amish girl.

"Will, come on now, and dry it up for a minute. I need to talk to you about this. It's very important that you tell me everything regarding your relationship with Naomi. And, I mean *everything*."

"I'm so glad to finally get it out in the open," Will sniffed, and surged on, "It's been driving me crazy to pretend that everything was all right when I was dying inside. Taylor's been a Godsend, since she loved Naomi too. But it wasn't the same for her—and she's a better actor than I am."

"Taylor is involved in all this?" I nearly squealed.

Will met my gaze and said, "Yeah. She was the only other person who knew about me and Naomi."

"No, Will. She wasn't. One of Naomi's friends, a girl by the name of Sandra, knew too. She's the one who tipped me off to you…and she thinks that you had something to do with Naomi's death," I said softly and slowly, wanting the words to sink into his skull.

He breathed in and then rushed the words out, "That's totally insane. I loved Naomi. I was going to take her away from the shitty life she was living. She was going to Montana with me, Aunt Rennie. I was picking her up that night she was killed, to take her away from here."

Damn. I took a deep breath and tried to process what he'd just said. When Daniel's voice filled the air, I snapped my head to look at him at the same time Will did.

"How did you ever get involved with an Amish girl in the first place?" Daniel asked, in a sensible voice.

"Who the hell is he?" Will asked.

"This is Daniel Bachman. His construction company put the new roof on my house last year. He's helping me out with the investigation, because he used to be Amish."

Daniel said, "I wish we could have met under happier circumstances, Will."

Will sat and studied Daniel for a few seconds before he said, "Yeah, me too." He sighed, stretching his long legs out in front of him and leaning back, "I began driving for some of the Amish to make extra cash during the summer. I had one particular run that I made in the mornings, picking up several girls and dropping them off at the butcher shop. I'd return in the afternoon for them. Naomi was one of those girls, and well, we sort of hit it off. Even with those horrible clothes, she was so beautiful. And she was really sweet too." Will wiped his eyes again with the towel. I let him collect himself for a minute before I plowed on.

"Exactly how close were you and Naomi? You know what I mean." I hated asking, but it was better to get the question over with quickly.

My nephew stared down at the glazed, tiled floor, and toyed with the towel in his hand. When he finally spoke, his voice was resigned. "As close as two people can get."

I sighed, catching the look of sympathy Daniel was sending me. It was strange to have a man whom I barely knew sitting there in my sister's kitchen, during a family crises and privy to everything. Yet, for all its strangeness, I felt perfectly all right with it.

"Do you know if Naomi was involved with any of the Amish boys?" I said.

Will made a huffing noise. "Oh, yeah. She was supposed to marry one of them."

At the same time, both Daniel and I said, "What?"

Daniel shook his head and motioned me to continue, which I did. "Are you sure that she was engaged?"

"Yeah, the wedding was set for spring, but they hadn't told anyone about it yet, except the parents," Will said in a voice still heated in anger.

Daniel spoke up, "They wouldn't speak of it to anyone else in the community. Amish wedding are usually kept secret until a couple of months before the wedding day. Only the immediate family would have known."

"Will, do you know the guy's name?" I said, holding my breath.

"Eli. Eli Bender," He said.

I looked to Daniel, who said, "Bender is a common name in the community, but I know Joseph Bender would be the right age to have a teenage son."

"Then that's where we go first," I said feeling more settled that there was another young man out there, other than my nephew, that might be the father of the unborn child.

"Why? Do you think he had something to do with her death? I read that it was an accident—a hunter that might never have known he hit her."

"Conveniently, our local newspaper chose to print its own theory," I said.

"Aunt Rennie, you're going to find the guy that did this, aren't you?" Will's voice was adult now, but it rang in my ears the same as the little kid he used to be, when he expected me to make everything all better.

But this wasn't a scrape from the pavement that I could bandage for him. My nephew was at real risk for being implicated in Naomi's death. And then there were the ramifications to my career I had to think about. I'd have to be very careful to walk a tight line on the investigation now that Will was involved. Mayor Johnson had been helpful and friendly thus far, but that could change in a heartbeat. The elderly man had served on and off as Blood Rock's Mayor for thirty years. He was an expert at making problems that would tarnish the small town's image disappear—along with the people involved. Once Tony's illicit affairs in the city came into the open, Mayor Johnson had thrown his support behind me in the election. But I wasn't fooled by his current friendliness. He'd shove me under a bus if he thought it'd benefit the town.

"I'm sure going to try, but there's a lot at stake here. You've done a good job keeping this secret up until now…and you're going to have to stay silent for a while longer. Don't discuss this matter with anyone outside of the family until I give you the go-ahead." I took a breath and spilled the words before I could change my mind, not procrastinating any longer. "Naomi was about six weeks pregnant. Is there a possibility that the child was yours?"

Will's eyes went wide with shock before he answered, "I was careful. I was, but maybe, I don't know—it could have been mine."

I stayed another half hour consoling my nephew, while Daniel blended into the room. He was so quiet and unassuming I almost forgot he was there. By the time we walked out the door into the bland sunlight of late autumn, I had convinced Will to tell his parents everything. We weren't Amish, and there was no need for them not to know about his relationship with Naomi. He'd done nothing wrong. And since I was coming back to the house after work to help Will along with the discussion, I'd explain to them the need to stay quiet about it until I'd found out more information. Will needed the support of his family right now more than ever, and that was a priority to me.

KAREN ANN HOPKINS

When we turned onto the roadway, I told Daniel, "You can drop me off at the department. I have some work to do. I won't be able to fit in a visit with every Bender family in the community *and* have my family pow-wow later this afternoon."

"When do you want to go looking for Eli?" Daniel asked, glancing at me for a second before turning back to the road.

"If it works for you, I'd like to go tomorrow morning."

"Okay," Daniel said awfully quickly. I turned to look at him.

"Are you sure I'm not keeping you from building things?" I teased.

"I have a reliable crew, and it's fairly slow right now. Don't worry about me. You've got me tied up with Naomi Beiler's death now. I'll stick with it until we find out what happened to her."

"Thanks, Daniel," I said, thinking again how I wished I knew how to flirt with a gorgeous guy.

"You're welcome." He paused and looked back at me with determination, throwing me off for a second. "Do you have any plans for dinner?"

I absorbed his words, saying them again in my mind to make sure I understood him.

"Why, do you?" I said.

"Actually, I do. I plan to grill a couple of these steaks I bought today, and I was hoping you'd help me eat them." He smiled crookedly for a second and then looked back at the road. When I didn't immediately answer, he added, "I think I have some red wine at the house too. After today's revelations, you could probably use a drink."

It took only a second more to decide. What the hell, you only live once. And, as poor Naomi proved, you never knew how long you have either.

"I don't have much of an appetite, but you're right about the drink. I definitely could use one today."

"So we have a date?" Daniel asked. We were stopped at a light and he was staring at me, waiting for me to acknowledge what I'd already said, which didn't make any sense. I rationalized in my head that even though he had said the word *date*, he couldn't have meant it like a real date. I just wasn't that damn lucky.

To appease him and get his eyes back on the road now that the light had changed, I said, "Yes, we do."

Daniel's focus shifted back to driving, but I could see that he was trying very hard to tighten his lips from a smile that was threatening to spread. He obviously was quite satisfied that he'd managed to charm another female. The thought that he might actually be sincere was pretty far from my mind.

All I could come up with was that the world was unpredictable—as poor Naomi had discovered.

12

NAOMI

September 19th

Naomi's thoughts drifted back to when Will caressed her hand before she got out of the truck on Friday afternoon. The touch had sent a jolt though her belly that even now, just thinking about it was reawakened. Guiltily, she glanced over at Eli, who was waiting for her look. He smiled sweetly, before turning back to the bishop's sermon.

The drone of Bishop Esch's voice lulled Naomi's mind, the boredom feeling like the torture of a thousand hands pushing her under the surface of a summer warm pond. Her eyes fluttered and drooped. For an instant, she experienced the freedom of blissful unconsciousness before the jab into her ribs jolted her awake. She didn't even bother to look her grandmother's way, already picturing the deep frown etched on Mammi's wrinkly face. Instead, she turned her attention back to the men's benches, catching David Lapp's gaze just before his head went swiftly straight again.

She sighed and pressed the pebbly fabric of her dress on her lap flat. Why wouldn't he just give it up, she wondered? He was an annoying one for sure—always spying on her with that look of longing that would disappear as soon as she met his eyes. She had no interest in him, she never had. Couldn't he see that as plainly as the cap on her head? It wasn't that David was bad to look at, more that her eyes passed through him uncontrollably. He certainly didn't have the strong, confident manner that Eli owned, or the easy going, friendly way of Will. David Lapp was just too darn emotional and it would take a special girl to put up with him.

Just as the thought entered her mind, Naomi noticed that Sandra, who was sitting directly in front of her, had tilted her own head subtly enough to also gaze in David's direction. When Naomi glanced between the two, she was shocked to see that they were indeed looking at each other. She let out a soft breath at the revelation and sank down on the bench. A part of her was happy that her friend had finally taken an interest in a guy, but the other side wondered about how desperate Sandra must be to even consider the oldest Lapp boy. Naomi decided that she would have to be extra careful of the words she spoke to Sandy on the matter. As the sermon continued, she tried to recall any unkind thing she might have said about David in Sandy's presence, becoming increasingly worried that the coolness that Sandy had shown her recently might be an indication that she'd offended her.

Although she wasn't listening much, the bishop's words occasionally broke through the imaginary wall she'd built to keep him out. His words were about surrendering self-will. Naomi certainly wasn't feeling like surrendering at all lately.

More and more, her dreams were filled with visions of Will, and not Eli. She feared what the future held, and she couldn't help shake the feeling that she had no control over what would happen next.

Little fingers brought her attention down as Emma crawled onto her lap. Naomi pulled the toddler up and pressed her close. Her little sister smelled fresh and soapy from the bath that she'd given her that morning. Naomi breathed her in, relishing in a scent that made her feel grounded for a moment.

The church service dragged on for another hour, before the congregation joined together in the last hymn. The men's voices from the other side of the aisle were the loudest throughout the soulful tune. When the song trailed off to silence, everyone started rousing from the benches, stretching their sore limbs as they moved. Naomi followed Mammi Beiler out into the bright sunshine with Emma's small hand snuggly in her own.

Feeling the soft tap of fingers on her arm, she slowed to find Sandra behind her. Even without her speaking, Naomi knew her friend wasn't feeling well. Sandy's paler than normal complexion and hand over her belly told her what Sandy would say before the words left her mouth.

"My brother is taking me home. I've had a tummy ache all morning and I'm afraid I'll be sick in front of everyone if I stay," Sandra said.

"Hope you feel better soon," Naomi told her before she turned to catch up with her grandmother. Even though Mam was really old, Naomi still had to stretch her legs to walk with the woman.

Before Naomi got very far into Esther Lapp's kitchen, Mamma appeared and passed her littlest sister, Beth, into her arms as she walked by. She went out the door to who knew where without a word or a backwards glance. Since Beth was only a year old, she received the most of what little affection Mamma had available. That's one of the reasons Naomi found herself mothering little Emma so much—she was the forgotten baby. Naomi glanced down to see Emma's lips pursed and trembling.

"No fussing little one, come along, you can help me with the sandwiches," Mammi said to the child, picking up her tiny hand. Mammi winked at Naomi as she crossed to the counter where a couple of the other older women worked to prepare the after-service meal.

Naomi made her way to the sink where Lydia and Melinda were filling cups of water. She shifted Beth's weight firmly onto her hip bone as she joined them. Lydia's eyes widened when she saw Naomi and immediately she whispered something into Melinda's ear.

Naomi ignored them. It was the same as usual. She'd always been treated as if she was an outcast by the other girls, but usually Sandra was by her side to help take the sting out of it. She wished that her friend hadn't gone home with a belly ache, leaving Naomi alone to face her tormentors. Deep down, she knew they were just jealous, but knowing that didn't make it any easier.

Lydia turned to Naomi with a fake smile, and said in a loud whisper, "It sure seems like Will Johnson has taken a liking to you, Naomi—the way he always insists on dropping you off last, even though he has to double back to get to town that way."

Just as Naomi's heart was dropping into her gut and the blood was draining from her face, Melinda added, after a quick look around for listeners, "I guess Eli Bender isn't enough for you, huh?"

Naomi swallowed down the spit that had gathered in her throat, and straightening her back, said, "I don't know what you're talking about, but you best not go spreading lies."

Lydia raised one of her eye brows sharply, "What are you going to do about it? Especially, since it's true that Will Johnson is after you."

Naomi took a step closer to Lydia, who leaned back into the side of porcelain sink with no place to go. She was ready to give her an earful when suddenly Mervin Lapp was at Naomi's side. The fifteen year old boy's chest was puffed out the same as a rooster.

"It isn't Naomi's fault if some English driver likes her," Mervin said, looking straight at Lydia and avoiding Naomi's shocked eyes.

Mervin spent quite a bit of time at the Beiler's place, hanging out with Naomi's younger brothers, so she knew him well. But for the boy to stick his neck out for her with the other girls was not expected, to say the least. He'd just proven that he had the forceful nature that his brother, David, lacked, and Naomi gazed at him with fresh eyes. Mervin may have the same straw colored blond hair that David had, but where David's eyes were a liquid blue that always seemed on the verge of tears, Mervin had green ones that were like shiny springtime grass. And Mervin's gaze didn't shy away when Naomi looked at him the way David's did.

"Why aren't you out playing with the little boys, Mervin?" Lydia said tartly.

"I just came in for water, not a cat fight," Mervin replied, placing his hands on his hips.

Mervin's voice was more mature than Naomi had ever heard before, and for the first time, she noticed that he'd grown taller than her without her realizing it. Even with the peppering of freckles on his smooth face, it was obvious that young Mervin was growing up, and after his display of bravery, Naomi reckoned he'd be a fine man someday.

Lydia picked up the tray of filled cups and without a sideways glance at Naomi, or Mervin, she slid past them and out the door with Melinda close on her heels.

Naomi turned to Mervin and said, "Gee, thanks, Mervin. You didn't have to risk Lydia's wrath like that by sticking up for me."

Mervin's gaze settled on Naomi's face for a second too long, and then she understood. Mervin had a crush on her, the same as his older brother. Of course, David had never come to her rescue the way Mervin had.

Before the boy spoke, he looked down at the wooden floor and shuffled his feet. "It was nothing. Those two are just jealous of you. You shouldn't let it bother you."

"Oh, it doesn't," Naomi frowned, "but I do worry about what might happen if they keep talking about that nonsense and some of the adults start to believe."

"Truth always prevails. At least, that's what Dat says," Mervin said with the sureness of someone far beyond his years.

Naomi watched him fill his water bottle. After a nod and a half smile her way, he headed out of the kitchen. She worked on the rest of the cups with Beth on her hip, the baby's fingers coiled around the strings of her bonnet.

At dinner, Naomi sat with her family trying not to look sullen. But she didn't think that she succeeded if the funny faces Eli kept making at her from a table away were any indication.

Just looking at Eli sent a stab of worry coursing through her. What if Lydia or Melinda said something to Eli about Will's attentions toward her? She would be dead for sure.

Sometime in the middle of the dinner, Mamma showed up and took Beth out of Naomi's arms. She was happy that she'd be able to finish her meal for a change and she tried to stop fretting about everything and do just that. The homemade peanut butter sandwiches, which were the usual for the plain Sunday meal, were sweet and salty at the same time. Since the Amish strictly practiced the bible's instruction that Sunday was to be a day without labor, the sandwiches, which could be made up the day before were the perfect choice. There was also the tradition of the simple fare on the holy day, and tradition was of utmost importance to her people.

Naomi brooded and chewed and swallowed until most everyone was finished before she finally got up. With little energy, she did what was expected and helped the other girls clean the dinner plates off of the tables.

Lydia and Melinda didn't say another word to Naomi, but several times they giggled and whispered between glances her way. How Naomi wished Sandra was there to distract her.

The nudge on her shoulder was unexpected and she swiveled to see Eli smiling down at her. He nodded toward the doorway. After a quick glance around to see that none of the adults were paying her any mind, she began to follow Eli. But before she escaped the building, her gaze was drawn to David, who leaned against the wall beside the doorway. Her body chilled at his scrunched up face. For the first time ever, he didn't look away when their eyes met. Instead he stared at her with open hostility.

Naomi didn't shy away from his glare. She narrowed her eyes and tightened her lips when she looked back at him. For a few seconds there was a standoff, each silently willing the other to look away first. In the end, it was David's face that turned. Naomi exhaled in victory and swept outside into the warm, fresh air.

She blocked David face from her mind. He was of no consequence to her. He'd have to get over whatever problem he had on his own. She had too many of her own issues to deal with. Again, the thought of how different the two Lapp brothers were entered her mind. How could one be so sweet, caring and brave, while the other was such an awful dolt?

Catching sight of Eli more than a dozen steps ahead of her, Naomi stretched her legs. He was walking briskly, but he glanced back every few steps to make sure that she was with him.

Naomi's mind fluttered with confused thoughts as she wondered what Eli was up to. He certainly seemed to have a plan as he made his way past the small groups of teenagers talking along the walkway.

When they left the people, buggies, and hitched horses behind, Naomi's mind started to fill with uneasiness. She searched the area with wide eyes, checking to see if anyone was watching them. But the coast was clear.

The breeze stirred the leaves on the tree at the corner of the shed, sending a rustling sound into the air. Eli turned the corner around the tree and disappeared. For a last time, Naomi looked back, before she disappeared behind the shed too.

A second later, Naomi was pulled tightly against Eli's chest, sniffing in the smell of his cologne and feeling safe in his arms. When Eli and Naomi were like that, she almost didn't think about Will.

"What's wrong with you today, Naomi? You've been pouting all day and you've hardly even looked my way either," Eli said, frowning down at her.

"Nothing, really, I'm fine," Naomi lied.

Eli lowered his head and his mouth sought hers. Softly, his tongue pushed into Naomi's mouth and for a few seconds, she was content enough, until he pulled back, frowning even deeper.

"Now, I know something's up. Your kisses are just as depressing as you are. Naomi, tell me what's wrong," Eli begged, as he leaned back against the barn boards, his arms crossed in front of his chest.

If it had been Will, Naomi would have told him in a heartbeat about the treatment from the other girls, but she couldn't say a thing about it to Eli. If he knew that an English driver was flirting with her, he'd stir up all sorts of trouble. Naomi thought quickly and told him something true that would suffice.

"Mamma's been worse than ever lately. She's always so depressed. Napping most of the afternoons away, and when I get home from the butcher shop, I usually end up having to make dinner." Naomi sighed and went into his arms, laying her face against his heart. "Guess I'm just tired is all."

"Don't worry, by spring you'll be out of there and we'll be starting our life together." He brought his face down close to her ear and said, "I've got good news for you, darling."

Naomi pulled back a little and looked up at him. "What news?"

"I talked to Mother and Father, and they're thrilled with our plans. They said we can stay in the guest room until we're ready to make it on our own." The smile on his face was so

full and genuine. Naomi wondered how she could be thinking about kissing Will Johnson all the time, when she had a
wonderful man like Eli ready to take care of her for life. She
felt drearier than ever, but she tried to put on an act for Eli,
and forced a smile back at him.

"That's wonderful, Eli. I feel my spirit lifting already,"
Naomi lied.

He believed her, and satisfied, he lowered his head again,
touching her lips with his. Naomi mumbled into his mouth,
"Aren't you worried someone will catch us?"

"I don't care anymore. You need me today—and I need
you," he said, his mouth becoming more aggressive and hers
taking up the challenge.

Eli's optimism was contagious and for a moment Naomi
forgot about everything else. She enjoyed the feel of his body
pressed against hers and the rhythm of their tongues dancing. But the bliss was short lived.

"What are you two doing?" the angry voice of James Hooley
called out from under the tree.

Eli's head popped up and he stepped away from Naomi
in a hurry. She felt very much alone as she stood there, the
throbbing of Eli's kisses still on her lips, and Mr. Hooley's disgusted look fastened on her.

"It was just for a minute, Mr. Hooley. I needed to talk to
Naomi alone about something important." Eli took a step forward, his voice anxious with fear.

"You weren't talking to her. I saw you two kissing with my
own eyes, I did." Mr. Hooley motioned for them to join him
under the tree. Eli marched forward quickly, while Naomi
dragged along, taking her own sweet time. She was in no
hurry for what was to come.

"We're going up to talk to your parents and Aaron right now," Mr. Hooley said in a stern voice that left no room for begging.

Eli walked beside Mr. Hooley and Naomi followed a few steps behind, grateful for the cover that their bodies gave her from the curious eyes of everyone they passed. When they reached the house, Mr. Hooley asked them to remain outside while he fetched the important people and dismissed the others from the house.

Minutes later, Naomi was seated on a plush chair in Ester's living room. Eli sat across the room on the couch, flanked on one side by his father and the other his mother. Naomi's parents chose to remain standing near the doorway. Naomi watched Joseph and Katherine's facial expressions as they were told that their son had been making out behind the old shed. Joseph seemed annoyed, but Katherine hid a smile in her hands. Naomi's parents, on the other hand, were seething with Mr. Hooley's words, especially Mamma, who looked at her daughter with hatred.

"Ach, why do the young disobey?" Bishop Esch said to the room, his hands spread out, his voice controlled. He looked from Eli to Naomi and back again, before settling finally on Naomi. "This is a serious matter. We have rules in place to save the virtue of our young people and keep them in line with the Lord's will. When the rules are broken, the sinners must be punished." The bishop took a breath and asked, "What do you have to say for yourself, Eli?"

The bishop shifted his gaze to Eli, and Eli, not having a brave heart, lowered his head and said, "I'm sorry, Bishop. I know we did wrong. My intention was to talk to Naomi, but I was tempted and could not resist. Please forgive us."

Naomi looked at the faces of everyone in the room. Eli's admission of guilt had done the trick. Their expressions had all softened at his words.

The bishop breathed out with satisfaction before he locked his eyes on Naomi and asked the same question. Naomi wasn't sure where the anger came from, but it bubbled into her throat, burning as she swallowed. Maybe it was the pure loathing Mamma was shooting her way, or perhaps it was the nastiness she had to deal with from the other girls on a regular basis. Wherever it came from, it came with a vengeance as she spoke to the bishop. "We we're only kissing. That's all. No one was touching anything and all of our clothes were on. We're eighteen years old. We shouldn't have to apologize for a little bit of kissing."

The silence in the room was louder than the birds chirping outside of the window or the children's laughter in the yard. The shocked faces of the adults, Naomi could deal with, but the way Eli looked at her, with disappointment, made her wish that she'd controlled her temper. Now, she'd really messed things up for them.

"Young lady, your attitude of defiance is beyond unacceptable. How your parents choose to punish you in their home is up to them, but from the church, you will receive several hours of counseling from me and the other ministers," here he paused thinking, and then continued, "...plus four weeks of shunning to begin after your sins are announced before the church members next Sunday. I pray that your heart will be opened and you will be filled with the will of God during this time of separation."

The words swirled around in Naomi's head. Somehow, she didn't see the faces of the others, she didn't need to.

Naomi already guessed that Katherine's would hold pity; Mr. Hooley's would be content, and the bishop's, resolved. Dat and Mr. Bender would still hold a mixture of shock and disappointment, and Eli's would be sad. The hair tingled on her neck when she thought of Mamma. She would be spitting mad. Naomi was sure that if she looked real close she'd see horns popping out of her mother's head.

Naomi barely even heard the bishop make the announcement of Eli's punishment, which was only two weeks of shunning, since he'd been contrite about his sins. Well, good for Eli. She guessed that if he was willing to sink to his knees, he should be rewarded. Of, course, part of the shunning meant that Eli and Naomi wouldn't be able to see each other during those weeks either. She was sure that Eli would be pained for that part...so maybe he was still being punished as severely as her in a way too. The bishop was going to make a lesson of Naomi for all the other young people of the community. And she knew that when she finally arrived home that evening, she'd get the whipping of her life with the switch that she was so well acquainted with. Even for all that, Naomi still felt lighter than she had all day long. They could all do what they wanted to her—she didn't care.

In the end, she'd find her freedom somehow.

13

DANIEL

November 14th

Through the table, I could feel the vibrations of Serenity's foot tapping the floor and I wondered how the woman could be nervous eating dinner with me when she spent her life apprehending criminals. Surely, I was pretty tame in comparison.

Again, I tried to catch her gaze, but she studied her steak so intently that I thought maybe she was trying to figure out the breed of cow it had come from. Suddenly, she looked up and said, "Why do you think Sandra was so hell bent on telling me about Will, and yet she failed to mention the Eli Bender boy completely?"

She had a point and I'd already been thinking about it myself. But dammit, couldn't Serenity stop being the sheriff for a moment and just be a woman having dinner with a man who found her highly attractive?

I sighed and leaned back. Obviously, this night wasn't going in the direction I had hoped it would.

Resignedly, I said, "I believe Sandra told you who she thought had a hand in the death of her friend. She's just a kid, Serenity. She's not looking at all the angles the way that we are."

"But why didn't Timothy and Patricia tell me about Eli when I asked them? What are they hiding?" she leaned in, daring me to give her an answer.

I could see where she was heading with her train of thought, but I couldn't buy it myself. Timothy and Patricia were good, honest people. Patricia may have her problems, but she wouldn't cover up for a person who might have killed her daughter.

"You need to understand that these people aren't going to rattle off every bit of information you want. They are secretive and suspicious of the outside world."

Serenity stood and began picking up the dishes from the table in a fit of anxious energy. I remained seated and watched her as I fought to keep a smile off my face.

"They certainly seemed at ease with all the outsiders donating money to their cause at the school house benefit auction," she said.

Feeling the need deep within myself to play the devil's advocate and defend my roots, I said, "They were comfortable with those people, because they'd probably spent years building up trust and friendship through business deals and just being neighbors. You come on the scene, a woman with a strong personality, and someone they don't have any knowledge of at all—of course they're going to be leery."

The doubt still lingered on her face and I added, "And besides, why worry right now when there's nothing you can do about it tonight anyway. Hopefully, in the morning you'll get your answers. Why don't we relax in the living room, where you can finish off that glass of wine that you've barely touched?"

I rose, waiting for her to move with me to the other room. She eyed me suspiciously for several long seconds. Finally, she picked up her drink and led the way to the couch. She made sure to sit at the far side, which bugged me, but then, I was grateful that she was sitting with me at all the way things were going.

Her behavior made me doubt what I was doing. Maybe I was wasting my time trying to get to know Serenity better. Although, there was a sparking current between the two of us that made me want to take the risk, there was something about her independent nature that scared the hell out of me. She was just the type of woman that I could fall hard for—and then she'd break my heart.

"You know, Daniel, I can understand why you left the Amish," Serenity said after she took a sip from her glass. Her eyes fastened on me and I braced myself for what she was about to say. "They are pretty damn creepy."

Her words sunk in and my anxiety disappeared. I began to laugh in earnest. I was expecting her to say something much worse.

When I'd finally calmed, I met her frown and said, "You're seeing them at their very worst right now. If nothing had ever happened to Naomi Beiler and you'd gone to the school house with me, meeting the Amish for the first time there, your perception would be very different. I guarantee it."

"Doesn't true character come out in a crisis? Besides, you and I would never have been there together if it weren't for Naomi's death."

I thought for a minute, staring out the sliding glass door into the darkness. I certainly couldn't tell her the truth—that I'd wanted desperately to ask her out when I'd worked on her roof a year earlier. I'd been intimidated by the beautiful police officer, who unlike most of the women I'd encountered over the years, completely ignored me after the initial consultation. I just figured that the only woman I'd crossed paths with since Abby, who I was truly interested in, didn't give me a second thought.

When I glanced up at Serenity's waiting face, I wondered what had changed since then. Maybe I was tired of being alone—maybe she was too irresistible for me to ignore any longer. Whatever it was that had prompted me to open my heart to the little sheriff, I knew that it wouldn't be easy to back out now.

"Yeah, you're right about that, but I'm glad to be helping you on this case. It's given me the opportunity to put my foot in the door with my family, and that's a good thing."

Serenity stared at me, her expression changing several times before it settled on hesitation. She sat up straighter.

"Do you know Tony Manning?" she asked in a guarded voice.

"Sure I do. Doesn't everyone in this town?" I said honestly, wondering where she was heading.

She huffed and rushed out, "I mean, are you buddies with the man?"

"No, not buddies, but he's never done me a bad turn. If you're asking, I did vote for you." I grinned. It hadn't been tough call for most of the people of Blood Rock to take a chance on the young woman with the exemplary career over the old codger who couldn't stay out of his own kind of trouble.

She twittered her fingers and then, amazingly moved closer to me. I stiffened, suddenly very much aware of her close proximity. If I shifted and leaned toward her, she was close enough to kiss now.

"I don't know why I'm telling you this—maybe I'm crazy, but I trust you for some strange reason." She breathed deep and blurted, "Tony implied that the Amish would take care of the situation on their own. I got the impression that he was talking about a vigilante type thing. What do you think about that?"

Her pretty eyes were glued on me, waiting. Although I didn't really want to talk about it, her question had brought up a particular incident in my head that I thought I should tell her—that I wanted to tell her about.

"When I was five years old, so we're going back about thirty years, there was one night that I will never forget. Aaron Esch was close to our age now, as were my parents. It was during a long, hot, dry summer when a young Amish woman, and I don't even know her name, so don't bother asking, had something very bad happen to her. At the time, I was too young to understand much of it, but later on, through the older boys talking, I figured out that she'd been raped by an outsider who lived within the area."

I paused to see that she was staring at me intently before I turned away and looked through the window into the darkness outside, the scene from my childhood vividly before me.

"It was after dark and I was in bed about to fall asleep, when I heard the clops of the hooves on the driveway. I remember climbing from the bed to search out the window. When I saw three buggies pulling right up to the house, I became alarmed and went to my brothers' beds to tell them what

I'd seen. My brothers were already gone. I found the three of them in differing positions of kneeling on the steps, their heads all turned in the direction of the kitchen, listening. I tiptoed past them down the steps, not really trying to sneak by, but it didn't matter anyway. They were so caught up with their own eavesdropping that they didn't even notice me.

"When I reached the kitchen, I hung back, just inside the doorway, peeking around the corner. Mother was sitting at the table, her hands tightly clenched while she stared up at the four men standing around the table. Father was there, along with Aaron Esch, and James Hooley. The other man was one of the ministers at the time, Abraham Yoder, and he's since passed. I listened for a minute to their rushed words about a pickup truck and the covered bridge on Route 27. The words all blurred together to nonsense in my five year old mind. But, one thing that I understood, and always stayed with me, is the blood."

Serenity interrupted, her eyes round like saucers, *"Blood?"*

"Yeah, blood. All four men had it smeared on their bare arms, where there shirts were rolled up. Aaron even had a scratch running down the length of his cheek. You can barely see the top of it still, if you look above his beard line. In those days, his beard wasn't quite as bushy, and the scratch more visible."

"What happened?" Serenity moved even closer, her eyes still wide.

"My mother looked up and saw me standing there in the shadow. She hushed the men loudly between clenched teeth. It took her a second to cross the kitchen and pick me up in her arms. With my trained little ears, I heard my brothers high tailing it up the steps ahead of us. By the time we reached the bedroom, my brothers were under their covers, feigning sleep. Mother tucked me in and kissed my nose. Before she left, she said loudly to the room, 'You best be forgetting what you heard tonight, and never speak it aloud, if you know what's good for your backsides.' She didn't have to worry about us saying a thing. My brothers understood more than I did, but we all knew that if we talked, we'd get Father into big trouble. We never spoke of it again. At least, I know this is the first time I've told anyone about it."

We sat silently for a minute, Serenity staring at the floor, and me staring at her. When she spoke, I was surprised.

"Was Tony hanging around with your Father at that time?" Serenity asked.

"I remember occasionally seeing Tony in the neighborhood when I was a kid. He worked at the stock yard in those days, before he became a cop, and then sheriff. But, he wasn't in the kitchen that night, and I don't remember him having anything at all to do with it."

"I didn't mean that...exactly. I just wondered if maybe he'd heard about it from somebody." Serenity was still deep in thought, her lips pursed and her eyes faraway.

"I think the adults in that room didn't speak about it to anyone. Any of the Amish who might have known about it would have kept silent, probably believing that whatever was done needed to be done."

"But Todd said your people were pacifists," Serenity said.

I laughed again, but not with as much vigor. Having Serenity beside me on the couch, looking all warm and sweet helped to keep my humor level in check.

"They're human too, don't ever forget it. My own Father had a temper like a summer storm when he was angry. It's just that we don't fight in wars against people that we don't personally have grievances with."

"Oh, that's a whole 'nother subject that we don't have time to talk about," Serenity said with a roll to her eyes.

I took the words as the only chance I might get. Leaning in close enough to her to breathe in her spicy scent, I said, "Why, is there something else you'd rather be doing, Serenity?"

I hoped that she understood the tone of my voice, but a part of me was worried silly that she'd jump off the couch and leave. Or, even worse, laugh at me.

She didn't do either of those things. Instead, she drifted closer and when her head tilted slightly, I pressed my lips against her plump ones. I couldn't help the sigh that escaped me as her mouth parted and I covered hers with mine. The rush deep down was exactly what I expected I'd feel kissing the beautiful woman.

Now that Serenity had loosened up, she slipped her arms around my neck, and I took it as the cue to pull her in tight against me. The electricity between us was tangible as our mouths began to work frantically against each other, our tongues wanting more.

Serenity's cell phone going off caused me to cuss, and I wasn't ashamed for the word I'd used when Serenity pulled away and looked at the number.

"Sorry, I have to take this," she said breathlessly before standing and walking into the kitchen.

When she returned, she had on the hard-faced expression of a sheriff again. I inwardly groaned at the progress we'd just lost.

"I have to go. There was a car accident on Route 45. There's a fatality, and I'm on call. So...I guess I'll see you in the morning," Serenity said as she reached for her leather jacket that was tossed over the back of the couch.

I caught her hand before she touched the material and stood, pulling her up against my body. Dammit, I wasn't going to let her escape without an acknowledgement that we'd shared a kiss. I began to lower my head, and could feel her sway slightly just before she shoved her hands into my chest and pushed away.

"Really, I have to go." She caught up her jacket and moved to the door quickly. "I'll see you in the morning—unless your plans have changed?" she asked, with a conflicted look hovering across her face.

"Nope, nothing's changed. We're still on for our search of Eli Bender," I said, not even trying to hide the smirk on my face.

Serenity nodded and plowed out the door like she was escaping a tornado.

But, then again, from the feelings I'd experienced kissing her, maybe she was.

14

September 25th

Naomi sat at the picnic table cradling her head on her arms, and hoping that anyone looking out the butcher shop windows would believe that she was truly sick. She hadn't felt guilty lying to Mr. Zook about having a belly ache. After all, he'd barely spoken to her since the announcement at church of her temporary shunning. She needed to be with Will—and this was the only way.

When Naomi heard the rumble of the diesel engine, she smiled, feeling happier than she had in several days. She peeked over her elbow to confirm that it was Will, before she rose slowly, continuing the act and making her way to his truck.

Will jumped out and ran to the passenger side, opening the door for her. He raised his hand to help her with the climb up, but she gave a sharp head shake, meeting his eyes for a second before she took the step in herself. The last thing that she needed was for one of the nosey girls to see Will touching her.

It was a mile down the road before Naomi let out a whoop of joy. Will jumped at her sudden victory cry and then turned in understanding with a wide smile.

"Have I just participated in the rescue of a damsel in distress?" Will asked, still grinning.

"Yes, Will. You sure did. I've needed rescuing since last week." She blushed at Will's intense look and turned to watch the farms drift by. Autumn's colors were beginning to sprinkle into the landscape. Naomi felt strengthened at the sight of the yellowing leaves. In her mind, the change of seasons meant that there were changes ahead in her life also. Even though there were so many obstacles in her way, Naomi still held out hope that she would be happy and free someday.

"I knew something was up, the way you ignored me all week, hardly speaking after I dropped the other girls off. I thought that you were mad at me," Will said.

"Mad at you? I could never be angry with you. I've been punished and I've had to be extra careful about everything I do."

"What are you in trouble for?" Will's voice was full of concern, and she loved the sound of it.

Naomi thought for a moment about lying, but decided that this was a good time to test whether she could talk to Will about anything—as she believed that she could.

Staring ahead, she said, "One of the ministers caught me and Eli kissing out behind a shed after Sunday service. Eli begged for forgiveness and got two weeks of shunning. I was stupid, and argued, so I got four."

Naomi risked a glance back at him to see him lost in thought. But his face wasn't angry.

When he looked at her again, he sighed, "I wish it was me kissing you out behind a shed, instead of this Eli dude."

Naomi moved closer and without thinking, rested her hand on his thigh. "I do too. You have to believe me. I cared for Eli at first, before I met you, and then I was sort of pushed into this whole engagement thing—"

"What! You're engaged to the guy?" Will exclaimed. His eyes were bright and full of fire.

Naomi shrugged, suddenly embarrassed. "We talked about it and he told his folks the news. It's supposed to happen in the spring."

Will quietly brooded, while Naomi stared out the window. Rain clouds were moving in and the air felt heavy with dampness. The weather was beginning to fit her mood.

When Will finally spoke, Naomi froze after so much silence. But her heart swelled at his tone, which was soft. How could he forgive her for being engaged to another man?

"Where do you want to go?" he asked.

Where? Naomi hadn't even thought about it. Just driving around was fine for her, as long as she was away from the Amish people for a few hours.

"I don't know. Since Mamma is visiting one of her sisters today in the next county over, I wasn't too worried about her finding out that I wasn't home when I was supposed to be in bed sick." Naomi looked back at him, wondering, "Where should we go?"

Will eyed her, and then turned his gaze back to the roadway before he spoke. "Well, we shouldn't go anywhere public that's for sure. The last thing you need is another few weeks tacked on to your punishment." He stalled, and then said tentatively, "We could go to my place. My parents are at work and Taylor is still in school. What do you think?"

Naomi's heart raced and she swallowed her anxiety down with a gulp. She would finally be alone with Will—what she'd dreamed about for weeks. Then why was she hesitating? Naomi almost asked Will to turn around and take her home, but when his eyes peeked over at her, shyly, she made up her mind.

"That sounds fine. I want to see where you live."

There was a crackling, nervous energy in the cab as they made their way closer to his home and more than likely, a dramatic change in their relationship. They sat in relative silence until Will drove into a cluster of houses that were all big and fancy. Naomi sat up straighter, peering out the window with interest, momentarily forgetting the butterflies swirling around in her belly.

"You live *here*?" she asked, noticing that the yards were all neat, the flower beds filled with mulch and lined with lights.

"Yeah," Will said as he pulled into the driveway of a house that looked like a small mansion to Naomi's bulging eyes.

For the first time with Will, Naomi was at a loss for words as she followed him into the garage and then the house. She barely noticed the shiny metal appliances in the kitchen as they passed through, or the childhood photos of Will and Taylor that lined the wall of the staircase that they climbed to the upstairs. It was just a fleeting wish in her mind as she glanced at a baby Will sitting on a furry rug smiling for the camera, that she had photos of herself when she was a baby. Being Amish, her family wasn't allowed personal portraits, and she suddenly wished with a sharp pain that she knew what she'd looked like as a little girl.

Will's room was darkish, with the blinds almost completely down. Only a faint shimmer of light from the cloudy afternoon came through the slits. He sat on the bed watching Naomi's every move as she wandered through his room, learning about his life.

There was a computer on a small desk with a cluster of typed papers scattered to the side of it. Posters of large muscled horses and rodeo riders filled the walls, obscuring the wallpaper behind them. Two piles of clothes littered the floor, and Naomi instantly picked out the clean one from the dirty one.

"What do you think?" Will asked her quietly.

One last glance around and she breathed out, "It's wonderful."

Will laughed, the sound strong and full of life. At that moment, Naomi knew that she loved him. She moved forward into his arms that were waiting for her. He pressed into her, his own head resting against her breasts, as they both sighed together.

"I dream about you," Will whispered.

"I dream about you too," Naomi said, a smile playing on her lips. She rubbed her face into his messy, yet sweet smelling hair.

Will turned his head up, and he was about to say more, but she pressed her finger to his mouth. Naomi didn't want to talk—or think. She just wanted to feel.

She leaned down and touched his lips softly. Will's hands came up and pulled her down to him. Soon enough, she was beneath him on the bed, his mouth traveling over her, his hands caressing her every inch.

It felt so right, but then why did a small part of her not want to let go? Eli was pushed far back in her mind, but he was still there, and Naomi felt a spasm of fear about what she was doing, and the consequences that she might have to deal with later.

Her mind became jumbled, until Will said, his face nuzzling her neck, "I love you, Naomi. I love you with all my heart."

Just as the gray clouds released a wave of raindrops that pounded the house with a thousand thumps, Naomi let go of her worries. Everything was all right now. She brought Will's face to hers and looked into his eyes.

"I love you too, Will."

15

November 15th

"You sure are spending a lot of time with Daniel Bachman. Exactly, how deep is the man getting into…the investigation?" Todd wore the most obnoxious smirk I'd seen yet.

I sighed in agitation, shaking my head. "Get your head out of the gutter. Daniel's been very helpful with the case so far." Looking up and seeing the same lopsided grin still stuck on his face, I added, "So, shut the hell up."

"Touché," he said, rolling his chair further away from mine.

"Can we get back to work, children?" Bobby said, with no hint of humor. I guess the old guy, well past ready for retirement, was growing tired of our banter.

When Mayor Johnson entered the room, I heard the soft sound of Bobby's growl. I looked smugly at the coroner, thinking it served him right for calling me a child.

Before the mayor opened his mouth, I rose and said, "Good morning, Ed, what brings you by today?"

The mayor's words came out as quickly as his feet moved him around. Even though he was well on in years, he still had the nervous movements of parakeet trapped in a cage.

"It would be a better morning if Bobby here, would get those damn reports to me quicker." He turned and leveled his mustached frown at Bobby, before he settled his gaze on me, "And another matter—I've got calls coming into my office from as far away as Indianapolis about this Amish girl. I thought she was shot in a hunting accident?"

"Bobby ruled the death was from a shot gun, but we're still..." Ed's hand shot up to silence me. Heat flooded my cheeks in annoyance with the impatient man.

"Look, I understand things are pretty quiet around here most of the time, but there's no need to go stirring up trouble where there isn't any. If the Amish are happy to close the damn investigation and label it a hunting accident, we should be too." The mayor's tone had changed during his speech to slow softness. He wasn't even trying to cover up the pleading in his voice.

Fire sparked inside of me. I couldn't stop myself from blurting out, "Have you been talking to Tony?"

Ed shuffled his feet and looked away for some seconds before he gathered the courage to face me again.

"He came by my office earlier to bring it to my attention that you've been harassing the locals with this nonsense." Before I had the chance to interrupt, he charged on, saying, "I understand your desire to follow all the rules on your first big case here in Blood Rock, but things are different in the country, Serenity. If something is as obvious as the nose on your face, you don't have to look past it. The poor girl was accidently shot by a hunter—case closed. We don't need to concern ourselves with the sordid details of her life within the Amish community."

Still fuming, I searched Bobby's face. The irritation was written all over it, but unlike me, he'd learned to deal with the mayor by simply refusing to speak to the man.

I drew in a deep breath and with a conscious effort to keep my voice level, I said, "I don't see it that way. The fact that you'd be taking advice from the likes of Tony Manning, is, to put it mildly, frightening."

"For once, the man makes sense. Let's get the case closed quickly," Ed's brown gaze locked on me and he said, "It's the best thing for your career, Sheriff. Trust me on this one."

The mayor turned to leave the room, but before he crossed the threshold he glanced back at Bobby and barked, "I want those reports on my desk by tomorrow, Bobby."

"What a prick," Todd mumbled.

"That's putting it mildly," I said flopping down in the chair.

Finally Bobby spoke. "Don't pay him too much mind, Serenity. He's all bark and little bite in the beginning. I guess you have another week, two tops, to come up with solid evidence that Naomi Beiler wasn't a victim of an accidental shooting. After that, he'll lean hard on you to close the case."

I nodded, accepting his words. Bobby knew the mayor better than anyone else. Not only had he worked on and off under the man for thirty years, they were also brother-in-laws.

"I thought I was prepared for some backward thinking when I returned to Blood Rock, but I wasn't expecting to be pissed off quite so quickly."

"Oh, trust me, this is only the beginning of the aggrava- tions you'll be dealing with," Bobby said with a slight smile as he pushed the accident report papers from the night before in front of me.

Just as I finished signing the last report, Jeremy peeked in and said, "Serenity, there's a couple of men here to see you."

"About what? You know, I'm pretty busy today—can't you handle it?" I said, trying to keep the sharpness out of my voice.

Jeremy shook his head, "You're going to want to talk to these two."

I rolled my eyes at Jeremy's choice of timing to be mysterious and said, "Fine, show them in."

Bobby leaned back in his seat with a drawn out sigh, while Todd continued to smirk. I ignored them both and waited while Jeremy led the two men, dressed in camouflage clothes and muddy boots into the conference room. At a quick glance, I knew that they'd come straight in from the woods, without even stopping home to wash up.

My curiosity spiked as the taller, middle aged man, said, "Sheriff, ma'am, Rodney and I were out bow hunting in the fields south of Burkey Road this morning when we found something that we thought you might want. Especially, since we read about that girl in the newspaper and all."

I stood up and moved around the table in a blink. Even Todd sat up straighter at the man's words.

"What's your name, sir?" I asked, staring at the hunter green back pack in the man's hand, my heart beating harder with each second that passed.

"Jimmy Huskey, ma'am." He tipped his ball cap at me.

"What do you have, Jimmy?" I said.

He held it towards me and I took it carefully. It was lighter than I'd guessed it was. I glanced at Bobby, who motioned for me to wait. He left for a minute and returned with plastic gloves, which he held out to me. Todd moved in close enough that I could smell his cologne and I wrinkled my nose, but didn't ask him to back up. Taking a breath, I pulled the string, opening it up wide and reached in. My hand clasped a soft, plush object and I pulled it out. The stuffed rabbit was patched together with several different colors of fabric and I immediately thought of the Velveteen Rabbit as I looked at its sad, button eyes.

I laid the rabbit gently onto the table and reached in again to bring out three pairs of woman's panties. They were plain white and size small. After laying them beside the rabbit, I went in again, knowing that it was for the last time. The denim purse I pulled out was hand stitched with a red bandanna pocket on the front. A quick glance into the purse showed that it was empty except for a couple of tissues and a tube of lip moisturizer, but turning it over in my hands, my heart jumped and I took a deep breath. The name *Naomi*, was stitched in cursive across the back, the red of the thread matching the bandanna. I stared at the word, registering the time it had taken to sew the name on so neatly, and with an artistic flare, too. The face of the pretty Amish girl rose before me and for the first time, I felt a real sense of loss. Why did Naomi Beiler have to die?

"Where exactly did you find this?" I asked Jimmy, not taking my eyes off the purse.

"Oh, it would be difficult to explain in words, ma'am, being that we were out in the fields."

I looked up at Jeremy, "Jeremy, take these men back to where they were hunting and go with them personally to the spot that they found this back pack. Comb the area for any other evidence." As he was turning to leave, I added, "And check out a map to see where the pack was in relation to Naomi's body."

"Sure thing, I'll get back with you later today," Jeremy said, motioning to Jimmy and Rodney to follow him out.

When they were gone, I turned to Todd and said, "Well, this proves that Naomi was running away."

"Which backs up what her parents told us," Todd said.

Bobby put on his own gloves and began placing the items carefully in the empty box that he'd gone out to get while we were talking. "It's rather sad, isn't it, that the only items the girl took with her were these. It speaks volumes for the Amish people's placement of materialistic value in their society," Bobby said.

"What's shouting at me louder is the question of why Naomi would have ditched her pack before she was shot. It makes no sense that if it were an accidental shooting, like we're supposed to assume, that the pack wouldn't have been with her body," I said, looking up at the guys, hoping that they finally would agree with me that something was not right about this case.

Bobby scratched his head and nodded. "Maybe we can get some forensics off of the items that will help us find the answer."

"How long will it take?" I already knew the time frame, but was so anxious, I asked anyway. After all, if Bobby was correct about the mayor, I only had a couple of weeks to find out what really happened to Naomi before the powers-that-be shut me down.

"I can put a rush on it, but it depends on the people in Indianapolis. I'd guess maybe a week," Bobby said.

Daniel's head popped in, and my mind froze, thinking back to the kiss the night before. I hoped that the blush I felt heating my face wasn't noticeable to the guys in the room. Just thinking about his warm, firm lips moving on mine sent a pleasant tingle through my groin that I wished to God I didn't feel.

"Are you ready to go, Serenity?" Daniel asked in an upbeat voice.

I'd actually forgotten about our trip to the Amish community and Daniel Bachman for a few minutes, even though the idea of it had plagued me most of the night before and into the early morning. How the hell was I supposed to act around him now that we'd swapped spit?

I did my best to dismiss the thought of his tongue in my mouth and said, "I'll be right out."

Daniel took the hint and disappeared. When I looked back at Bobby, he shrugged, shaking his head.

"What?" I demanded.

Bobby paused in the doorway, and said gently, "Be careful when mixing business with pleasure, my girl. It usually backfires." Then he was gone and I was alone with Todd who was smirking again.

"Do you want me to go with you and Daniel out there today?" Todd asked.

Too quickly, I said, "No. You can file the accident report."

For once, Todd didn't have a catchy comeback for me. Maybe he was learning to keep his mouth shut.

Later, after I told Daniel about the back pack and was sitting in his Jeep traveling down the country roads toward the Amish community, I couldn't help but think back to the story that Daniel had told me the night before. Hell, if I was having this much difficulty gathering information for a possible crime that happened a few weeks ago, I could only imagine how impossible it would be to solve an Amish cold case.

"You're awfully quiet this morning, Serenity. What are you thinking about?" Daniel asked. He didn't say my name any differently than anyone else did, but when the word slipped out of his mouth it sent a shiver through me every time.

"Oh, I have quite a lot on my mind," I managed to say, continuing to stare out the window. It was another wet, dreary day in Indiana. I began to feel the tug of depression that kind of weather always brought on. And to think, we still had five more months of it.

It had been just such a night three years earlier when my outlook on life had changed dramatically, triggering my move back to Blood Rock. Naomi's death and Will's involvement with her had distracted me enough to keep the memory away. But now, watching the drizzle fall beyond the window, it came into sharp focus once again.

I walked slowly toward the body lying on the pavement. Ryan had my back, but training and experience wouldn't allow me to let my guard down. When I bent down, I felt the tingle of foreboding. I didn't want to push the hood back, something inside me made me hesitate...

Daniel cleared his throat, pulling me out of the past. "Are you going to pretend that we didn't kiss last night?"

His words shocked me. I hadn't expected him to mention it, and the fact that he so brazenly brought it up raised my hackles. Within a couple of weeks, Naomi's case could be closed and then I wouldn't see Daniel again. Unless, I decided to have a garage put on the house. I certainly wasn't interested in a one night stand. I had way too many other things going on to deal with that kind of crap.

I leveled my glare at him, and said, "It wasn't a big deal. Let's just blame the wine, and forget about it."

His eyes changed, becoming darker and a look of disbelief flitted across his face. I realized then that I'd hurt his feelings and I wanted to take it back, but it was too late.

"If that's the way you want to handle it, fine by me." He stared straight ahead and I could feel the friendly, fun connection that we'd shared for the past week snap. What a damn fool I was. But I certainly wasn't going to admit it out loud.

Daniel pulled into a driveway that led up to a two story, white sided house on a knoll. We passed the barns before we reached the house and Daniel slowed to wave at several teenage boys who were working at various chores in the barn yard. I looked closely at each of them, wondering if one might be Eli.

When we parked and I opened the door, I was hit with the sharp odor of wood smoke burning and I could see the tentacles drifting from the chimney. I zipped up my jacket at the brisk, wet air and followed Daniel, who was now completely ignoring me, up the front steps to the doorway.

He rapped firmly on the door and then we waited in uncomfortable silence. I stared at him for a second, trying to get him to look my way, but he wouldn't, so I looked back down at the barns. I spotted the bearded man who was walking slowly up the hill to the house. My pulse quickened with nerves as I sensed the apprehension in the man from his posture. He obviously wasn't looking forward to talking to us.

When the door opened behind me, I swiveled to see an attractive Amish woman holding a small baby in her arms.

Her eyes were the lightest blue and her skin was as pale as milk.

"Hullo, what may I help you with?" the woman said, her voice huskier than I'd expected.

"I'm Daniel Bachman. Do you remember me, Katherine?" Daniel asked the woman.

Before she said a word, I knew she remembered him well, the way her eyes quickly passed over him in an admiring way, before shifting to me. Her ivory skin reddened and I felt a stab of jealousy. It didn't matter that the woman probably had six or seven kids with a man who she was surely happily married to. All I could think about at the moment was that she had noticed how gorgeous Daniel was, causing the green eyed monster to rise up in me.

"Oh, yes. I do. I saw you at the school house the other night. This is your girlfriend?" she asked, eyeing me from head to toe.

Daniel said, "Yes, this is Serenity Adams."

"I see that Joseph is on his way. Why don't you wait here in the house? It's nippy out today," Katherine said.

We walked into the warm room and I was immediately overcome by the smell of fresh-baked cookies. I couldn't help lifting my face and inhaling the pleasant aroma.

Katherine, who must have noticed my gesture, said, "I just made cookies, would you like one?"

I couldn't deny that I hadn't had breakfast and was probably going to begin drooling if I didn't accept her offer. I said, "Yes, please, they smell wonderful."

Katherine motioned to the counter where the cookies were still warm on the trays. I ignored Daniel's glance and picked two off the nearest tray. I slid by him and sat down in the first high backed chair I came to at the kitchen table.

Katherine and Daniel began speaking in their language which I thought was rude, but I decided to treat my inability to join the conversation as an opportunity to look around the house. Besides the baby that Katherine was holding, there was another bigger one sleeping on the couch in the adjoining room and two more toddlers playing on the floor with wooden blocks.

The house was almost uncomfortably warm and I unzipped my jacket, realizing, as I looked up, that the gas light that was hanging above me was where the heat was emitting from. The inside of the home had a cozy feel, with homemade quilts lying across the chairs and a tweed rug covering the hardwood floor.

The sudden sound of a toddler wailing snapped me out of my daze. The child's scream was enough to get Katherine hurrying across the room.

I sat nibbling on my cookie not bothering to get involved, when Katherine did the unthinkable, handing the baby off to me as she passed by. What the hell, I thought, as I gripped the blanket encasing the baby without moving a muscle.

A quick look at Katherine told me that she would be busy for at least another minute consoling the other child, so I darted a pleading look at Daniel, hoping he would rid me of the infant.

Now, instead of ignoring me, he was grinning from ear to ear. Either, he had decided that he wasn't angry with me any longer, or more likely, he enjoyed seeing me squirm.

I wondered if the pink-cheeked baby was a boy or girl, but I wasn't going to unwrap it to find out. I'd only shown interest in my nephew and niece when they were able to walk around and talk a little bit—then they were my best buddies. But when children were this small size, they completely freaked me out. I held the baby stiffly for another minute until Katherine finally had the child on the floor calmed and came back to claim her little bundle from me. I passed the baby off, sighing with relief. I didn't bother to look Daniel's way, knowing that he was probably laughing at me on the inside.

Joseph arrived with a rush of cold air. Daniel and I rose to greet the man, who shook both of our hands and then settled into the stoic look of a man not wanting to be there.

Katherine managed to hustle the small children from the room, even waking the sleeping baby to do so. I would have liked it if she'd stayed, feeling that Katherine was a woman who might actually have talked to us honestly—or have allowed her facial expressions to give her away.

Daniel spoke to the other man in Pennsylvania Dutch while I waited. I tried to look patient, but more than likely, failed to do so.

Probably sensing my growing frustration, Daniel turned to me and said, "Eli Bender is Joseph's son."

"Can we talk to him?" I asked.

Joseph answered, "I do not see the point of it. I've told Daniel that Eli courted Naomi for a few weeks before they quit each other. The relationship was not serious."

I stared at the man, anger swelling in me and said, "Really, not very serious? That's not what I've heard."

Daniel shot me a warning look that I ignored. He was pissed at me, so who knew whose side he was on anyway.

"I have to get back to shoeing that horse now. You two have a nice day," Joseph said, picking up his hat from the counter.

I had had about enough of being blown off. The stress of having only a couple of weeks to discover Naomi's truth was beginning to fray my insides. I was just about to let Joseph Bender have it when Daniel stealthily came close and put his arm around me. The tight pressure of his arm told me to shut up. Reluctantly, I remained quiet.

Once we were back in the Jeep I rounded on Daniel and hissed, "I am through being the silent woman at your side. I appreciate the help you've given me so far, but really, all this cloak and dagger nonsense has to stop. The Amish don't need to be treated as if they're bombs that are going to explode if I push them a little bit."

Daniel didn't answer me, instead, turning around and silently driving back down the gravel to the roadway. He waved at Joseph as he passed the open barn doorway where the man could be seen hammering on a shoe held to an anvil.

Once we turned onto the road, Daniel finally turned to acknowledge my presence in his vehicle.

"Are you quite finished?" he said in level voice.

His calm demeanor made me feel foolish, and I leaned back against the seat and sighed. "Yeah, I guess so."

"I'm taking you to the welding shop where Eli works. You can grill the kid there," Daniel said.

"Oh. Is he eighteen?"

"Yes, Serenity, old enough to talk to you without an adult present, but young enough to still blab his mouth if we catch him in the right frame of mind," Daniel said, letting his gaze flick over my face briefly before turning back to the road.

From the look that passed, maybe I still had a chance with him. But did I want to bother with a relationship with a known woman collector? People could change, I knew, but the man on the seat beside me frightened me more than any other male I'd encountered. I guess my heart knew that it really could be broken if I fell hard for Daniel.

Once we arrived at the welding shop, I waited in the Jeep while Daniel went in. He'd mumbled something about how breaking the ice would be easier with him alone and I agreed, not wanting to rile the man any further. I was definitely in foreign territory here.

When Daniel finally emerged some ten minutes later, he was accompanied by a tall, young man who I had to admit was good looking. Not as handsome as my nephew, but damn close. The boy's straw hat covered longer hair than I'd seen on the other Amish boys, and as he climbed in, his blue eyes flashed arrogance.

Daniel introduced us, "Serenity, this is Eli Bender, Joseph's son."

I turned to the young man who sat sullenly in the back seat. Forcing a nonchalant demeanor, I asked him, "Eli, would you mind telling me about your relationship with Naomi?"

He sat quietly for a minute, and then he looked straight at me and said, "I loved her…more than she did me."

I softened a little toward the boy when I saw the sorrow attempting to distort his features, but he held it in, taking a sniff and staring back at me. I noted how differently Eli was handling his grief from my nephew and I suddenly wondered which boy Naomi had really loved.

"I'm sorry, Eli. I know this must be difficult for you, but I need to ask you a couple more questions." He looked back at me resignedly and I plowed on, "Were you and Naomi planning to marry?"

"We had been talking about marrying in the springtime. I'd told my parents, but I don't think she'd told hers yet."

"How long had the two of you been together?" I asked, watching the shift of his eyes for lies, but so far, he seemed to be telling the truth. Or, he was a very well trained liar.

"Guess we'd been courting about six weeks when Naomi and I got in trouble with the Church. We quit each other during our punishment," he said, his voice gaining some hardness.

Daniel, anticipating my question, said, "He means they broke up. That's what the Amish kids call it—quitting each other."

"Why did you break up with Naomi?" I asked softly, knowing I was treading in painful territory, but I still wasn't expecting his reaction.

Eli said loudly, "She done quit me. Not the other way around. But I was so angry 'bout it that I let everyone think it was me who didn't want her no longer."

Dread was beginning to wash over me when I asked, "Eli, why did she quit you?"

Without hesitation, he said, "For an English guy. Naomi was seeing one of the English drivers behind my back. What the others were gossiping about was true."

The sadness that Eli had exhibited earlier had disappeared, to be replaced with simmering anger that I could see just beneath his cool demeanor, waiting to ignite. I suddenly felt the prickling of concern that this boy had the motive and the anger to do his ex-girlfriend in, especially, since she did the unthinkable by dumping him for an English boy.

Watching his face very carefully, I said, "When did you see her last?"

"Why, I saw her the same day she died."

"Where?" I asked, expecting him to tell me that he'd seen her at some Amish event.

"In the cornfield—I saw Naomi while she was running away in the cornfield," Eli said, sending me into a tailspin.

16

NAOMI

October 1st

Naomi sat across from Bishop Esch as he read from the Bible, hardly hearing anything the man said. She'd been tortured in this way for the past two hours and she inwardly prayed that the bishop would run out of air and just be done with it.

The last week had been nearly impossible for Naomi. She thought about Will morning, noon, and night. And, after their time together in his room, the few minutes that she was able to hold his hand and whisper a few loving words in the afternoons were not nearly enough for her. How was she ever going to live with Will being so close, yet so unbearably far away?

"Naomi! Focus, girl, and stop drifting away with the autumn leaves outside the windows," Bishop Esch said angrily. He closed his Bible with a thump.

Naomi met his stare defiantly, although her voice was contrite, "Sorry."

"That's the problem, young lady, you aren't really sorry in the slightest way. You have rebellion in your heart. I've seen it before, and I know it now." He leaned forward and crossed his arms on the table, telling her that he wasn't through with her yet. "It has been brought to my attention that you've been flirting with your prettiness to the boys in the community... and outside of it. What do you say to that?"

Naomi knew who'd brought it to his attention—Lydia. The reckoning might have finally arrived.

"I have done no such thing. Some people might be jealous, spreading rumors to be vicious," Naomi offered.

The bishop flattened his beard with his hand and said, "Don't you wonder at the reason that you don't get along with the other girls? Maybe it's your own fault that jealousy is upon you."

Naomi glanced over at James Hooley. His head was tilted back, his mouth gaping into the air. The sound of his heavy breathing could be heard clearly from across the table, and she hated him for it. She hated both of the men for making her suffer these lectures daily after she'd already worked an eight hour shift at the butcher shop, with still several hours to go of being bossed around by Mamma after all that. *Why won't they all just leave me alone?* Naomi screamed in her mind.

"You should think on what we've talked about. We'll meet here again on Wednesday," the bishop said, finally giving up—at least for now, his eyes said.

His dismissal had her up and out the door in a heartbeat. The cooler air was welcome and she left her coat unbuttoned. It took just a minute for Naomi to untie Cisco from the hitching rail, and climb into the buggy.

She snapped the reins and sent the bay gelding trotting onto the road, leaving the black canvas door open. The feeling of oldness that had covered her while she'd sat in the schoolhouse across from the grumpy men was washed away with the sudden rush of air.

The hours spent listening to the droning sound of the bishop's voice as he'd read from the Bible and lectured her about her rebellious ways, had done nothing but make Naomi more withdrawn. Rarely did she engage the bishop in conversation, instead, only choosing to speak when she was asked a direct question. Every time she gazed into his steely gray eyes, she remembered him standing before the congregation with his arms spread wide and reciting her many sins to the entire congregation. While he'd announced her punishment, she'd sat on a bench beside him facing the crowd. The faces of her family, neighbors and friends were a blur before her, and even now she couldn't recall any of them, except for little Emma. The child had been staring at her with total unconditional love and maybe that's why Naomi had seen her face.

Following the service, she'd driven home with her family, but they acted cool toward her, speaking only when necessary. After a few days, she became accustomed to taking her meals before the others at the table alone. That part of the punishment wasn't too difficult for her to handle. It suited her just fine to have the quiet time. Even though her father and siblings treated her silently, Mamma still found her tongue when she needed something done or just wanted to be mean to her. Naomi did feel sorry for the littlest ones though. Nathan, Emma, and Beth didn't understand why their older sister was being treated so differently. When Emma was forbidden to join Naomi at the table the night before, the little girl had cried for an hour, until she'd finally climbed onto the sofa completely exhausted and fell asleep without eating her supper at all.

Arriving at the steep hill on Mulberry Road, Naomi slowed Cisco to a walk. She hated that particular intersection, already feeling the queasy nerves spreading through her. Even with a strong horse like Cisco, it was difficult to stay stopped on the hill for long, and then get the momentum up again to make it safely across the busier road crossing.

Naomi listened carefully, fanning her head back and forth. Cisco took a step back, pushing the buggy backwards with his movement. Her vision was limited with the deep bend in the road, but hearing no oncoming traffic she flicked the reins, and clucked the horse forward. They were nearly across when the small white car came out of nowhere, flying down the roadway toward them. Naomi's heart froze, but her hands worked, flapping the reins harder to urge Cisco on. The car shot out around them, a slew of obscenities coming from the open driver's side window.

She almost had an opportunity to breathe when the horn of the car blared after it was past, the sound sending Cisco into a rear within his harness. The horse was usually dependable, but occasionally something would set him off. And nearly being hit by a car and topped off with the loud noise of the horn had done him in. Naomi could see the white of his left eye as he turned in the harness and rose into the air again, this time falling backwards into the buggy.

Somehow, Naomi's legs got moving and she leaped from the buggy, landing in the ditch with a rough roll. She wasn't safe yet though. Cisco, being a large horse, could do a lot of damage when a fit came upon him. He was scaring himself now, the buggy being the enemy, and he lurched forward to escape it. But he'd broken one of the shafts when he'd fallen backwards and now the buggy dragged behind him scaring him even more. The horse and buggy came down together in a blur, crashing into the ditch. Naomi didn't have time to think—only react. She curled into a ball, fearing that death was upon her. But a guardian angel must have been protecting her. Cisco missed her by mere inches and she was able to scoot away in the tall, dry grass while he thrashed and kicked the buggy to shreds.

It only lasted a few seconds more before Cisco was free and standing beside the wreckage that he'd created. Sweat covered his quivering body and several long, bloody gashes stretched down his hindquarters and legs, but otherwise, he seemed all right.

Gathering her wobbly legs beneath her, Naomi stood and tried to calm her pounding heart as she made her way to the horse, grabbing the reins, which were still attached. With nothing else to do, she began leading the trembling horse home.

She had about two miles to go and Naomi silently fumed, thinking how stupid it was that she couldn't drive a car, instead having to rely on a flighty horse to get her around. She worried what Dat and Mamma would say about the wrecked buggy too. They would surely be furious with her, not even thinking twice that she could have been killed or that it wasn't her fault. There'd been several accidents in the community over the recent years between buggies and cars and she'd been luckier than the rest who had been involved. At least she didn't have to go to the hospital.

The cool air now felt warm with her exertion and Naomi took her coat off and tied the arms of it around her slim hips. Seeing the farm on the right come into view, she sped up, wanting to get by it in a hurry.

The last thing that she needed was to be noticed here.

Her luck seemed to have run out when she'd cheated death and wasn't crushed by the horse. With a heavy sigh and a roll of her eyes, she waited as Eli ran down the hill full tilt to the road. By the time he reached her, he was panting. He skidded to a stop and grabbed the reins from Naomi with one hand, and used his other hand to brace her body.

"What happened? Are you okay?" Eli shouted in between breaths.

Naomi was angry with the world and wasn't too kind to Eli. "I'm fine. You shouldn't be near me, Eli. You're breaking the rules. Better wait a few weeks to call me and then you can ask how I'm doing."

Eli's gaze narrowed and he said, "Don't be silly. This is different." He began looking Cisco over, trying to put distance between himself and her bad mood.

When he was satisfied that the horse wasn't about to fall over and die, he asked again, with a softer voice, "What happened?"

"Cisco got spooked when a car almost ran over us. He went crazy and kicked the buggy apart. It's in the ditch near Mulberry Road," Naomi pointed back the way she'd come.

"Come on up to the house. I'll get my buggy hitched and take you home," Eli said firmly.

Naomi didn't like his bossiness, and after what she'd done with Will, she certainly didn't want to be trapped in a buggy with Eli and her guilt. Her emotions were frayed and she took it out on Eli.

"I'm fine, really. I'll walk the horse home." Naomi began to tug Cisco into motion, but Eli's strong arm held the reins, pulling them back from her. "Let go," she shouted.

"What has gotten into you? Just be reasonable, let me help you." Eli's voice was pleading now, but she ignored the sound of it.

"Yeah, like I should have been reasonable and admitted my guilt to Bishop Esch too, huh? Just the way you did—lie down and give up. I'm tired of it. And, you know what?" Eli's face paled with the onslaught, and he took a step back. "I don't think we're good for each other anymore. You can go and find yourself a goody, goody girl who won't disappoint you."

Naomi gave a greater tug, and finally freed the reins from Eli's hands. He seemed to have lost the desire to fight with her harsh words. She watched him turn and walk quickly up his driveway without a backward glance. She wasn't sure how she felt watching Eli walk away, but with the sun dipping down low in the sky, she knew she'd better get going if she wanted to make it home by nightfall.

Naomi was sure that if she changed her mind, Eli would have her back. But, at that moment, she didn't think there was a chance of that happening. She was already making plans for a very different life.

She'd show Eli—she'd show them all.

17

DANIEL

November 15

When the words were out of Eli's mouth, I turned to look back at him, wondering if the kid had any idea of what he'd just done to himself. Serenity was almost completely backwards now, her mouth dropped open.

She regained her composure quickly and said, "Were you following her, Eli?"

He shook his head. "No. I'd planned to talk to her that night about us getting back together since her shunning was up. I figured she'd be at the ball game. When she didn't show up, I went to her house and she wasn't there either. She's been acting so temperamental lately that I was worried about her. I thought she might go to the cornfield to hide, like she always did, so that's where I went to look for her."

His voice sounded true and I was already guessing why the cornfield when Serenity, who still had no clue, asked him,

"Why on earth would you look in a cornfield for your former girlfriend?"

Eli's cheeks turned a deep red and he looked out the window. When he finally turned back, he stared at me and not Serenity. I felt sorry for the kid, but I really couldn't help him on this one.

"Well?" Serenity pushed, losing any patience that she might have had left.

"It was the place that Naomi and I went to be alone. You know..." Eli trailed off, and I watched as understanding graced Serenity's face.

Maybe for the first time in her life, Serenity was at a loss for words, so I jumped in and continued the questioning before Eli got tired of us and left the Jeep.

"What did she say to you, Eli? What happened when you found Naomi out in the corn that night?" I asked.

"We argued. She told me she was running away to be with the English driver named Will. She said she was sick of the community and a bunch of other stuff." He was losing interest in the conversation and I worried that Eli was ready to bolt.

Serenity's voice came out strained and she said, "Was she alive when you left her?"

The change in the young man's face was quick. His eyes widened and his mouth opened wide. "Why, of course she was alive. You don't think that I shot her, do you? I loved Naomi. I never would have hurt her."

I believed him. But, Serenity must not have, because when Eli flung the door open and stepped out of the Jeep, she was faster than him and met him as he stood up. By that time, several of the boys had gathered in front of the welding building, along with Nathaniel Schrock, the owner of the business.

Serenity pressed her hand into Eli's chest and informed him that he was being brought in for his failure to disclose information linked to a questionable death or words to that effect. She efficiently had the cuffs on the boy as she told him his rights in a few heartbeats.

The rain had turned from a misty sprinkle into a proper down pour. Through the loud droning of the rain pelting down, Eli cried out that he was innocent and how he'd never hurt Naomi.

When Nathaniel came to me with a face full of distress and questions, I tried to speak to the man and calm his worries, but before I could say much, Serenity called me back to the SUV.

"Look, Daniel, we're taking him to the station. Now, you can help me get him in the Jeep and make this easier or I'll stand out here in the rain with him until Todd arrives. Which will it be?"

I didn't think Eli Bender shot Naomi, but Serenity needed my help and that was my priority. I stepped forward and placed a hand on Eli's shoulder. "Listen, everything is going to be all right. But you have to come into town with us. Fighting is only going to make things worse."

Eli said, "Nathaniel, will you call my folks and let them know what's happening?"

"Of course, Eli, stay strong. The Lord is with you," Nathaniel said. He turned and ran into his shop to make the call.

Serenity had the door open and Eli in the back seat a second later. She climbed in next to him and I ran around the Jeep and jumped in.

It seemed like the drive to the little police station in Blood Rock was the longest of my life and not just because I was chilled from being soaked in the rain. I continued to glance in the rearview mirror at Eli, who was hunched in the corner, staring out of the window. Serenity never took her eyes off of him and her hand was poised on her holster. The quaint investigation had turned suddenly ugly and I didn't like the feel of it one bit.

Todd met us in the parking lot when we pulled in. He disappeared with Serenity and Eli for about an hour before I saw them again. I waited in the uncomfortable chair in front of the dispatcher's desk with a million thoughts racing through my head. I needed to talk to Serenity and I'd wait for her, even if it took all night.

When Serenity finally came around the corner and saw me, her eyes widened in surprise, but only briefly. She motioned for me to follow her down the hall, which I did. When we were both in her small, gray hued office, she closed the door and turned to face me.

"Thanks for all your help. I'm sorry that you had to be there for that. I thought if I waited, the Amish people would have spirited him off to some hidden community that he would've blended into easily and we'd never have found him."

"Do you really believe that he shot Naomi—*really*?" I said, reaching out to catch her arm.

She looked down at my hand and squinted. I let go. The brief contact with her skin had distracted me, almost making me lose the energy to argue.

She took a deep breath and said, "He has the motive. He was with her right before she died. And his community went to extreme lengths to keep his relationship with Naomi a secret. That's enough evidence to hold him for more questioning, especially with his failure to bring pertinent information to our attention about the crime."

"You still don't know for sure there was a crime committed," I said, running my fingers through my hair and wondering how the hell I became so emotionally invested in all of this.

"I'm going with my gut on this one. If that girl died completely from an ill-fated accident, then why the hell is everyone constantly lying to me? There are two important things that we know for sure in this case. One, Naomi Beiler was shot and two, she's dead. I'm not going to brush this under the carpet because Tony Manning, the mayor...or *you* want me to take it easy on the Amish. This entire investigation has been a fiasco from day one. No one is acting the way they should."

Serenity's face was flushed and her lips pouted as she glared up at me. At that moment, I found her completely irresistible. This was likely the last time I'd be working with her on the case now that she thought she had her man. In an instant, I decided that she could ignore the fact that we'd shared a kiss, but I wouldn't. Dammit, it had been a lifetime since I'd felt so drawn to a woman. I aimed to leave her with something to remember me by.

I stepped forward and before she could back away, I caught her waist and pulled her closer. I only fleetingly thought about her gun and her ability to use it, before I brought my mouth down to hers. She was ridged with shock, but I continued to move my mouth against her lips until they softened and finally received my tongue. Her stubborn body melted into mine as her mouth hungrily accepted my kiss. At the point when I knew she was completely mine, I stepped back.

I looked into her eyes, which were now dark with passion and said, "Try to forget that one."

It was difficult, but I turned and left the room. Maybe I was being immature, but, man, did it feel good. I was betting that kiss would finally wake Serenity up and she'd realize that she wanted me.

Besides, I believed to the core of my heart that Eli wasn't her man. She'd be calling me when she discovered her mistake. And she'd be remembering that kiss when she dialed my number.

18

NAOMI

October 14th

Lydia glanced over her shoulder while she walked with her sister, Rosemary, up the stone path to their house. Her puckered mouth and narrowed eyes made her look like a sick squirrel. How glad Naomi would be to never have to see her again.

Will's hand reached over and grasped hers in a tight squeeze. The feeling that his touch evoked was different this time. Oh, the dancing butterflies were still there, but there was also peaceful warmth spreading through Naomi. All she needed in the world was Will. He would take her away from all this and love her forever.

"What are you thinking?" Will's voice pushed through the dreamlike haze.

Naomi gazed back at him with eyes full of love. After a deep breath, she said the words that had been on the tip of her tongue the entire time since he'd picked her and the other girls up from the butcher shop.

"Can we go to Montana now?"

"*Now*—are you serious?" Will said, almost stopping the truck in the road.

Naomi nodded her head vigorously. "I'm ready to go. My shunning is up next week and then I'll have more freedom to sneak out."

Will appeared to be thinking hard and then he nodded softly. "Yeah, we can do it next week. My parents will be surprised, but they'll understand. They've been expecting it for a while." His gaze became serious. "Are you sure you're ready to do this? I mean, once we get out west, I won't be able to bring you home easily if you change your mind."

"Yes. I'm absolutely sure. I want to be with you. And there's no way that's going to happen if I don't run away. Besides, I've always wanted to go places and see things—together we can do that."

The following few minutes were not nearly enough to properly make their plans, but they tried anyway, deciding on the day and place. By the time they pulled into Naomi's driveway, her heart was leaping in her chest.

Naomi brushed her hand softly over Will's before she clutched the door handle in her hand. "Thank you for taking me with you."

Will grinned. "Hell, I can't leave the woman I love behind, now can I? Be careful over the next several days and don't go getting into any more trouble."

When Will winked, Naomi melted a little more inside. She wished that they were leaving that day instead of the following week. But she had to be patient. They had the rest of their lives ahead of them after all.

Even before her hand turned the door knob, Naomi felt a prick of uneasiness. When she did step into the kitchen she wasn't surprised to see Bishop Esch sitting at the table with her Father and Mother. She straightened her back feeling braver than she ever had. All Naomi had to do was survive the next six days and she was out of there for good.

Before Naomi could speak, Mamma said, "You best be sitting down over here, Girl."

Mamma pushed a chair away from the table and Naomi moved quickly to take it. Once she was seated with three pairs of eyes watching her closely, Naomi said to the bishop, "Hullo, what brings you by today?"

Bishop Esch sighed, and after scratching his beard for a second, he said, "I was discussing your attitude during our counseling sessions with your parents. Quite frankly, Naomi, I don't have the feeling that you are at all remorseful for your actions with Eli. And now, after all the sinning, you've gone and quit the boy. I'm confused by your behavior, and see this as a sign of trouble brewing for you."

Naomi processed what the man said quickly in her mind, taking in the disapproving look from Da. She didn't even need to glance at Mamma to know how enraged she was. There wasn't much she could do, except try to hold things together a little while longer.

Naomi bowed her head and in her saddest voice she murmured, "I know. I've been very tired lately, what with all the work at the house and the butcher shop combined." She raised her eyes to meet the bishop's gaze, which if she wasn't imagining it, might have softened a wee bit. "I am feeling overwhelmed with my duties and I think that it's affected my attitude lately."

The bishop glanced at Dat who was nodding his head slightly in understanding, but Mamma sat silently with the steely look of a woman who had no sympathy left in her.

"We all work hard, Naomi. That is our way in life, especially the women. But, even so, we can help you if you are having difficulties dealing with your situation." Bishop Esch turned and said to Dat, "Timothy, do you know of a way that this girl's load could be lightened for a while?"

Naomi couldn't believe what she was hearing and she brought her bottom lip back up as she glanced at Dat who was straightening his beard, looking very uncomfortable.

Before her father could say a word, Mamma's hand shot out, pointing at Naomi. "Why, this is just an excuse the girl is making to get out of her duties."

"Now, Patricia, I'm not saying that Naomi should be excused from her chores or her job. I'm simply suggesting that you both take into account what she has told us today. It is my position in the community to assist our people, even the young ones, when they have problems."

Mamma rose from her chair and for a second, Naomi thought that she would leave the room, but instead, she pointed her finger once again at her. "I tell you, this girl has the devil in her. She's always sassing me and sneaking around. I don't trust her."

Naomi absorbed the words in shock—*the devil?* Mamma was losing her mind, Naomi reasoned to herself. But even though she understood that the woman who had given birth to her, and never had more than an ounce of affection to share, was insane, her heart still wilted at her mother's statement. The knowledge that Mother didn't love her at all slammed into her gut. Naomi sucked in a deep breath and wiped the tears that were beginning to trickle down her cheeks.

The bishop motioned for Mamma to sit, but she ignored him, and said, "I have spoken my mind on the matter." She turned and left the room. It seemed, with her exit, all the anger and hatefulness left too.

Dat remained silent, but the bishop shook his head and said, "Timothy, I do not agree with your wife. Naomi is rebellious, but that is all." He stood in a fluid motion not expected of a gray bearded man and said to Naomi, his eyes dead serious, "I'll continue to counsel you, Naomi, until the shunning is complete, but I expect to see improvement in your willingness to obey and be submissive."

Bishop Esch walked to the door in long strides, followed closely by Da. Just before he stepped out, he turned and said, "And you really should reconsider your relationship with Eli Bender. Settling down with a fine young man might be just what's needed to sow your wild oats."

When Naomi was finally alone, she exhaled. Her mind raced with the craziness of it all. The bishop was pushing her into a marriage with Eli, her Father couldn't find his tongue even though Naomi's life was crumbling around her...and her mother hated her. The excitement she'd felt earlier when she knew that she'd be escaping was thoroughly drenched now.

The touch of Emma's small hands on her knees brought Naomi's head down. Without any thought at all, she pulled the small child up and hugged her tightly. What would her little Emma do when she was gone? As the child's hair tickled

Naomi's noise and her fingers kneaded her arm, the doubts came rushing in.

Naomi was suddenly terrified about what she was planning to do.

19

SERENITY

November 17th

I pushed the ice cubes around the cup with the straw, thoroughly disgusted with myself. No matter how I tried to rid Daniel from my mind, the feel of his lips pressed against mine kept invading my thoughts. As it was, I was operating on only about four hours of sleep, and now, when I needed to be focused, my brain was a jumbled mess.

Bobby's voice broke through the cloud. I looked up to stare at the old man who had paused from eating his burger to talk to me. "I would think that you'd be in a finer mood, Serenity. After all, the judge agreed with you about the Amish boy at the arraignment today."

It wasn't the words he said, more the tone he used that put me on the defensive. I glanced at Todd, who was munching on his fries, acting disinterested, but I knew better. Very little conversation got by Todd.

"I know what you're thinking, Bobby—that I got into too big of a hurry to bring Eli Bender in," I said and leaned back in the booth. I watched the other patrons in Nancy's Diner, thinking how nice it would be to be one of them, just enjoying the greasy cheeseburgers without all the stress that had my belly tied in knots.

"That's not it at all. I'm more interested in how you're going to handle the news if Eli isn't the unborn child's father," Bobby said with a thoughtful rise of his eyebrow.

Leave it to Bobby to hit it right on the nail. Todd was looking at me with mild sympathy, bringing me to my senses and reminding me of what the bishop said at Naomi's funeral. It is what it is.

"I certainly hope it wasn't Will's child, but if it turns out to be his, I don't believe the fact would change the charges against Eli," I said.

Todd said, "How long will it take, Bobby, to get the results back from Indianapolis?"

"A few days, maybe a week, I'd say," Bobby answered.

The longest damned week of my life, I thought, taking a bite of my sandwich. We sat silently for several minutes before a nagging question finally made its way out of my mouth.

"Bobby, do you recall any strange incidents that happened within the Amish Community, oh, say, about thirty years ago?"

Bobby pulled his attention from his lunch and looked at me with an intensity that I usually didn't see on the laid back old man's face. "Why ever would you ask such a question?"

The tickling of foolishness vanished and I plunged in. "I heard a story that happened around that time, and I was curious if you knew anything of it. But, I guess it was told to me in confidence, so I don't want to give you the particulars."

Bobby drew his brows together, thinking for a few seconds and then said resignedly, "The Amish settled here in Blood

Rock about thirty-five years ago, and I remember the hoopla within the community about their arrival. Most folks didn't really mind having the Plain folk moving in, but others were quite bothered by the idea of having to rub elbows with a group who were so different from them. People were more prejudiced back then, especially about things they didn't understand."

"How did you feel about them?" I interrupted.

"Oh, I had no problem at all with the Amish. As a matter of fact, I was captivated by their lifestyle at first. There is quite the appeal of their simple ways and strong family ties. I became friendly enough with some of the local men by visiting their businesses. Did you know that the house that Mary and I sold a few years back was Amish built?"

"No, I didn't. But, you said, *at first.* What did you mean by that?" I stared at Bobby hoping that if his words didn't answer my question, his expression would.

"Don't go getting me wrong. I still don't have any problem with the Amish, but I've seen things over the years that have made me reconsider that their way is really simpler. In fact, my observations have led me to think that their lifestyle is a way of self-inflicting punishment. The young people seem to have it the worst. They're expected to take on the work load and responsibility of an adult at the age of fourteen or fifteen."

"Yeah, but those kids are a hell of a lot more mature than our teens," Todd interjected.

Bobby shook his head softly, and said, "No, it doesn't matter what culture the child is brought up in, the desire to have fun and be free is universal." Bobby paused and turned back to me. "Getting back to your original question, Serenity, there was one tragedy that sticks in my mind as if it were yesterday."

Bobby searched around for prying ears, and seeing that the diner's noon day rush was past and most of the booths were empty, he settled back against the seat, his hands folded on the table.

"I was still an assistant to the coroner, Billy Jones, at the time. I wasn't in charge, but Billy was quite the drinker and many of his responsibilities fell directly on my shoulders. That's why I was personally called out to the railroad tracks that day. You see, Billy was on a binge somewhere and Sheriff Connelly couldn't locate him. Anyway, it was a young Amish woman who was hit by the train." Bobby thought for a second before adding, "I do believe that her name was Rachel Yoder."

Todd interrupted, "What's the big deal in that? Even now, we occasionally have to pull someone off the tracks."

Bobby looked form Todd to me before he answered. "It wasn't the fact that she was hit by the train. It was that she purposely stepped in front of it."

His words registered, and a chill swept over me. I blocked the mental picture out. "How do you know that it wasn't an accident?"

"It was in broad daylight, and a motorist stopped at the crossing saw the Amish girl walking alongside the tracks. When the train was almost abreast with the girl, she took the step in front of it. It was no accident—the girl wanted to die."

"Why would she do such a thing?" I asked.

"That's the part that makes that case similar to this one. No one would talk to Sheriff Connelly about it. The Amish people were as tight lipped in those days as they are now."

Bobby swiveled in his seat and called out, "Nancy, come on over here, and help refresh my memory."

Nancy was an older woman who was extremely vibrant, despite her wrinkles. She dyed her hair the bright red that I'd been told had been her natural color before she'd ever received her first gray strand. When she moved about, her hips swung in a motion that many younger women couldn't pull off, me included.

She stopped wiping down the counter, flinging the cloth aside to make her way over to our table. With no shy bones in her body, she slid into the booth beside Bobby and across from me.

"What can I help you with, Bobby?" Nancy drawled the question out, making it sound as if she was offering something very inappropriate.

Bobby must have thought so too. He blushed before he turned slightly to the woman, "Do you remember when that Amish girl got herself killed by the train?"

Nancy nodded. "Sure do. That was a long time ago, but I remember it pretty clearly. I was working at that dive out on Route 44 where the sheriff and his boys used to hang out. He was pretty pissed off with them Amish people and how they acted."

The cloudy day outside the windows suddenly seemed to brighten when I realized that there might be a common pattern with the two events.

"How were they acting, Nancy?" I asked.

Nancy brought her darkly shadowed green eyes to me and said, "Why, they just didn't seem to care much that the girl did herself in. And they wouldn't give the sheriff any information about why she'd do such a thing either."

"None of the Amish people were at all helpful?" I pressed, instinctively knowing this was important somehow.

As if Nancy had just stumbled over a thought, her eyes widened, "There was a sister that was talking a bit, until the rest of 'em quieted her."

"Do you know her name?" I asked, thinking it was a long shot.

"Course I do. She's a friend of mine now—goes to the same church I do."

Confusion must have lit my face, because Nancy laughed, and said, "She ain't Amish any more, Serenity. Mary Yoder turned English a few years after the train took her sister's life. She's married to Mike Clark and they have a few grown."

"Do you think Mary would talk to me about her sister?" I asked, suddenly excited that I knew two people who used to be Amish.

Nancy nodded. "Let me give her the heads up that you'll be contacting her, but yeah, I believe she'll talk to you."

"Can you call her now? If it's okay, I would like to visit her today." I tried not to sound too anxious, but probably failed miserably.

Nancy raised her eyebrows. "Today? Why, you must be a curious girl to rush over there." When I didn't say a thing, only holding my breath, she continued, "All right then. Let me wait on that tall, handsome piece of pie first."

Nancy winked. When I peeked around the booth behind me, my heart stopped. It took just a second for Daniel to hone in on me and when his gaze met mine, he frowned slightly. The look got my heart started again. His face cleared of emotion and he walked leisurely to our booth.

"Oh, great," I sighed, thudding my head back against the bright red plastic cushion.

Todd half stood, looking in the direction of the door before I could tug him down. When he seated himself again, he chuckled, "Looks like you have a stalker."

In the few seconds it took Daniel to arrive at our table and take the seat beside Bobby that Nancy had vacated, I'd regained my composure. I hoped my face was neutral when I chanced a glance back at Daniel.

Without taking his eyes off of me, he said, "How did Eli's arraignment go?"

When I stubbornly refused to speak, Todd answered for me. "The judge agreed that we can hold him for questioning while we wait for the DNA evidence to come in."

"I take it that you're no longer in need of my services?" Daniel directed the question at me, and unless I wanted to look like a juvenile to Bobby and Todd, I had to answer him.

"I'm not sure, but I think we've got things covered for now," I said meeting Daniel's gaze and feeling weak kneed just looking at him.

My response obviously hurt his feelings, although he was careful to conceal it when he abruptly rose. "If you need anything further, Sheriff, don't hesitate to call me."

Daniel left us to join his crew at the counter. When Todd, Bobby and I passed him on our way out, he didn't even look up, instead staying in conversation with his buddies. I could hardly blame him for ignoring me. I'd been quite the bitch.

The cold air cleared my hot thoughts and I looked at Bobby as we neared the patrol car. "Do you want to head over to Mary's with us?"

"No, I have some paperwork that I need to get caught up on if I plan to take Thanksgiving week off."

"All right, we'll drop you off at the department and Todd and I will go meet Mrs. Clark."

Before Bobby slid into the back seat, he turned to me and asked, "Why is it so important for you to talk to this former Amish woman about an incident that happened thirty years ago?"

I didn't really have an answer for him—at least, not one that made any sense. I just felt the pull to follow through with it, almost as if I were being guided by an invisible force to do so. But, hell, I couldn't tell Bobby that.

I gathered my wits, and said, "The more I can learn about the Amish the better. I'm sure other situations will arise where the knowledge will come in handy. And I've already discovered that the best place to learn about the Amish is from those who used to live among them."

Bobby was satisfied with my answer and questioned me no more. Once we dropped him off, Todd and I headed to the south side of town where Mary lived with her husband. Todd was rather subdued during the drive, and against my better judgment, I turned and said, "What's going on with you? You haven't said one rude thing to me today."

Todd slowed the vehicle and glanced over. Seeing that he was about to spill the beans, I silently kicked my curious side.

"Heather's pregnant," Todd said firmly, right before he began rubbing his hand over his buzzed hair in distress.

That was the last thing I was expecting him to say. I was trying to figure out how to respond when he began talking again.

"Now she wants me to marry her."

"You were planning on marrying her anyway, so what's the big deal?" I oversimplified it for sure, but I had more important things on my mind.

"That's not the point. Before, I had a choice in the matter. Now, she just expects me to do it. *Everybody* expects me to do it." Todd sounded really depressed and for the first time in twenty years, I felt sort of sorry for him.

I put Naomi, the Amish, and Daniel out of my mind for the moment. "Todd, Heather is your high school sweetheart. You've been with her, on and off, for all these years. Really, you should have popped the question a long time ago."

"Yeah, maybe, but what about you—you're not married either."

Why on earth the conversation had drifted into my personal space, I had no idea, but since Todd wasn't cracking any jokes, I decided to be honest with him.

"I guess it's because I haven't met anyone I felt right about marrying yet. I mean, I've dated a few guys seriously, but not one of them I'd want to spend the rest of my life with. You and Heather are different though. You two have already shared a life together, and even when you've gone your separate ways, you both always ended up back together again. I think that you're just being stubborn about the whole marriage thing."

"Do you really think that two people could be meant to be together—like soul mates?" Todd asked.

I gazed out the window and thought for minute. My parents had been married for forty years and I certainly couldn't see either one of them with any other person. And, Laura and Ryan had been together for about twenty years and they were still going strong. Maybe, what Todd said was true. But, certainly, I wasn't a relationship expert. I couldn't even begin dating someone without screwing it up completely.

Glancing back at Todd's anxious frame, I decided to be nice. "Yeah, I do. And, I think you and Heather are two of those people."

Todd nodded and said, "You know, I think you're right. When I get home tonight, I'm going to ask Heather to be my wife. I'm really going to do it."

I was glad to get it out of the way before we met with Mary. Now, Todd should be able to concentrate on his job. A couple of minutes later we pulled into the Clark's driveway. I thought that the little, one story cookie cutter house fit perfectly into the usual idea of American living—and, how it was a far cry from the type of Amish household that Mary probably grew up in.

The dried out orange Mums in pots to each side of the doorway caught my attention while we waited for someone to answer the door. The cold winter was fast approaching and all of nature was bracing for it. Already, I missed the blazing sunshine of warmer days.

"Hello, Sheriff. I just got off the phone with Nancy, but I wasn't expecting you so quickly," the woman at the door said. She had a head full of dark hair that was lightly streaked with gray. Her eyes were bright and friendly.

I held out my hand and Mary lightly shook it. "You must be Mary Clark. Please call me Serenity. This is Todd."

After the introductions were made, we found ourselves seated around the table in Mary's blue and yellow kitchen. I looked around the room, taking in the country décor, while Mary poured a cup of tea for herself and me. Todd was already sipping the cola that she'd given him.

"Nancy said that you wanted to ask me some questions about my sister, Rachel. Is that true?" Mary said, finally taking a seat across from me. Her face was still open, but her body had tensed with her words.

"Yes. Bobby Humphrey told me about Rachel's death. I must admit, I became intrigued with the story. You see, I'm investigating the death of another Amish girl and I thought that the information about your sister might help me understand the Amish psyche better," I said.

Mary absorbed my words and sighed.

"I must say that there isn't a day that goes by that I don't think about my sister and how she took her own life, but I haven't talked about it for, oh, so many years. Did Mr. Humphrey tell you that Rachel killed herself by stepping in front of the train?"

"Yes, he told me that part. Do you have any idea why she would have done such a thing?" I asked softly. Mary's eyes met mine and they were moist. I suddenly questioned my visit with the woman, realizing how painful the memories were to her. I hastily said, "If you don't feel comfortable talking about this, I understand."

Mary sniffed, "No, no. This is a conversation that I've been waiting to have for almost thirty years now. It's long overdue. I believe I owe it to Rachel to tell it." Mary took a sip of her tea and settled into her chair before she continued.

"Rachel was the prettiest girl in the community. All the boys were after her, but she wasn't interested in any of them. Instead, she had her eye on an English boy who lived up the road from our farm. I admit, he was a handsome young fellow, and a hard worker, always helping us put up the hay or bring the crops in for some extra money. But he was also a

187

rowdy character, and it didn't take long for the leaders in our community to see it and restrict the Amish youth from interacting with him. Well, my sister had her own rebellious ways. Even though she knew it was forbidden to mingle with English boys in general, and this boy particularly, she went ahead and started up a relationship with him anyway." Seeing my eyes widen at her words, she smiled. "Yes, it was quite the scandal. I won't get into all the details, but in the end, when Rachel was caught, she did the most horrible thing imaginable. She lied, telling the bishop and ministers that the young man had attacked her.

"Rachel was young, and she said what she did in a moment of panic and fear. Our father had a violent temper and she was terrified of what he would do to her if he knew the truth. What Rachel didn't think about, was what our father and the other men of the community would do to her English lover.

"To this day, I don't know exactly who was in on it, but I do know that the boy did pay for his accused sins."

Mary paused, looking out the window, while I tried to slow my heart. My God, I knew who did it. Daniel's story was weaving into Mary's, giving me the picture of an incredible Shakespearian type tragedy.

Mary's voice pierced my runaway thoughts. "That's why she took her life with the train. The guilt pestered her for days, until it was too much for her to live with. I tried to talk to her about it but failed, being angry with her myself for her destructive ways and decisions. But I never dreamed she would commit the ultimate sin."

Mary's voice trailed off and she dabbed her eyes with a napkin. After glancing at Todd, whose own eyes were wide, I swallowed and asked the questions that had been nagging me since Mary began speaking. "Who was the boy, Mary? Did he die?"

Mary's face firmed and she sat up straighter. I could tell that she was weighing in her mind whether she should tell me. After an uncomfortable minute of near silence, the only sound being the tick-tock of the wall clock, she looked me straight in the eye, and said, "No, he didn't die. As a matter of fact, he's still very much alive today."

I whispered, "What's his name?"

"Anthony. Anthony Manning," Mary whispered back.

20

October 20th

The bellowing finally stopped after the shot gun's *boom* blasted through the room. Naomi squeezed her eyes shut for a few seconds trying not to think about the cow that was now lying dead in the adjoining room. All too soon, chunks of the animal's meat would be beneath her hands, ready to be wrapped. She swallowed down the queasiness that suddenly hit her belly, wondering why, after a year of suffering though this horrible job, she was just now becoming physically ill from it.

When Naomi opened her eyes and saw the men tying the rope around the cow's hind legs so that it could be hoisted up and cut open, her insides rolled and hot bile rose in her throat. Dropping the knife, she pulled the plastic gloves off and covered her mouth as she sprinted from the room. She flung the door open and ran to the side of the building, where she vomited into a clump of green grass. Just as Naomi was straightening back up, Sandra's hands were on her shoulders.

Sandra's voice rang in Naomi's ear. "Are you all right?"

Sandra handed Naomi a paper towel. She pressed it to her mouth, wiping the wetness away. Her stomach was still wavy, but not like before. She took a trembling breath before she answered Sandra.

"I guess I'm getting sick. My belly's been rocky all day."

"You probably just need some fresh air," Sandra said as she wrapped her arm around Naomi's shoulders and guided her to the picnic table. "Let's see if you feel any better after sitting for a minute."

Naomi's legs were still wobbly, and she was happy for the help from her friend's strong hands. Once they were seated, Naomi lifted her head to the cool breeze, letting the brush of air dry the dampness from her forehead. After a minute, she opened her eyes and looked at the only friend she'd ever had. Naomi felt a deep sadness that she'd be leaving her behind. Seeing the concern in Sandra's eyes, the pull to confide her plans became too strong. In a second of reckless trust, Naomi made the decision. Glancing over her shoulder to make sure that they were completely alone, and seeing that they were, she turned back to Sandra, who was waiting patiently for her to say something.

"Sandy, I have a secret to tell you. But if I do, you have to promise to never speak to anyone about it." Naomi said it in such a serious voice that Sandra's eyes became as round as saucers as she leaned in close.

"Course you can trust me, you know that. So what's the secret?"

Naomi swallowed down the sudden misgiving and whispered, "I'm running away. I'm leaving Blood Rock and never coming back."

Sandra's jaw dropped and she grabbed Naomi's hand squeezing it tightly, "What are you talking about? *Are you crazy?*"

"No, I'm perfectly sane, maybe the only one, besides you, in this entire community. I can't take it anymore. The way Mamma treats me and how the elders are against me. This is for the best. I know it is."

"How are you going to do it?" Sandra's voice was half panicked and half in awe.

Naomi looked around again before she whispered to Sandra, finally allowing herself to speak the words to her friend that she'd wanted to for so many days.

"Will Johnson is taking me to Montana with him. He loves me...and I love him. I'm going to become English."

"My goodness, you *are* crazy!"

"No, I'm not. I've thought it all out. I'm not Amish material," Naomi said with sureness that must have convinced Sandra, because after the girl absorbed her friend's words, she nodded slowly.

Sandra whispered, "When is this going to happen?"

"Tonight—I'm leaving tonight. All I have to do is cross-over the cornfield to Burkey Road, where Will will be waiting for me."

Sandra took a deep breath, "Oh, my. I can hardly believe it...but I do understand. You have it even worse than the rest of us it seems, with your crazy mother. But are you sure that you can trust Will?"

With no hesitation at all, Naomi said, "Yes. I trust Will with my life. Don't you go worrying about me—I'll be fine for sure."

"I'll miss you," Sandra said with glistening eyes. It took all of Naomi's inner strength not to begin tearing up herself.

"After I've settled in, I'll send you a letter. Maybe if we're real careful, we can stay in touch that way. And, who knows, maybe someday we can see each other again."

"Oh, I hope so. I don't know what I'm going to do without you."

Naomi put her hands over her friend's. "I'll never forget you, Sandy."

Sandra smiled sadly and now the tears flowed down Naomi's cheeks unchecked. Naomi knew deep down that she was doing the right thing—but then why did it feel so terrible, she wondered?

21

SERENITY

November 17th

My head was swimming as I walked into my sister's kitchen. The warmth of the lights and the steam rising from the pot on the stove instantly calmed my nerves. Laura was bent over Taylor at the kitchen table, helping my niece with her homework. Their heads popped up at my entrance.

"I wasn't expecting you, Serenity. What's up?" Laura asked, leaving Taylor at the table and approaching me with a concerned look on her face.

That was the thing about my sister—she could read me like an open book.

I shrugged and averted Laura's gaze by opening up the fridge and searching the interior for nothing in particular.

"How's Will doing?" I asked, trying to avert attention from me.

Laura leaned against the counter top. "He's still a mess, but he'll survive. He went out and worked his horses today. That's a good sign."

Grabbing a cola, I shut the fridge door and faced my sister. "You know, he's going to internalize this for a while and that's what you have to watch for. Keep the lines of communication open. I'm sure he really wants to talk about it, but it hurts too much right now."

I glanced at Taylor. She was pretending to do her homework, but in reality, her ear was tilted our way, listening. I crossed the floor and sat beside her, placing my hand on her back and rubbing her the way I always did.

"How are you holding up, kiddo?" I asked, cringing when I saw the advanced algebra questions in front of her.

Taylor was a tough little cookie, reminding me of myself when I was her age. There was sadness in her eyes, but she had it under control, just as I expected her to.

"I'm all right, Aunt Rennie, but poor Will is heartbroken. You know, he really loved Naomi. I think they would have gotten married and everything."

I sighed, again wishing that I could have met Naomi before she died. "I believe that you're right, but now we have to help your brother get through this."

"By loving him a lot, right?" Taylor said, her upbeat nature shining through even in tragedy.

"Yep, we'll all smother him with hugs and kisses. I'm sure he'll just love that," I joked.

Taylor giggled and slammed the text book shut. "I'm finally done."

After Taylor left the kitchen, Laura took a seat and stared at me with a worried frown. "Have you heard anything about the paternity test yet?"

"No, and I don't expect to for a few more days." I was toying with the edge of the table cloth, my mind drifting back to my conversation with Rebecca Clark. If I settled my thoughts on it for too long, goose bumps rose on my arms and my heart sped up. I still hadn't decided what the hell I was going to do with the information—and how I could even confirm what had happened that night to Tony Manning. The question that had me in a confused tizzy was why the ex-sheriff was so buddy, buddy with the Amish after they'd tried to kill him.

"I think the part of all this that bothers me the most is that I can't do anything at all to help Will. This situation is completely out of my hands. There are no soft words of encouragement that will make this any better for him or heal his soul," Laura said.

"Yeah, I know what you mean." I was as deflated as my sister looked.

"No, Rennie, you can't understand exactly what I'm talking about. It's like..." here Laura paused and sniffed a little before going on, "...I can feel his pain and it's killing me too. I wish I had the power to change everything—make it all better for him. I can remember every time that boy hurt himself on the playground or riding his bike. And it doesn't seem to get any easier when they grow up."

Looking into Laura's face as she dabbed a stray tear with the napkin, I suddenly knew who I needed to talk to about the incident with Tony Manning.

Mothers remembered everything.

"You'll be staying for dinner won't you?" My sister's voice sounded far away, but I answered her anyway.

"Sure. But I have to be quick about it. There's somewhere I need to go later."

Daniel was already pissed at me, so it shouldn't really matter. But I still worried that when he found out where I was going he'd want to ring my neck for sure.

22

NAOMI

October 20th

Naomi sat at the table between her younger brothers, Samuel and Elmer. The mood was light, and Naomi thought, possibly even joyous. The shunning was finally over.

She had no appetite, but Naomi forced herself to keep shoveling forkfuls of food into her mouth. She'd need the energy for later that night when she planned to sneak away. The thought still sent spasms of fear through her, but as each hour had passed during the day, she'd become more resolved—especially when Will had brushed the side of her face with his hand and told her he loved her before she'd stepped out of the truck.

She waited anxiously for the sun to dip low in the sky and her family to go their separate ways, some going to the ball game at the Schrock's, others heading to the school house for the meeting. Naomi wasn't interested in either event. She knew that the ball game would be a bore, as usual, and the decision of who was going to be the new school teacher would be a long, drawn out affair. The only part of the plan that Naomi worried about was whether her parents would buy her feigned illness when the time came, allowing her to remain home.

Nine year old Elmer's voice boomed in Naomi's ear, bringing her back to the kitchen. "Will ya help me, Naomi?"

Naomi blushed, having no idea what her little brother was jabbering about. "What do you need help with?" Naomi said, acting as interested as she could manage.

"The new pony—I want to ride her to the ball game, but she's a stubborn girl. Maybe you could work her for a while first?" Elmer questioned. His eyes were wide with pleading.

"Why doesn't Samuel...or Marcus do it?" I suggested, not in the mood or having the time for such nonsense this evening.

Samuel blurted, "I can't do it. I done told the Schrock's that I'd be over there early to help set the nets up."

"I'm going with him," Marcus said at the same time he stood up, gathering his plate and cup into his hands.

"You have not been excused yet, young man," Mamma scolded with the usual scowl fixed on her face.

Avoiding Mother's glare to stare at the table top, Marcus said, "May I be excused?"

"You may," Mamma said. Once she stood, the rest of the children were able to move about and several of them bounded from their chairs, heading for the door.

Naomi watched Marcus grab his coat and hat quickly up, while Samuel, who was fifteen, worked at a more leisurely pace to get dressed for the chilly outdoors. She couldn't help but sigh at the mess of dirty dishes left on the table. The one

Beiler boy willing to clean up after himself was Marcus, who she figured had so much of an abundance of energy that he couldn't help himself.

The only people still sitting at the table were Da, Elmer, herself, and little Emma, who had abandoned her seat to climb onto Naomi's lap.

"So will ya ride the mare?" Elmer begged.

Naomi hardened her heart, knowing that there wasn't enough time. "No, I have too much to do in the kitchen before we have to leave."

Mamma's voice drifted across the room from where she was standing at the sink and Naomi nearly fainted at her words.

"You go on and help your brother. I'll clean up here."

Naomi glanced at Da, who nodded at her. "Well, okay, if you're all right with it?" she said, hesitating.

Mamma rounded on her oldest daughter and said in a shrill voice, "I told you I'd do it. So you best get going, 'fore I change my mind."

Naomi quickly deposited Emma onto the floor and made her way to where the black coats were hung neatly on pegs in a row. Slipping her favorite corduroy jacket on, Naomi pulled tennis shoes of the same color onto her feet and left the kitchen, just one step behind Elmer.

The cold air pricked Naomi's face and she dipped her head down to shield her cheeks. Elmer skipped along ahead of her and she couldn't help but smile at his enthusiasm. After all, it hadn't been that long ago when Naomi herself would have been thrilled to ride a new pony. As her feet began to sink into the sticky mud in front of the barn, a shimmer of excitement went through her.

Naomi willed the thoughts of escape to disappear as she focused on the jet black, shaggy pony that Elmer was tugging out of the stall into the hallway. It was a big pony, and the small, dished face and flaring nostrils told Naomi that the animal would be a high strung ride indeed.

Silently, Naomi worked beside her brother, brushing the fluff until it shone brightly on the animal's side facing the open doorway and the lowering sun. Once the pony's hooves were picked out and the saddle secured, Naomi slid the bit into the mare's mouth and pulled the headstall up over her ears.

"Now, you be careful, Naomi. Blackie gave Samuel quite a ride the other day," Elmer said, concern pinching his face.

Naomi took up the challenge as easily as she would have picked up a broom. "Oh, did she now?" she said, gathering the reins into her hands and lightly stepping up into the saddle.

She felt the quivering movements of the mare's powerful muscles beneath her, but Naomi relaxed her body and held the reins softly, telling the spunky little beast that she would ride it with respect and dignity. Ten minutes later, after taking the pony through the walk, trot and a bouncy canter in the back yard, Naomi felt confident that Elmer could take over the mare without getting killed.

When she stopped beside him, Elmer's eyes were wide and his mouth round. "How'd you do that? She's a different horse than she was the other day."

Naomi stopped and slid off the saddle in an easy motion, handing the reins to Elmer. She fixed a serious look on her little brother and said, "You know that Samuel is too rough with the horses and most of them are afraid of him. If you want a horse to be your friend and work well for you, then you have to be patient with them." She paused patting the pony on its thick neck before continuing, "You have to be kind to them and give them some freedom."

Elmer had straightened his back while he listened to Naomi's advice. When he climbed into the saddle himself, he remembered her words and softly nudged the pony forward on a loose rein. When the pony began walking down the driveway leisurely, Elmer swiveled in the saddle and shouted out to Naomi, "Thanks, Naomi—you done a good job."

Naomi waved back, smiling. Oh, how she'd miss her little brothers and sisters. She knew deep down that they all still needed her. The tightness of indecision began to grip her insides as she stood in the driveway, the cold breeze penetrating the jacket and flattening her dress hard against her legs.

Once she left, that would be it. Dat and Mamma would forever hate her, and they'd do everything in their power to keep her siblings away from her. But the alternative to not leaving was staying. The prospect of living her life in the Amish community was worse than all her anxieties and worries about running away put together.

Naomi sucked in a deep breath and made her way slowly to the house, her feet dragging on the hard ground.

All she had to do was convince Mamma that she was really sick—and then she would finally be free.

23

SERENITY

November 17

It was strange driving to the Amish community alone, I thought, as I carefully passed the buggy, admiring the shiny dark horse in the evening light. I had to admit that I was content with the solitude. Thoughts of the two young Amish women, Naomi and Rachel, and their early, tragic deaths had been peppering my mind all day. True, they had a lot in common, both being involved with English men, and leading secret lives, but their circumstances were also quite different. Naomi was running away to be with her boyfriend, while Rachel chose to lie and hide the relationship with hers.

The fact that Tony Manning was Rachel's ill-fated lover still shocked the hell out of me. As hard as I tried, I couldn't imagine Tony's hard features softened with youth—and I certainly couldn't picture him being interested in an Amish girl either. Maybe all the years in between had changed the man into the ruthless asshole he was now.

I slowed as I approached Rebecca Yoder's farm. I guessed that Daniel's sister's house was the bigger one that sat further off the road, while the small, rectangular home near the road belonged to the older Bachman couple.

The sun was nearly down and I suddenly began sweating at the thought of what I was doing. Maybe the Bachman's weren't even home—or perhaps they were in the middle of dinner. The little, tiny reasonable voice in the back of my mind told me that I should back out of the driveway and forget the whole thing. Of course I couldn't listen to it. The much louder voice of determined curiosity pushed me to put the car into park and shut the engine off. No, I wouldn't be able to sleep tonight if I didn't follow through and at least try to find out what happened that night, some thirty years ago, when the Amish had taken the job of policing the neighborhood into their own hands.

When I stepped out into the brisk air, I zipped up my leather jacket, thinking that it was time to put the lining back in. Again, the scent of wood smoke was in the air and I lifted my face to breathe the pleasant odor in deeply. The old Border Collie on the porch half-heartedly barked at me as I approached the house. There was a dim light emitting from the corner window. Someone was probably home after all.

The dog rose and greeted me at the door in a friendly manner and I reached down to stroke its head, glad for the distraction before I rapped on the wood. There were muddled voices speaking foreign words on the other side of the door before it opened a slit. I was met by Daniel's father and his long grey beard.

"May I help you?" Mr. Bachman asked, opening the door further after a quick appraisal of his visitor. He definitely recognized me.

I swallowed the butterflies and said, "Yes, I hope so. I really hate to bother you on such short notice, but I wanted to talk you about some of the history of your community." I paused, holding my hand out toward the opening in the doorway, "I'm Serenity Adams, the sheriff here in Blood Rock."

Mr. Bachman hesitated only for a second before he opened the door wider and reached out to grasp my hand firmly. "Yes, of course. Come on in. It certainly is too nippy this night to have a conversation on the porch."

I followed Mr. Bachman down a short hall and into the kitchen where the lingering smells of dinner wafted in the air. Mrs. Bachman, a petite woman, with dark, gray hair, was just finishing the wiping down of the counter when we entered. She turned to stare at me with an incredulous expression.

"Anna, the sheriff wants to talk to us. Why don't you brew another pot of coffee?" Mr. Bachman said.

"Oh, don't go to the trouble on my account. Really, I'm fine," I said, with a wave of uneasiness as Anna continued to stare at me as if I had two heads.

After a few more uncomfortable seconds, Anna ignored my words and got to work on the coffee. Mr. Bachman pulled out a chair at the round table and motioned for me to take a seat, which I did quickly.

Once Mr. Bachman was seated I said, "Mr. Bachman…"

"Please, call me Mo—short for Moses. That's what everyone calls me," Mo interrupted.

I took the opportunity to really look at Daniel's dad and I felt a slight chill at the close resemblance between the two men. There was no mistaking that they were father and son. Mo was a handsome man even in his elderly years and I could picture him with darker hair and his frame tall and strong with youth. But, unlike Daniel, Mo had shiny dark eyes that held pinpoint focus, giving me the impression of a man not to be messed with. I decided that Daniel's father was indeed more intimidating than Bishop Esch was and I finally understood Daniel's inability to reunite with his parents after all these years.

Clearing my throat and my thoughts, I said, "Mo, the reason I came out here tonight was to ask you some questions about an incident that happened here in the Amish community some thirty years ago."

There was no mistaking the stiffening of Anna's back as she poured the hot liquid into the cup, some of it sloshing onto the counter. Mo's face didn't change. He remained calm and cool, even settling back further in the chair as if he had no cares in the world. He was going to be a tough egg to crack—if not an impossible one.

"That was a very long time ago, Sheriff. I have a difficult time remembering the events of last week, but I'll do my best to enlighten you."

Yeah, right, I thought, before I plunged in. "I recently learned about a young woman named Rachel Yoder who died on the rail road tracks around that time. Do you remember the incident?"

Mo tilted his head, thinking, and then looked me square in the eyes and said, "Why yes, of course. Rachel was a niece of mine. She committed the ultimate sin that day, taking her own life."

"Don't you think the ultimate sin would be to kill someone else?" The words slipped out of my mouth before I could stop them.

The small smile that lifted on Mo's face prickled the hair on my arms.

"Yes, murder is indeed a grievous act, but there would still be time to ask God for forgiveness, whereas, if a person takes their own life, they die a sinner." Before I had the opportunity to respond, Mo went on to say, "Do you understand that our people would never use deadly force, even to protect ourselves or our families?"

When I shook my head, Mo said, "It is our belief, that each and every day, we are prepared to meet our heavenly father. But what about the man who breaks into a home and commits violent acts? Do you think he would be ready for salvation at that moment? Our people believe not. It would be a sin for us to put another person into the situation of being damned. Therefore, it's better for our kind to allow violence to be done upon us, without attempting to defend ourselves."

When Mo finished speaking, a cold silence fell on the kitchen. Anna had turned around. She stood as still as a statue. Her face was the same stony shade of one too. My mind tumbled the information around in my head, wondering what exactly it meant, and why the hell he'd said it to begin with.

With the narrow stares of the couple keeping me on edge, I said, "So the Amish would never act on a violent urge…such as in the punishment of someone they believed had done a very bad turn on one of their own—something like, maybe hurting a woman, perhaps?"

Mo didn't lose the composed look as he leaned in closer across the table to me. I had no idea what Anna was doing at the instant. I was so mesmerized by her husband's black eyes. "You missed the point entirely, Sheriff. Punishment is not the same thing as murder. Our God not only allows for punishment of sinners, he condones it."

The cold air sweeping into the kitchen from the hallway as the door was flung open, immediately reached the three of us. It temporarily erased Moses' strange statement and his penetrating gaze.

The words flying out of the teenage girl's mouth were completely unintelligible to me, but the sight of Daniel's brother-in-law carrying a limp toddler in his arms certainly wasn't. I leapt to my feet and covered the kitchen in two long strides. The child was a girl and she was sopping wet and covered in mud. Her chest was still—she wasn't breathing. I looked into her father's eyes with my arms stretched out.

After a few more foreign words between Moses and Reuben, the child was placed into my arms. I dropped to the floor with her and immediately tipped her head back. I began to perform CPR on her, careful not to press too hard on her little chest after each breath of life I pushed into her lifeless body.

I'm not sure how long I was on the floor with the girl, and I completely blocked out the sounds of distress and crying coming from Rebecca, Anna and the teenage girl in the room, focusing on the job at hand. I only paused long enough to pull my cell phone out and speed dial 911, handing the phone to Moses, who of course was the only somewhat composed person in the room. But in that instant of passing the phone, I did see fear in his eyes, and I made a mental note that this Amish family was definitely acting the way I'd expect them to behave under the circumstances. The thought that the girl that I worked on was probably Daniel's own niece invaded my mind for a second, but I forced that aside, putting all my energy into trying to save the child.

When the girl gurgled and a little rush of water flowed out of her mouth, the haze in my mind lifted. I brought the girl into a sitting position and the faces and voices pressing in close became crystal clear. Rebecca was crying and moved in closer with a pleading look. I nodded in return and she lifted the child from the floor and cradled her against her breast. Anna held the two of them and the teenager gently rubbed the child's cold little hands between her own.

I didn't know if the girl would suffer permanent damage from the ordeal, but for the moment, she was taking small gulps of air and her eyes were dilated. I stood up, wiping the mud onto my jeans that had transferred from the girl to my hands. I turned to Reuben.

"What happened to her?" I was still experiencing a major buzz of an adrenaline rush through my veins and it made my voice stutter a bit.

"Christina was following the other children in the dark, playing, when she slipped into the hole that was dug for the new ice house. The recent rains had filled the hole with water and before the other children realized that Christina was no longer with them, she'd gone under. Rebecca and I were on the porch enjoying the cool air when we heard the shouts. Anna has the gift of healing, so we came here, not even knowing that my in-laws had company until we saw the car."

I took another breath. "The EMP's should be here soon. Anna, please bring a thick blanket and get her wrapped snuggly," I said. The older woman quickly got to her feet and scurried out of the room.

I turned to Mo, "I think I could use that cup of coffee now."

A ghost of a smile briefly lit the man's face before he turned and went to the counter. After I had the strong brew in my hands, I sat quietly, observing the loving interactions of the family as I tried my best to mold into the chair that I sat in.

Another fifteen minutes passed before the ambulance finally arrived to the remotely located farmstead. I greeted Beth and Raymond, filling them in on the details. They had Christina, who was now babbling toddler nonsense, onto the gurney and loaded into the van with her mother in no time at all.

Since the rest of the family couldn't drive to the hospital in a car the way anyone else would, I offered to take them into town so that they could be together while Christina was evaluated. Before I crossed the threshold outside into the night, which was far darker than the well-lit streets where I lived in town, Mo's voice called me back.

I turned to face the man, who had chosen to stay at the house and wait for the return of his family. He looked as if he'd aged from the ordeal with his granddaughter, his eyes not quite as bright and his stance not so straight.

Gruffly, he said, "Thank you for saving my little Christina's life—for there is no doubt in my mind that when Reuben brought her in, she was very close to being with our Lord Jesus. But our Lord wasn't ready for her and we weren't ready to let her go. Thus, you were with us this night. Sheriff, did you feel the hand of God guiding you here?"

I swallowed, "Maybe, but not to perform CPR on a child who'd nearly drowned. Actually, I came here to talk to you about Tony Manning. Do you know him, Mo?"

The kindness left Mo's eyes to be replaced with steely determination. "Well, the Lord works in mysterious ways, indeed. I'm glad you came, Sheriff, for my granddaughter's sake, but mind that you listen to me well. I have nothing to say to you in regards to events of the past."

Dammit, if saving a member of his family wasn't going to get the guy to open up, nothing was. Frustrated, I turned to leave. I'd only made it two steps off the porch when Mo's words echoed a previous speaker, sending a chill down my neck.

"Leave this thing with the girl well enough alone. You'll soon learn that we take care of our own."

I looked over my shoulder and was about to march my butt back up the steps when Reuben's slight cough, obviously trying to get my attention, did the trick. I glanced at his distressed face and decided to let Mo's comment go—for now anyway.

I turned back once more to see Mo as he went into the house. The sight of the closed door made an impression on me, but I couldn't worry too much about it. At that moment, I had to figure out how I was going to squeeze Reuben and the five children who'd appeared out of nowhere into my little car.

As I walked to the car, my own determination strengthened. The goal of finding out what happened to Naomi was at the forefront of my mind, but not far behind was the resolution that I'd also discover Tony Manning's secrets too.

24

NAOMI

October 20th

Naomi peeked out her bedroom window and watched the buggy pull out onto the roadway heading to the schoolhouse. She let out a long sigh as she sat on the edge of the bed and took one last look at the stark, pale blue interior, collecting her thoughts. Unlike Will's, Naomi's room had no posters adorning the walls or anything at all that told of her love of horses and the outdoors. The only personal item displayed sat on her dresser in a delicate porcelain frame. It was the Lord's Prayer. Without thinking, Naomi crossed the room and picked it up. She silently said the words in her head. She was a believer and becoming English would not change that.

When she finished, she carefully set the frame down, and feeling a sudden rush of adrenaline, she scurried back across the room and went to her knees. Reaching far under the bed, she found what she was looking for and pulled it out. The pack was hunter green and as plain as everything else in her life. Thankfully, it was also light weight and she slung it over her shoulder easily.

Even though the house was dead silent, Naomi still tiptoed soundlessly down the stairs. She slowed at the entrance to the kitchen to look around before she entered. Her heart beat furiously, and no amount of swallowing or breathing would calm her nerves.

She passed through the kitchen as if she was a ghost, hardly seeing the long wooden table with its mixture of chairs and benches. She purposely ignored the line of coats hanging on the pegs and instead focused on hers as she put it on. Naomi didn't want any last minute reminders of who she was leaving behind. If she thought too much about sweet little Emma or rambunctious Marcus, or even surly Samuel, she wouldn't have a strong enough heart to be able to do what she was about to.

Naomi blocked out the faces of her dear siblings, and after repositioning the pack onto her back, she reached for the door and turned the knob. Hesitating only a second, she glanced back into the kitchen, lit only by the dim evening light coming through the window. She pushed the door open, leaving the house in a rush. Naomi didn't want to give herself any time for second thoughts. Worried that she'd change her mind, she took two steps at a time, skipping off the porch and heading toward the barns.

The cold air bit into her face and glancing up, she saw the dark, wintry clouds piling high atop each other. It certainly wasn't the best weather for hiking a few miles through fields to meet up with Will, but Naomi also knew that the harsh weather would keep folks close to their hearths and the safety of buildings, which suited her needs just fine.

She didn't slow for the few chickens still pecking around outside of their coop, instead, she jogged through the middle of them, sending them squawking away in all directions. When she reached the gate leading to the back field, she shimmied over it fluidly, and took off at a run through the short grass of the cut hay that afforded no cover at all.

When Naomi reached the hedgerow, she parted the brush with her hands and entered the thick foliage without a backward glance. She breathed easier once she was hidden again and her heart began to settle when her thoughts returned to Will and the strong possibility that she'd be kissing him by nightfall.

If Naomi had turned around to gaze one last time at her family's farm, she might have noticed something that would have crushed all her plans. But she didn't. The Amish girl was free in her thoughts of escape, joyfully making plans in her mind about the bright future that was laid out ahead of her as she cut a path through the thick foliage beneath the trees.

When Naomi disappeared into the tawny autumn leaves of the hedgerow, her Mother stood silently watching from the window of the chicken coop. Patricia's face showed no emotion, being as still as her feet were. Then one single tear drop slipped from her eye. She hastily wiped it away, giving her body life once again.

25

DANIEL

November 18th

I rapped on the door impatiently, trying to see in through the drawn curtains in the window beside it. My heart had been pounding since I'd received the call from my sister some thirty minutes prior. Rebecca's voice was still sharp in my head, telling me how thankful she was that my girlfriend had been visiting with our parents when my youngest niece had fallen into the water filled hole and nearly drowned. I'd listened to her tell the story of how Serenity had performed CPR on the child, bringing her limp body back to life. Of course, that whole part of the story was wonderful and I was thankful that Serenity, with her emergency training, was present. But what was piercing my mind like a sword was the question that my sister couldn't answer for me—what the hell was Serenity doing there in the first place?

I knocked on the front door with more force just as it finally burst open. Serenity was a sight to behold, wrapped in the unexpected pink robe, which barely covered up the cleavage showing from beneath a lacy black camisole. Her blond hair fanned out around her in messy disarray, leaving me without words. Unfortunately, Serenity didn't have the same problem.

"What the fuck are you doing banging on my door at six o'clock in the morning?" she hissed out.

Her nasty response to seeing me shattered any romantic thoughts and I said, "Yeah, I could ask you the same thing about why you were at my parent's home last night."

Serenity's mouth dropped open and her eyes were wide with frustration. "You've got to be kidding me—that's why you're putting dents in my door?"

Her voice was still turbulent, but it had come down a couple of notches, and I reined in my own anger, saying, "You have absolutely no right to be sneaking around behind my back, harassing my folks."

Serenity pulled the robe up tighter around her neck, blocking my sight of her lovely skin. She turned and said over her shoulder, "It's too damn cold to talk outside."

Taking her words for an invitation inside, I followed her and closed the door behind me. I stayed on her heels until she plopped down on the suede looking sofa and crossed her legs beneath her robe. She looked up at me with agitation for some seconds before she jerked her head to the other side of the sofa, indicating that I should sit down.

I was stubborn and remained standing for a minute more, avoiding her eyes, which had suddenly changed. They were now regarding me with amusement, making me feel even more uncomfortable than when they were shooting fire.

I looked around the room, ignoring Serenity. At a glance, the pictures on the walls were all of faraway places. I recognized the Eiffel Tower in one of them and the Golden Gate

Bridge in another. The palm trees and beach scene above the couch captured my eyes for a longer time. I envisioned walking leisurely along such a beach with Serenity beside me.

"I didn't know that you were such a travel buff," I said, trying to erase the hostility of the previous moments.

"There's a lot that you don't know about me," Serenity said smugly.

I looked away, wondering at the coy, almost flirtatious expression that she was now giving me. Feeling stupid standing there in the middle of the room, I finally sat down, purposely settling into her space and causing Serenity to move sideways to keep from touching me. I could almost feel the warmth coming from her skin. I distracted my thoughts by staring at the shaggy black rug.

Remembering the way she'd kissed me, melting against my chest as if she were born to be there, I became brave. "Yeah, it's too bad that you're such a difficult girl to get to know. God knows I've been trying."

Seeing Serenity's eyes widen was worth the comment, but I was disappointed at the way she sidestepped the conversation.

"Why is it such a big deal to you if I visit with your parents anyway? It's not as if you're seeing them on a regular basis."

Why was she being so damned difficult? I wished that I was pressing myself into her, instead of talking about my parents.

"I think you at least owe me an explanation as to why you went out there last night."

Serenity puckered her lips to the side in thought before she finally answered. "Oh, all right." She locked her gaze on me and said in almost a whisper, causing me to lean in closer to hear her. "That story you told me about your dad, the bishop and the other guys...well, I did a little bit of digging and I found out some interesting information to go along with it."

Sweat beaded on my neck as I remembered back to that night and the way I'd felt when I'd seen my father covered in blood. I shivered and said, "Go on."

"At about the same time that went down, a girl named Rachel Yoder killed herself by stepping in front of a train in broad daylight. After talking to her sister yesterday, I found out that Rachel was the girl from your story—only she wasn't really raped. Her relationship with the English man was consensual. She couldn't live with what she'd inadvertently caused to happen to her lover—so she did herself in with the train. And, that means, that there was no justice at all in what a few members of your community did to the man."

I sat quietly digesting what Serenity had said. Vaguely, now that she had brought it up, I recalled an accident with a girl and a train—I could even remember staring at the casket that held her body, which was too mangled to be opened for family and friends.

Serenity went on, pulling me back into the present.

"Do you know what the real kicker is? I found out who the guy was, and you're not going to believe it."

With real apprehension, I asked, "Who was it?"

"Unless there are two guys with the name from the same town and about the same age, it appears that Rachel's English lover was none other than Tony Manning."

"No way!" I exclaimed, trying to put the puzzle together in my head. I remembered Tony working at the stock yards and occasionally driving a pickup truck while the Amish loaded hay or produce onto it. The guy always had a dangerous feel about him and the youngsters stayed well out of his way. I could slightly recall a few of the teens hanging around with Tony, and then, only until it was forbidden to do so. I couldn't recollect anything at all connecting Tony to the girl hit by the train.

After the shock of learning that the recipient of my father's beating was Blood Rock's previous sheriff, another thought flooded into my mind, and I looked angrily at Serenity and said, "So you went to talk to my parents about that night—and what happened? Even though I told you the story in confidence, you still wasted your time on it."

"How do you know that it was a waste of my time?" Serenity growled, her eyes throwing daggers my way.

"Obviously, it wasn't a waste since you saved my niece, but why the hell didn't you talk to me about it? I could have saved you the trouble of going all the way out there for nothing, because that's what I'm sure you got out of my father—nothing."

Serenity scrunched up her face. "What good would you have brought to the discussion? You haven't spoken to your parents in fifteen years. Besides, you were pissed at me."

Again, my blood was reawakened by the sight of the ivory skin at Serenity's collar bone and lower, which was now exposed due to her outburst. I leaned in, close enough to smell the warm vanilla scent coming from her, and said, "What makes you think that I was pissed at you?"

Serenity rolled her eyes and began to rise when I made my move. I reached out and grasped her wrist. "You didn't answer the question," I said before bringing my mouth a breath away from hers.

Her words were somewhat ragged as she said, "You seemed pretty angry with me."

"You know what? I'm not angry anymore," I closed the distance and covered her lips with mine. The jolt I experienced touching her scared the hell out of me, but I didn't stop. The only way I could stop now was if she insisted. But I didn't think she was going to do that.

I pressed Serenity into the sofa, as my left arm went around her waist and my right hand touched her face tentatively. She was kissing me back with enthusiasm, and I felt I could begin breathing again. I was confident that she wasn't going to bolt. My tongue delved inside her mouth, and I loved the feel of how her tongue laced in and out of mine in perfect rhythm.

Serenity's raspy intake of breath made me bolder still, and I slipped my hand into the robe, pushing the material away. Her breast was full, but not too large, and I held it in my hand, running my thumb over the material that covered the nipple in stroking movements until Serenity moaned, saying, "Oh, please, Daniel, please..."

I lifted my head and said in my own, barely controlled voiced, "Please, what? Tell me, Serenity. Tell me what you want from me."

I stared down into Serenity's lustful eyes and wondered what they would look like if they were filled with love. Would I even know the difference? I wanted Serenity to acknowledge that she wanted me—that she was ready to surrender to me fully, or I wasn't going any further.

"Don't be silly, Daniel. You know what I want," Serenity said, trying to reach up and bring my head down to hers again, but I wouldn't let her.

"No, I need to hear the words." I began stroking her nipple again at the same time I lowered the weight of my groin onto the soft place between her thighs. Serenity spread her legs, clutching me around my hips. The feel of her wrapping around me made me want to forget about my stupid verbal requirements. I was almost going to say so when she spoke again.

Serenity's eyes were open and sure now. "Daniel, I want you to…"

Before the last words tumbled from Serenity's mouth, her cell phone went off. Her eyes cleared in an instant as she looked towards where it sat on the coffee table, lighting up with each new ring.

"No you don't," I told her.

"It could be important. Get off of me so I can answer it." Serenity was all business now, and I rolled away cussing out loud as I did so.

Serenity grabbed up the phone and brought it to her ear as she fluttered away into the other room. I was left with a yearning deep within me and a racing pulse. I decided that the next time I tried to seduce her I'd hide the damn cell phone beforehand. The hell with how pissed she got about it—it would be worth it.

And, I knew with complete certainty, that there would be a next time.

By the time Serenity came back into the room, I was sitting up. Her words completely undid me again, but in a not-so-enjoyable way.

"That was Bobby. He has the forensic report back from Indianapolis. He's waiting for me before he takes a look." Serenity blushed as she pulled her robe tighter around her, trying to cover up what I had just been touching. "Wait here while I get changed. It will only take a sec."

"You actually want me to come with you," I asked, even though I was inwardly afraid of her answer.

A smile played at the corners of Serenity's mouth, "Yeah, I do."

26

NAOMI

October 20th

The squishing sound Naomi's shoes made in the damp ground bothered her—it was too loud. Even here on the edge of the cornfield, with the tall, dry stalks shielding her from any prying eyes, she was a nervous wreck. She glanced over her shoulder again, not really expecting to see anyone, but not taking any chances either. Just a little over a mile and she'd be on Burkey Road, and finally free from the Amish community. Will would be there, waiting for her. *He would be there.* He was the kind of steadfast man that would not let her down.

The breeze picked up, bringing with it cooler air and the sound of the stalks scratching against each other. Naomi held the top of her coat tight at her throat with one hand while her other hand pushed the sharp leaves out of the way. With each step she took, she felt more confident of the decision she'd made, and she picked up her pace. As a sign of her determination, she'd ditched her bright white cap a while back in a dried up creek bed, happy to be done with the bothersome head covering forever.

Moving the backpack to the other shoulder, Naomi thought how telling it was of her life that she could fit the only things that she needed or wanted into such a small space. She wouldn't have use of any of her frumpy, polyester dresses where she was going. No, she had left all her clothes behind. The canvas bouncing against her back held a few pairs of panties, garments that would soon enough find their way into a trashcan as soon as she visited a fancy lingerie store. Her favorite home stitched jean purse and the toy cloth rabbit that Mam had given her when she was a small child were the only other items in the pack.

After cutting through the rows for a few minutes, Naomi found the grassy tractor path deep in the cornfield. She hurried on, eager to reach her destination, but also wanting to separate herself from the memories that this particular place held for her. Even with the rush of prickly autumn air on her face, she remembered the last time she'd been there, when the stalks had been vibrant and green and the pockets of hot air caused the skin under her dress to be sticky with sweat. She hadn't been alone either. Eli Bender's face flitted before her. She remembered how tingly her lips had felt as his mouth crushed against hers, exploring. And how weak her legs had gone when he'd lowered her to the ground, into the soft tall grass. It had been quicker than she thought it would be—and somewhat of a disappointment. Sandra had told her it should get better with practice, and thankfully, she'd been right.

Naomi was almost to the turning point, the stalks bending with the force of the wind, showing her the way, when she heard the *swash swash swash* of footsteps that sent her heart leaping into her throat. She turned quickly, fanning her eyes back and forth, searching. The path behind her was clear. Maybe she'd imagined the sound. She stood perfectly still and tilted her head, listening. But the only noise reaching her ears was the friction of the stalks and the whistle of the wind.

Even though her eyes and ears promised that Naomi was alone, she could not ignore the prickle on the back of her neck warning her of danger. Holding her breath, she became a statue, except for her eyes, which continued darting wherever they could reach without turning her head.

Finally, Naomi breathed out a sigh. She giggled nervously, thinking how silly she was. No one knew where she was—or cared for that matter. Dat and Mamma were at the school house meeting, probably in the thick of a heated debate about whether Bessie Yoder should take over as head teacher, replacing old Jory Raber. Everyone else was at the ball game.

Naomi relaxed, turning back around. She didn't get one step when she heard the sound of footsteps again and then there were hands on her shoulders.

"What are you doing out here all by yourself?"

She didn't need to look to know who the voice belonged to. Her heart sank in instant despair. She was so dead.

"Answer me. What are you doing out here with your hair uncovered," and as if he just noticed the backpack, he added, with even more heat in his voice, if that were possible, "...and with a backpack?"

Naomi finally met his gaze in the misty grey darkness of near night.

"Don't you go talking to me that way, Eli Bender. I won't have it. You hear me?" Naomi matched his tone, straightening her back and lifting her chin defiantly. There was no way that she was going to allow Eli to ruin all her plans.

His face wavered a bit, telling Naomi that her bulldog posture had worked. Eli was still mad, but uncertainty flashed across his features.

"Explain yourself," Eli demanded, still holding her shoulders in a tight grip.

Naomi ignored his question. "Were you following me?" she nearly shouted, struggling against him with her hands pushing on his chest.

He released her, but followed when she stepped back, leaning over her with his tall frame. "No, I wasn't following you. It was just a crazy hunch that you'd be out here in the cornfield. When you didn't show up at the ball game, and no one knew where you were, I got worried and came looking for you in the only place I could think that you'd go," he said with a whining tilt to his voice that frayed what was left of Naomi's nerves.

"We done quit each other. Remember that? There was no need for you to come looking for me. This isn't your business," Naomi thundered, trying to be heard above the swaying corn stalks.

Eli's voice softened a tad, and he said, "Are you running away?"

A part of Naomi felt like dirt. Eli was her first guy after all, and probably the nicest fellow in the whole community. He was definitely the most handsome one, with his chestnut brown hair that was always a little too long, by the Ordnung standards. Even now, he had to keep brushing it out of his face to see her properly with the wind.

She tried to think quickly of a way to get Eli to back off. She knew that if she gave him even the inkling that they would get back together, he'd never let her leave that night. No. Her only chance was brutal honesty. Eli would be in his own heap of trouble if his folks knew that he'd been meeting with her secretly in the cornfield, and there wasn't a way for him to tattle on her unless he fessed up about where he'd found her. Naomi trusted that Eli's need for self-preservation would keep her safe. At least long enough for her to get far, far away.

"Yeah, I am running away. I'm not going to put up with this community any longer." Naomi narrowed her eyes to slits and jabbed a forefinger at Eli's chest. "And you better not try to stop me."

"Who's helping you away? Are all the rumors true? Have you been messing with Will Johnson?" Eli's face was stone, but his eyes showed pain.

Naomi couldn't let those eyes affect her. She just couldn't.

"What's it to you? You were so ready to take up with the bishop and the others against me. Why would you care if I left and never came back?" she hissed the words out, both angry about the direction her thoughts had gone and impatient to be on her way.

Eli reached out and touched Naomi's shoulder, but she shrugged him off. His voice was pleading when he spoke. "I never took up sides, Naomi. I just wanted what was best for you. That's all."

"I don't see it that way." Eli's face softened even further. Naomi dove in, knowing there was no turning back now. "Can't you get it through your thick skull that I don't love you anymore? I have a new guy and he's going to take me places that you can't. Just go away and leave me alone."

Naomi bit her lower lip to punish herself, swallowing the salty drop of blood. The look of shock that Eli gave her would forever be cemented into her mind.

"You *are* the little whore that they accused you of being," Eli said in a low voice that felt barely controlled in the cool air. His lip curled up, and Naomi readied herself for the onslaught, closing her eyes tight. But it never came.

When her eyes popped open, she saw Eli's back as he made his way hastily up the tractor path. He didn't even look back at her before he disappeared into the tall corn.

Naomi breathed out, hugging her arms around her belly, trying to stop the shivering that had suddenly come upon her. She'd burned her last bridge, and now, forward was the only way to go.

27

SERENITY

November 18th

I stared out the conference room window at the dreary day outside. The clouds and hint of cold rain suited my pensive mood. If Bobby would just come through the door, I could get this over with.

Even though I wasn't looking at him, I could feel Daniel's eyes on my back, his hot gaze boring into me. My face warmed and my groin tingled, thinking back to earlier when he'd been lying on top of me. I shivered, not daring to turn around. I imagined the smug look of satisfaction that was probably on his face, and seeing that expression, even imaginary, sobered me, bringing me back to my senses.

"All righty then, I do believe I should have a few minutes without interruption," Bobby entered the room briskly, with Todd a few steps behind.

I turned around, and ignoring Daniel, who I could see from the corner of my left eye was still watching me, directed all my attention on the older man as he plopped into a chair.

"What do you have for me, Bobby?" I said, hoping the anxiousness wasn't evident in my voice.

Bobby shuffled through the small stack of papers in his hands until he reached one in particular that he pulled out and handed to me. With a quick examination of the sheet, I saw that it had nothing to do with paternity.

Before I had a chance to question Bobby, he said, "That's the forensics on the pack that Jimmy Husky brought in. The findings were interesting. There were several strands of hair on the bag, which matched Naomi, and smaller ones that were close enough to match her siblings. But there was one strand of long brown hair that didn't belong to either Naomi or any relative of hers."

"Is there any other information that was gleaned from the hair?" I asked, thinking it would be a long shot indeed that the hair would be of any use determining who shot Naomi. There were too many long haired women in the community and they regularly frequented each other's homes. And then there were all the beards.

"Just that the hair was probably from a middle aged woman—sometimes forensics like this comes in handy weeks or even years after the initial investigation. The DNA will be kept on file," Bobby said, while he began shuffling the papers again.

I hoped no one could hear the pounding in my chest. When Bobby handed me the second paper, I knew it was the paternity test results just from the lift of his eyes. I wondered if he'd already peeked at it.

Oblivious to the others in the room, I read the words carefully. Finally, I breathed a sigh of relief. I couldn't help slapping the sheet down on the table. Eli was the father. Now my nephew could move on with his life without any real connection to the Amish world, besides his memories of Naomi.

I immediately sent Laura a text telling her the news, trusting her to relay the information to Will in a thoughtful manner. Then I turned to Bobby and said, "Is there anything else that would be useful to the investigation?"

Bobby said, "No. That's it," he hesitated. I could tell by the way that he twirled the side of his mustache that he had more to say, so I leaned back and waited several more seconds before he spoke again. "Have you decided what to do with the young Eli?"

Damn. I'd known that's where he was heading. Did I still think that Eli had done his ex-girlfriend in? Yes. Was I absolutely certain? Not really.

"We have enough to hold him a while longer without filing murder charges. I believe we should wait and see what he says when he learns the truth about the baby. Maybe he'll have a moment of clarity and spill the beans."

Bobby huffed loudly, snapping my head up.

"What?" I asked, becoming defensive.

"The longer you hold the boy, the more the Amish community will turn against you." Bobby paused and pointed his head at Daniel, who'd been sitting so quietly that I'd almost forgotten he was even there. "What do you think on the matter, Daniel? You were one of them. Surely, you have feelings on the subject."

"Yes, you're right about the community not taking kindly to Eli being held in jail. The longer that it goes on, the less likely that Serenity will ever be trusted among the Plain people," Daniel said.

"They certainly trusted me to perform CPR on your niece though didn't they?" I couldn't help the venom that oozed from my words. I was so spitting mad.

Daniel smiled. "I'm sure they are very thankful for your help with the girl, but that won't change the fact that they won't be very receptive to you in regards to other matters. The Amish take care of their own—and you're attempting to hurt one of them."

"Funny, your father said something similar last night. But I'm not out to win a popularity contest among the Amish. I could care less what they think. My duty is to Naomi and finding out who shot her dead in that cornfield."

I searched each man's face, seeing solid support in Todd's expression and resignation in Bobby's. Unfortunately, Daniel's face showed rebellion. He was sticking to his roots on this one and supporting his friend's son.

"Is everyone in agreement that that's what our duty is?"

Bobby and Todd nodded, while Daniel looked away, ignoring my statement. He said, "Will you at least allow me to tell the kid about the baby? Considering the differing cultures, it would be more appropriate for me to talk to him about it."

I glanced at Bobby, who nodded in my direction. Damn. I was out numbered on this one. Even though I could override their opinions all together, I was reluctant to do so. If I was going to last as the sheriff in Blood Rock, I had to have Bobby and Todd's support. As far as Daniel was concerned, I might need some work done on my house someday, I reasoned to myself. Seeing his ultra-serious face made me think how different he'd looked when he'd been all over me on my couch.

"All right—but we'll be monitoring the questioning room. I want to hear what he says, and watch his reaction," I told Daniel.

Daniel nodded, "All right, sounds fair enough."

It didn't take long to move Eli from his cell in the adjoining building to the small square, windowless room where we did our questioning. I stood shoulder to shoulder with Bobby and Todd, studying Eli's face through the one way glass as Daniel began by making small talk with the young man, developing a friendly atmosphere before he dumped the unfortunate news into Eli's lap. Or, so I thought. When the words changed into the unintelligible German language, it was swift and smooth. I had only a second to catch Bobby's raised brows and Todd's, *what the hell*, look before I was through the door. But I was too late. Daniel had spoken quickly and I assumed thoroughly by the hard, unswayable expression that met my gaze when I looked at Eli.

"What do you think you're doing?" I asked in a low voice. I was determined to control my temper, even though it was damn near impossible to do so.

Daniel turned and what I saw written on his face scared me. His dark eyes lacked any emotion at all. But even worse than that, was the steely stubborn resolve that I saw there— just like his father.

"I beg your pardon?" Daniel said, with the attempt at confusion lighting his face.

I lowered my voice still further. "Why did you switch from English to German?"

"Uh, I'm sorry. I guess I misunderstood you about the procedure I was to follow while speaking to Eli. It's more comfortable for him to have the news delivered to him in his birth language—more understandable and softer in a way, I guess you'd say."

I stared at him, daring him to turn away. He returned the favor with a self-righteous glare that I knew I couldn't sway. He was lost to me.

Todd was standing so close to my back that I could feel his presence without even seeing him. "Todd, please take Eli back to his cell," I said.

Watching Todd escort Eli from the room, I noticed the kid's straight back and chin thrust forward. Eli was keeping his emotions locked inside of him, instead displaying a puffed up rooster demeanor of someone who'd just received more than a few words informing him that he'd almost been a father.

Bobby stood in the doorway, waiting for me to make my move. His stoic look wouldn't betray his thoughts. Speaking to the wall, I said, "You may go now, Daniel. I won't be in need of your services any longer," I faced him again and added, "—for anything."

Daniel suddenly looked very much like Moses, a man who could easily hide his thoughts from the world, and a very cunning one at that. After Daniel had swept out of the room, his heavy boots could still be heard thudding down the hallway.

When there was silence, I dropped into the chair that Eli had vacated and huffed out, "That bastard. I never dreamed he'd sink so low as to speak German to Eli."

Bobby fiddled with the corner of his beard. "I can't say that I'm really surprised. Even though he's been away from the Amish for quite a while, he's still one of them at his core. Maybe, we should give him the benefit of the doubt though, and choose to believe that he did just accidently slip into his old tongue."

"No way, Bobby—he knew exactly what he was doing. His eyes told me that much. He completely undermined my authority." I sighed in frustration, "I just wish I knew what the hell he said to the kid."

"There is a way of finding out. We have him on the recorder," Bobby said in a soft, musing way.

"The last I knew, no one in the department speaks Amish. How are we going to translate?"

"Give me a little time to look into it. I wouldn't ask anyone local of course, but if you'd be willing to pay incentive money, I might be able to get the translation. It could be done."

"Really—do you think you could find someone who'd do it for us?" I asked, only half believing we'd be so lucky.

"I have more resources than you might imagine, young lady. The person would have to remain anonymous of course… and don't go thinking that we'll have a new contact into the Amish world. It won't work that way."

I suddenly gained several more pounds of respect for Blood Rock's coroner. He was a man who wasn't afraid to step out of the boundaries of protocol occasionally to get the job done. And that's exactly what I needed at the moment.

"Okay. Do what you can, Bobby. And be quick about it."

After Todd headed over to the court house on a different matter, I left Bobby at the table and walked down the hall to my office. Walking through the doorway, my heart stilled as I was met by the smirking expression on Tony Manning's face. His face usually pissed me off, but the fact that he was sitting in the chair behind my desk totally undid me.

"What the fuck do you think you're doing?" I said, just short of a shout. Inadvertently, I placed my right hand next to my gun holster. When he rose slowly, laughing, I suddenly felt like an idiot. This was the twenty-first century—not the OK Corral. Damn, being around the Amish, caught up in their time warp must have messed with my brain. Tony motioned to my chair with flourish, and said, "It's all yours, Serenity. I was just keeping it warm for you. You know, having a little blast from the past you might say."

I remained standing. When Tony saw that I wasn't going to sit down he strolled toward me, getting close enough that I had to tilt my head up to look at him.

"You still haven't told me why you're in my office."

"No, guess I haven't, have I? But, then, maybe I don't much want to," he said, his mouth ending in a tight grin, his sky blue eyes sparking.

Before my patience left the building, Tony began talking again. "It's been brought to my attention that the pretty little sheriff has been asking about me—prying into my past, digging up dirt that's better off left buried in the ground."

"It's a free country. I can ask questions about who ever I want, Tony. Even if I wasn't the sheriff I'd have that right."

Tony nodded his head slowly as he leaned his tall frame back against the desk. He crossed one foot over the other one, appearing to be staying awhile. Any anxiety I'd felt when I arrived in the room to see my arch nemesis sitting in my chair disappeared. I placed my hands on my hips and said, "I've discovered that only people with something to hide care much about questions."

"That's definitely true, but that still doesn't erase the fact that sometimes the nosey person finds themselves in a whole heap of trouble for doing so."

"Is that a threat?"

He left the desk in a blur. Suddenly, I was looking back up into his angry face. I held my ground though. Having no doubt that Tony had his own gun somewhere on his body, I estimated that I would definitely reach mine first if the guy was having some kind of mental break down and snapped.

"No, it's a promise. My past is my own, and no one will tell you a damn thing anyway. But I'll be damned before I allow you to continue snooping around in my business. I'll string you up to an oak tree first."

He held my eyes in a deep stare for several seconds, telling me that he meant what he said, before the half grin returned to his face and he walked out the door.

Well, damn. Maybe I was living in the Wild West after all.

28

DANIEL

November 18th

I paused, looking around my sister's kitchen and realizing that this was the first time I'd ever sat in the room. I couldn't keep my heart from racing, the silent stares of my childhood friends affecting me more than I wished to admit.

Joseph and Katherine had taken the news that they'd almost been grandparents better than most people would have—just a small sniff from Eli's mother and the solemn nod from Joseph that said that he had suspected the news before I had delivered it to them.

Against my own advice, Joseph had gone to the phone box and called my sister and her husband, along with Lester and his wife, Esther. The two couples had arrived quickly, positioning themselves around the table, a pot of coffee with its strong brewed scent sitting in the center, beside a vase filled with dried flowers. I focused on the autumn hues of the flowers. I didn't really want to be staring at the blooms, but the alternative was meeting the eyes of the people I'd chosen to leave behind years ago.

My mood had been resolved all day until this moment, when the scent of the candle that Katherine had burning on the window sill drifted to my nostrils—*vanilla*. The warm smell instantly reminded me of Serenity and thoughts of how my day had started stirred my blood.

I'd made a mess of things between me and the sheriff, and I was fairly certain that I couldn't rectify the situation. But, as much as I hated the thought of losing the possibility of a relationship with the most intriguing woman I'd ever met, I knew deep down that I'd had no choice. I owed it to Eli Bender and my childhood friend. I had regrets, but not for what I'd done, only for the consequences with Serenity.

"Daniel, you may be sitting here among us, but you are not with us, my friend," Lester said softly.

I straightened in the chair. "I'm sorry, what did you say?"

The others laughed, and Joseph slapped me hard on the back. I suddenly felt very at ease, almost as if I was a teenager again and being Amish was still an option.

"We were all agreeing that from what you've told us, the sheriff doesn't have enough to continue holding Eli much longer, and that soon he'll be back with us. Then we can forget this unfortunate time and go forward," Joseph said, optimism shining in his eyes.

I said, "I believe that's a good assumption."

Joseph glanced at Katherine, and then nodded toward the doorway leading into the family room. The interplay was extremely subtle, but I caught it, as did the other women, who rose in unison with Katherine and left without further words.

Once the room held only me, my brother-in-law, and my two closest childhood buddies, I breathed a little easier and looked questioningly at Joseph, who appeared to be the leader out of the men.

Joseph's voice came out in a whisper and he leaned in closer to me as Lester moved to take the seat beside me.

"Aaron is holding a secret meeting with a few select men of the community tonight. It'll be after dark at the old Ramsey barn. Daniel, I'm worried that they will take matters into their own hands."

The worried look on Joseph's face slowed my heart's beating and I glanced over to Lester, who nodded and said, "If Eli is going to be released soon, then it would be better for everyone concerned if our people quietly waited for it to happen. God only knows what might happen if they lose their patience."

"What do you think they'll do?" I looked between the three men, but Joseph answered with a sigh as he leaned back in the chair.

"I don't reckon I know for sure, but there's been a lot of talk among the men folk. And it hasn't been meek either. Katherine and I have prayed on the matter and we both feel confident that Eli will be returned to us soon. I don't right know why so many of our people are more upset with the English than we are. He's our son."

I hesitated, but spoke my mind anyway. "What do you think happened to Naomi Beiler, Joseph?"

Joseph ran his hand through his beard thoughtfully before meeting my gaze. "It probably was just a random accident." He paused and pressed in close again. "A tragedy for sure, but really, not unexpected, when the girl's rebellious ways are taken into account. I only wish poor Eli didn't get involved with her in the first place."

Suddenly, like a slap to the face, I remembered why I'd left the Amish. The narrow thinking and complete lack of compassion for anyone with different views or goals in life was the way of many of the Amish people. That's why I'd wanted no part of their world. Even though the men seated beside me were once my close friends, I knew that it would be impossible to renew those relationships. I'd drifted too far from my roots to ever embrace the ideals of the Amish again. But then, why did I risk betraying Serenity? The best answer I could come up with is that at the time, I'd thought that it was the right thing to do.

"And you, Lester? What do you believe?" I asked, turning to my boyhood friend. Searching his face, I saw the creases at the corners of his eyes were deeper and his skin was tighter over the bones, but otherwise, he appeared very much the same as he had as a teenager.

Something passed across Lester's face that raised the hairs on my arms. It was almost as if his usual blue eyes had darkened to cobalt in foreboding. The muscles around his mouth twitched and his lips parted. I remembered that look. It was the expression his face always had right before he'd shared a secret with me.

Lester wasn't given the opportunity to speak. The shuffling was heard only an instant before Esther appeared, bringing all our heads turning in her direction.

"We should be on our way, Lester. I have too many chores at the house to remain here idle for long." Esther spoke the words calmly, but her posture was stiff and poised to take flight out the door.

Lester's face cleared and was completely blank of emotion again as he rose and reached out to grasp my hand. "It was good to spend time this afternoon with you old friend. I only hope that soon enough, we'll be able to enjoy each other's company without so much ill news between us."

A flutter of *something* sparked in Lester's eyes once more, but was gone so quickly, I wondered if I'd imagined it. My time away from the Amish had definitely changed my perception of their behavior. Stray looks and silent, but meaningful glances were the normal back then. There was a secret body language that all the Plain people instinctively knew that allowed them to communicate, without actually uttering any words—the perfect way to protect oneself from the sin of lying when being questioned by the bishop and ministers. I'd grown accustomed to speaking my mind and dealing with those who did the same, but still, even after all these years, I'd recognized that Lester was about to tell me something important. The moment was gone now, thanks to Esther.

Feeling suddenly out of place, I said my goodbyes to the others, welcoming the brisk air that met me when I stepped out onto the front porch. Several of Joseph's children brushed past me in a hurry to enter the warmth of the house, and it softened my mood when they each took the time to slow down enough to greet me by name.

Just when I reached the Jeep, I felt a light touch on my shoulder. I would have jumped out of my boots for anyone else, but the feeling was familiar and I instantly knew who'd snuck up on me. Rebecca was the only person in the world capable of doing that to me, and here, some fifteen years later, she still had the talent.

"Daniel, wait," Rebecca called out. I turned around to see the breath coming from her mouth in a puff of cold air. "I wanted to speak with you in private."

I was suddenly worried. What would bring my sister rushing up to me in the cold, while her husband sat in the buggy some distance away?

"What do you need?"

Rebecca glanced off for a few seconds, staring into the corral where two horses were munching on a pile of hay. She hesitated, shifting on her feet, before looking back at me again.

"I'm sorry to ask this, but what you told us about Eli and the investigation makes me wonder about your relationship with the sheriff. Are you truly a couple, Daniel—because, I have the gut feeling that all is not what it seems between the two of you."

I sighed, stalling my hand on the door handle. I really didn't want to have this conversation, but I also wanted to discuss the matter with someone—someone who might even understand.

"As always, your ability to sense the truth is right on." I met her eyes. "Serenity and I are not a couple. We pretended so that Serenity could learn more about the Amish ways and possibly discover what happened to Naomi."

I felt better that I'd spoken.

Rebecca reached out and squeezed my arm. "Things may well have started out as a lie, but I think that there is much to salvage if you are willing bend your pride."

I smiled, thankful that my sister cared enough to push her way into my business. Before I could decide how to answer her, she gave me a quick hug and headed to her waiting buggy. She looked over her shoulder and as she waved, she called out, "Enough time has passed without my little brother in my life. Come by and see us sometime. Our door is open to you."

My throat became tight and I quickly got into the Jeep to break myself away from all the sentimental feelings that were bombarding me.

Maybe after all these years, I could actually have a relationship with some of my family members. As I turned the key in the ignition and the engine came to life, I felt solid for the first time in a long while.

At the roadway, I hesitated, and after a moment of indecision, I turned away from town, and my home. I had another family member to speak to this day. The happy feelings I'd experienced moments before were quickly turning cold with apprehension.

I didn't expect this meeting to be as pleasant as the one with my sister and my old friends. Nope, it would probably have been easier to face a firing squad, but I knew I had to do it. It was a long shot, but if what Serenity had told me was accurate about Tony Manning, then dammit, I wanted to find out what had happened that night when I was just a kid, and whether there was a connection between that incident and Naomi's death.

29

SERENITY

November 18th

Heather's hand shot up from the booth and Todd made a beeline in that direction while I followed grumpily behind. I was having a difficult time dealing with the fact that Daniel had betrayed me. Hell, how could the guy be making out with me in the morning and then selling me out before lunchtime? Daniel's obnoxiously over confident personality had always ruffled my feathers, but I never dreamed that he'd turn on me the way he did.

When Todd reached the booth, Heather rose up and planted a big kiss on his lips. I watched with cynical disdain as the two mumbled a few words quietly to each other before Heather turned to greet me. She was one of those women who had enough meat on her bones to make her extremely voluptuous, without being chubby. At one time, I would have wished for boobs that big, but now, I figured that they were extremely impractical.

"Hey, how's it going, Serenity?" Heather smiled cheerfully.

I should have lost the mood, but I couldn't shake it. Sitting down, I replied, "Just peachy."

Heather glanced at Todd who only snorted loudly before she took the seat beside him. She was a smart girl though, and she took my curt answer as a signal to change the subject entirely.

"Have you heard the news?" Heather asked.

When I looked up and saw her beaming face, I knew what she meant. But she was so excited to tell me herself that I played along. "What news?"

"Todd and I set a date for the wedding—New Year's Day." She bumped into Todd's shoulder when she said it, and the action made me feel even more miserable deep down inside. I certainly wasn't jealous, but I had to admit that being around a joyously-in-love couple was the last place I wanted to be at the moment.

"That's great," I muttered.

Heather seemed to be waiting for more, but I sat silently staring out the window at the cloudy day. The trees were completely stripped of their foliage and the sight of the gray street, buildings and sky made me shiver. I could feel the cold outside even though it was warm and snug in the Diner.

Todd must have felt sorry for his fiancé, because he quickly said, "Don't mind Serenity. The Amish have been giving her a hard time here lately."

I narrowed my eyes at Todd, who only shrugged. It was pretty obvious that when Nancy suddenly appeared at the table to take our orders he was relieved for the distraction—like I needed him making excuses for me.

"Did you get over to talk to Mary?" Nancy asked me with an intense stare that said that my interest in the thirty year tragedy was the talk of the town.

"Yes, I did. Thanks for putting me in contact with her."

Nancy wasn't satisfied with my answer and she tilted her weight to her other hip and said, "I'm kind of surprised that she would say very much about it. The Amish are pretty tight lipped."

I smiled, "But, she's not Amish any longer."

"Oh, sweetie, don't you be fooled. They never lose all their ways when they come over to our side." Nancy winked at me before taking our orders and moving on.

Yeah, she was right. Daniel was proof of that.

"I must say that I've had some strange experiences with them myself," Heather said. The bright beam that had glowed around her a minute before had suddenly dimmed.

My curiosity was piqued and I looked at Heather. "Like what?"

"Well, for one thing, about a year ago, I was caring for a woman in the recovery unit at the hospital. She'd come close to dying from some kind of infection that had turned into pneumonia." She giggled uncomfortably before proceeding with her story, and I caught the tight smirk on Todd's face indicating that he'd already heard it.

"When I pushed open the door to the woman's room to check her vital signs, I heard the squeaking of the bed. I didn't think anything of it, figuring that she might have been struggling off of it to use the restroom, and I hurried toward the sound." Heather paused again and blushed deeply, a color that I'd never seen on her before, even after some previous bawdy conversations. "When I pulled the curtain aside, I discovered the woman's husband on top of her...and the noise that I heard was the bed moving from his...well, you know."

"You've got to be kidding me—what did you do?" I said, not quite believing what she was telling me. My memory flashed to the Amish people at the benefit school house dinner and I wondered which couple it might have been.

"The man looked over his shoulder and his eyes only met mine for a split second, before I hurried out of there. I gave the paperwork to another nurse and went on break."

Todd said, "Can you imagine? What a horny dick that man must have been to be fucking his wife in her hospital bed."

I was absorbing the story and ignoring Todd's comment when Heather went on to say, "And then, just about a month ago, an Amish woman brings her teenage son in and he's wrenched his leg pretty good. She's acting kind of strange, avoiding eye contact and nervous like, when I ask what happened to him. At the same time the boy began to give his version, she cut him off and said that he'd fallen from a tree. I'm no fool, Serenity. I deal with people all the time, and when my eyes met that boy's, I knew his mother had lied to me."

"What do you think happened to him?" I asked processing the information and feeling something nagging my brain about it.

Heather sighed, "I don't know for sure. Maybe she'd done something to him and was covering her ass. But then, the leg injury didn't indicate any kind of abuse. It was just weird as all get out. The whole scene bothered me for the rest of the day."

The tingling push at my brain finally opened up and my heart leaped. "Did you say this happened a month ago?"

"Yeah, about that," Heather leaned in close and asked in a whisper, "Why, do you know something about it?"

I was already standing up and was out of the booth when I answered her. "I might. Do you know the woman's name, Heather?"

"Oh, yeah, I remember it clearly. But really, I'm not supposed to say anything about patient's personal information. I could lose my job," Heather said quietly, but gazing at her face, I knew she was seriously thinking about spilling the beans.

Todd said, "Go ahead. Tell Serenity what she needs to know. I'm sure it will be okay since it's the police department doing the asking."

"No, Todd. Don't worry about it right now. I believe that I already know who she's talking about. Let me check it out and if I need anything further, I'll call you, Heather."

"Do you want me to come with you?" Todd asked. He was already moving to stand up, but Heather's hand caught his arm.

"We're supposed to go sample the cakes at two. Remember, you took the afternoon off to come with me." Heather's voice had a pleading ring to it, and although I would have welcomed Todd's company where I was going, his fiancé needed him more than I did that afternoon.

"It's all right, Todd. I can handle this one on my own."

Todd reluctantly sat back down, but not before I caught the roll of his eyes. I realized then that he was hoping that I'd rescue him from a few hours of wedding preparation. No such luck, Todd, I chuckled to myself as I turned and headed for the doorway.

"Why, you haven't had your burger yet, Serenity," Nancy called from behind the counter.

"Todd will get the bill. Maybe I'll be back for dinner," I said, not slowing down for her answer.

The blast of cold air seemed to charge every cell in my head as I made my way through the parking lot.

Was it just a coincidence, or was there a connection?

Briefly, I wished that I could call and speak to Daniel about my suspicions, but that door was nailed shut now. I'd handle this on my own—just like I did most everything else in my life.

28

DANIEL

November 18th

Ma was bent over working in her flower garden and I couldn't help but admire her for her gumption to do the task on such a blustery, cold day. Of course, once spring came along, she'd have the prettiest flower beds in the county and I was sure that alone was worth the work to my mother.

I was able to walk up behind her unnoticed since she hadn't paid any mind at all to my vehicle pulling in. She probably figured that her son-in-law had business with an English man. Ma certainly wouldn't expect me to show up.

My heart sped up when I reached her. I took a deep breath before clearing my throat and saying, "The beds are in excellent shape."

Ma slowly turned around, her eyes growing rounder as she rose up to a standing position. She collected herself quickly though, and wiping the dirt from her hands on her apron, she answered me in an even tone, "Well, they ought to, as much time as I've invested in them this past year."

Leave it to my mother to be practical and unemotional when speaking to her oldest son for the first time in fifteen years. I guess it was better than if she began balling her eyes out.

"Where is Father? I need to speak with him."

Her eyes squinted as she considered my words. Finally, she relaxed a bit and said, "He's walking in the back field. We have about ten acres of feed corn out yonder that still needs to be cut. You'll find him if you're willing to use the energy to get there."

Yep. Ma hadn't changed much. She was still using little disparaging remarks to hurt and manipulate me. She'd always believed that I'd taken the easy way out, by going English. She couldn't fathom that anyone outside of her world actually worked hard.

But I was just happy that she was talking to me at all. It was a start.

"I'll be heading out there then. I hope to see you again, Ma," I said quietly, before turning and heading toward the fields behind the house. Before I got far, she called out to me to wait, and I did so, wondering what she was up to.

Minutes later, she came out of the house with a canister in one hand and a basket in the other. She unceremoniously handed me the items and said, "There's hot chocolate and fresh made cookies to bring to your Father."

Mother turned and left me standing alone at the edge of the yard. Moving the gingham cloth aside, I counted eight large oatmeal cookies—my childhood favorites. There were way too many for one man to eat. Ma might not openly give me a big hug at this point, but the cookies were her way of doing just that.

Taking a bite and savoring the delicious taste that only my mother could put into a cookie, I began walking the fence line.

2

I walked for almost an hour, circling the cornfield. I finally stopped, admitting to myself that Dat might have snuck by me and headed back to the house. The time wandering around the field, tramping through overgrown dried weeds and over clumpy earth was not ill spent though. I enjoyed the time alone, letting my mind wander. Serenity was at the forefront of my thoughts and I wondered if there was still any possibility of getting together with her. Only once before had a woman taken hold of my heart the way she had, and that had nearly ruined my life. But the fact that I actually felt the sensations of first love again still amazed me. I could imagine spending my life with Serenity, raising a family with her and growing old alongside her. Yet, for all my day dreams, I was not at all confident that she wanted any of those things, with or without me. She truly might be the type of woman who'd be content to focus on her career and be single, and free.

The rough corn stalks towering over me also brought Naomi to mind, and it dawned on me how desperate she must have been to take the gamble of running away from her Amish home. Walking a few miles through the loneliness of the fields was only a small part of the obstacle, I knew. The really difficult part for the girl was to leave her siblings, the few friends she had and her entire way of life. A person had to be extremely motivated to follow through, or desperate.

Just when I was about to pull another cookie from the basket the sharp whistle that I knew so well rang out. I followed the sound and saw Father high up in a tree, looking at me from the hedgerow. Seeing him agilely make his way down from the branches, I silently wished that I'll be in such a spry condition when I was his age.

Walking to him, I felt fairly calm. The cookies and drink from Ma had done the trick. Maybe Father would be easier to deal with than I'd originally imagined. I wasn't holding my breath any longer. I was more confident as an adult than I'd been as a wary teenager. Regardless of what my father said, I could turn around and leave. I was no longer a captive to his world or his ideas.

When Father was just a few strides away, I said, "Mother sent you cookies and hot chocolate." I held out the items to him as if they were a peace offering that would save me from torture and death. A slight smile tickled my lips at the thought.

Father glanced at the items and after taking the basket from my hand he motioned for me to follow him. Silently I did so as he led me back near the hedgerow and a large log that was the perfect size and shape for a place to sit.

Once we were seated on the log, he pulled out the cups from the basket and poured them full of the still warm liquid. Although I was used to my father's long silences, the sun was dipping down low on the horizon. I wanted the opportunity to speak to the man while we were completely alone and away from all distractions.

Attempting to break the ice, I said, "Ma's cookies are still amazing."

"Of course they are. She puts only the finest natural ingredients in them. And a whole lot of love too. I think that's what really makes them special." Father took a sip of his cocoa and looked at me with a more serious expression before he went on to say, "But you didn't come all the way out here today to talk about Ma's cookies, did you?"

After a quick breath, I said, "No, I didn't. I was hoping that you might talk to me about something that's been on my mind for thirty years."

Father sighed loudly. "Well, go on and spit it out. I'm not getting any younger waiting on you."

Again, I met his gaze, feeling some of the same apprehension that I always did when Father pointed his black stare at me.

"One night, when I was close to five years old, I walked into the kitchen late in the night to discover you, Aaron, James and old Abraham gathered there. I heard talk of punishment and business, but what stuck in my mind the most was the blood that was on your clothes, and the other's too. What happened that night, Da?"

Silence followed my question. Only the rustling of the stalks and the occasional late afternoon call of a crow could be heard in the field. I waited though, knowing that there would be no rushing Father. He would speak when he was good and ready, or not at all.

Some minutes later when Father finally spoke, his voice sounded tired. I searched his face and saw an old man for the first time.

"We made a blood oath to keep the events of that night a secret, Son, and I won't be divulging any information now."

"Could you at least tell me if Tony Manning was involved?"

Father's head spun toward me and his dark eyes narrowed. He hissed, "Don't be mentioning that name again. It's none of your concern what happened all those years ago… or with whom. Some things are better off left alone."

"Yeah, and some things haven't changed much have they?" Father's brow raise questioningly and I said, "Just look at poor Naomi Beiler and everyone's unwillingness to talk about her and what happened out in the cornfield that day she was shot."

Father's face changed and I could almost touch the anger that emitted from him. He said in a louder voice than I expected, "That silly girl brought on her own demise. And putting the blame on Eli Bender certainly won't bring her back."

When Father slid from the log and began marching back to the house, I was quick to pursue him. "But someone shot her—and she didn't deserve it. There's no denying that."

My father rounded on me so suddenly that I almost bumped into him. His words held venom and I remembered all too clearly why I'd never come home before.

Father pointed his boney finger at me and said, "This is Amish business, not the outer worlds'. We will deal with it in our own way and within our own time." His face twisted as he continued, "It seems to me that you should focus on your own ungodly life and not be meddling into our affairs."

"Ungodly? Who are you to talk to me about such things when you obviously were involved in the beating of a man—an innocent one at that. And now you're supporting the cover-up of a possible murder."

Father shook his head roughly, "I will answer to my Lord when the time comes. But not to you."

He began walking away again. When he'd only gone a few steps, he stopped and over his shoulder he said, "Oh, and by the way, any fool could tell that the sheriff is not your woman. That you would stoop so low as to lie to your people with such a ruse is inexcusable—and it shows your level of ignorance to once again trust an English woman. I would have thought that you'd learned your lesson with that Abby girl."

I watched him stomp away, making no attempt to follow. The anger that heated my soul was spilling out into every inch of my body as I replayed Father's words in my head.

No, Da, I didn't lie to *my people*, only the Amish.

31

SERENITY

November 18th

Bingo—I was in luck. I parked my car and watched the teenager that I'd seen the night of the benefit dinner limp his way across the barnyard heading for the house. I quickly opened the door and jumped out, grabbing my jacket off the passenger seat as I went. Slipping the jacket on, I walked briskly on a collision course with the boy.

When he saw me, his eyes widened and he turned away, actually making a run for the porch steps. Holy shit, I couldn't believe it, but my legs were ready and I put them into motion. I caught the boy just before his feet hit the steps.

"Hey, whoa, why are you running from me?" I exhaled in irritation and from the short run. I rested my hand on the boy's arm, feeling the shaking of his body beneath his wool coat.

"Sorry, I got to get to the house is all."

"Why?" When the boy shifted quietly on his feet, avoiding my gaze, I surged on, "Your name is Mervin, right?"

Mervin nodded his head, but still avoided looking at me.

"Hey, I didn't come here to scare you. I just wanted to ask you about your injury." He glanced at me for a second—long enough for me to see his bright green eyes and the freckles covering his nose.

"How did you hurt yourself?" I said softly. My heart sped up when he turned back and met my gaze fully. The kid had a kind face. He also had the expression of a boy about to tell a secret.

"Get off this property." The woman's voice blasted. I looked up to see Mervin's mother, Esther, standing on the porch, glaring at me. Her pointy face was pale and dry looking—and very unhappy.

"Esther Lapp, isn't it? I'm sorry to come over unannounced, but I had a couple of questions to ask you." I began to move forward, hoping to calm the woman, but I stopped dead in my tracks when she continued to rant.

"I won't be talking to you, Sheriff. You can be on your way now."

The picture before me certainly wasn't the stereotypical Amish woman that most people imagined. Esther's face was frozen in a scowl of anger that seemed at odds with the neat bonnet and navy blue dress she wore. Her behavior left me no doubt that she had something to hide. The only problem was that my gut instinct and a conversation at the Diner wasn't enough to bring the woman in for formal questioning.

I let my hand drop from Mervin's arm, and he glanced up one last time before he leaped the steps, two at a time and disappeared into the house. The almost pleading look he'd sent me in that instant was enough to make me sure that Esther

Lapp was definitely hiding something, and that her son didn't want her to.

Ꙅ

I tried to process the encounter in my mind as I drove. I'd already passed several buggies and slowing down, I prepared to be patient as I came to another one on a steep grade. I brought the car to a crawl and let some space develop between me and the buggy, hoping not to intimidate the driver into asking too much of his horse on the hill. It still amazed me that there were people nowadays using horse and buggy as a mode of transportation. But here I was living in a place where it was mainstream to do so. The world was a funny place.

The ring from my cell startled me, and I grabbed the phone.

"Aunt Rennie, it's me."

Will's voice sounded abnormally subdued. "What's wrong, Will?"

"Nothing serious, I just wanted to talk for a while."

"Where are you?" I asked, anxiety growing inside of me.

Will didn't hesitate, but answered with a stronger voice, "I'm parked on Burkey Road."

"*Why?*"

"This was where I was supposed to pick up Naomi. I guess I thought hanging out here for a while might make me feel closer to her."

Without much thought, I said, "I'm nearby—wait for me and I'll be there in a few minutes."

"All right. Thanks, Aunt Rennie."

My patience at following the buggy that was going about two miles an hour was over. I sucked in my breath and tapped my foot on the floor waiting for the damn thing to crest the hill so that I could pass.

The top of the hill finally came, and after checking that the coast was clear, I pulled out around the buggy. Glancing over, I spotted Bishop Esch's long snowy beard. I almost waved to him, but changed my mind when he didn't look my way. As his buggy was growing smaller in the rearview mirror, I saw him pull off the road.

I tried to remember what I'd seen there when I'd passed, but the only image that sprang to my mind was an old tobacco barn that sat quite a ways off the road in a stand of vine covered trees. The driveway had been more like a path, dotted with large puddles along the way. With the darkness almost complete, I wondered what the the bishop would be doing in such a place. Then again, my mind reasoned, maybe he was just turning around.

I lifted my foot from the gas pedal and moved it toward the brake for a second, feeling the urge to turn around myself. If Will hadn't been waiting for me, I would have. Letting the strange vibes go, I pressed the gas down and sped up.

Turning onto Burkey Road, I spotted Will's truck alongside the road. I parked behind the dually, and not waiting for him to come to me, I left my car and jogged up to his. Slipping in the passenger side, I quickly judged Will to be emotionally sound with a glance. A soft country crooner song was coming from the radio and I gritted my teeth wishing he'd either turn it off or change the station. But I didn't tell him that.

"What are you really doing here, parked on the side of the road alone?"

Will smiled the same smile that probably made Naomi fall in love with him. "I'm not alone now."

"Seriously, what do you hope to accomplish here?" The roadway was dead quiet. I couldn't help the shiver that touched my skin when I peered sideways and into the corn.

"I could ask you the same question. After all, you were pretty damn close by."

He had me there. "Watch your mouth, Will. Remember, you're not supposed to cuss around relatives."

He laughed, and it sounded genuine, lifting my own spirits. "But, you're not a relative, just Aunt Rennie."

"I'm the sheriff. Really, you ought to show more respect," I said, feigning anger.

Will was silent for a minute and I was about to speak when he finally opened his mouth. His words made me sit up straighter and stare at my nephew.

"Will you take a walk with me to the place where Naomi died?"

"Whatever for?" I spoke the words carefully and slowly. I didn't need any more surprises today.

"I don't know for sure. It's as if I have this pull to be there, you know. I don't understand it myself." He shook his head, looking confused.

"It's already dark outside. It would be impossible for us to find our way out there now." I looked at the corn plants again, seeing a dark wall that looked impenetrable.

Will's voice grew excited as he said, "No, we could do it. See the moon is out, and I remember that the night Naomi died was very much like this one. Please Aunt Rennie, will you go with me?"

I met his gaze and I knew for certain that if I didn't go with him, he'd end up going alone some other time. The last thing any of us needed was for him to be traipsing around where his girlfriend was shot.

My mind made up, I touched the door handle. Before I got out, I told Will that we'd pull the cars up the tractor lane which ran between the corn and the hedgerow. I said that that it was to keep the vehicles safe, but in actuality, I was worried that someone, especially an Amish someone, would spot the vehicles and raise questions.

I made sure my gun was loaded and in the holster beneath my jacket and that my cell phone was on vibrate in my pocket, then the two of us started up the tractor path, following the soft spray of moonlight that lit the way. After a few minutes of hiking, my eyes were accustomed to the low light and I could actually see fairly well.

Will stayed close beside me, his arm occasionally brushing mine as we walked. I couldn't help but think how creepy it would be to be out here all alone, and again the picture of the pretty Amish girl invaded my mind.

"You never did tell me why you were driving around in the Amish community?" Will asked in a loud whisper that made me smile.

"It's not a big secret or anything. I was checking up on a lead—*attempting* to question a couple of Amish people."

"They wouldn't talk to you?"

"Nope, I've discovered that they're all a bunch of tight lipped..." I almost said something that was not kind at all, but a thought occurred to me and I stopped instead. "Whoa, Will. Wait a minute."

I looked around trying to get my bearings right. When we'd driven the vehicles to the place where Naomi was found, we'd come this way and then turned, and crossed over the cut part of the field to get to the body. I knew that we were in the right place. If we headed to the left, we'd be at the spot that Will wanted to go in a few minutes, but I hesitated, more interested in the other direction.

"What's wrong?" Will asked, moving to stand closer.

"Nothing, I was just thinking. Todd, Jeremy and I traced Naomi's possible trail back to her farm. It made perfect sense, and wasn't really an issue, but..." I paused looking to the right at the small trail that was not glaringly open, but definitely was there if you looked for it. "None of us noticed this trail before."

"What's the big deal? I'm sure there are dozens just like it along this hedgerow." Will's words were skeptical, but his voice wasn't. He'd already taken a step in the direction of the opening and was now facing me with an expectant look on his face.

"Well, for one thing, it's in a direct line to where we found Naomi, which means that the person who shot her could have followed the same path to get to the tree stand where Bobby believes the bullet came from. Secondly, it looks fairly well used—as if someone has worn it out recently."

Just saying it caused my heart to begin racing. But from fear or excitement, I wasn't sure. What I did know was that I was suddenly ready for a longer hike than I'd originally anticipated.

I eyed my nephew up and down, seeing a strong young man before me. "Are you up to this Will?"

"You know I am."

I nodded and looking back one last time in the direction of the shooting, I stepped ahead of Will and into the darkness of the tangle of branches.

32

DANIEL

November 18th

I wasn't surprised that Serenity wasn't home—already figuring that she wouldn't be there. As I drove through the quiet streets of town, the street lamps lighting the way, I blew out a nervous breath. She probably wouldn't even talk to me. Saying I was sorry or that I'd made a mistake wasn't going to cut it with Serenity. But I had to try anyway. The pretty little sheriff was wrong about Eli. I knew it in my heart. Now I just had to convince her of it.

Pulling into the police department, I noticed that only a few cars were left in the parking lot, and Serenity's was not one of them. Disappointment flashed through me, but I parked anyway, determined to at least find out where she was. My feelings for Serenity ran too deep to simply walk away now. I'd made a blunder for sure, but I'd followed my gut with Eli. Remembering how she kissed me back the other morning and how willing her body had been in my arms, I hoped that I could make amends with her. Maybe if I handled the situation carefully, she'd forgive me.

Walking into the brightly lit hall, my eyes had to adjust to the shock of it. The dispatcher didn't know where Serenity was. Just when I was about to give up, I spotted Todd turning into a room down the corridor. I quickly walked that way, and after a rap on the frame of the open doorway, I proceeded in. Todd looked up, showing no surprise at seeing me.

"Good to see you, Daniel. What brings you in so late?"

Todd's voice held a hint of sarcasm, which I ignored. "I'm looking for Serenity. Any idea about where she'd be?"

Todd pushed the papers away from him and leaned back in the chair, his hands folded on his belly. The smug smile was annoying, but I had no choice except to wait for him to answer if I was going to have the opportunity to get things straightened out with Serenity that evening.

"Hmm, I'm not really sure where she is. You know, Serenity is a busy girl."

Sighing, I prepared to leave, not interested in playing mind games with Todd. My talk with the sheriff would just have to wait until morning.

When I was almost through the doorway, Todd spoke again, "Wait. I might have an idea," he paused, as if debating whether to tell me, and said, "Today at lunch, my fiancé said something about an Amish family that piqued Serenity's interest. She hauled butt out of the Diner. I assume to go talk to the people."

"Which family?" I asked as my heart slowed.

"I don't have the foggiest idea. Heather knew though, but wasn't comfortable divulging information about a patient. Funny thing was that Serenity seemed to know who Heather was talking about. Sort of like some pieces of a puzzle fell into place for her."

"And you haven't heard from her since? Isn't that a bit strange to you?" I said, looking out the small window at the cold, dark night. My mind was getting jumpy with all kinds of worried thoughts.

Todd nodded slowly and looked up to meet my gaze soundly. "Yeah, actually it is little weird. She always touches base with me throughout the day. Course, I didn't have an ordinary afternoon myself—spent it wedding shopping. You wouldn't believe all the shit that's involved with getting hitched; a cake, flowers and the goofy little things you give away at the place settings."

I partially ignored him, not interested in the least about his wedding, except to feel sorry for any fool girl stupid enough to take vows with the man. What was bothering me more was the fact that he didn't know where Serenity was.

"Have you tried her cell?" Todd asked.

"I wanted to talk to her in person. Why don't you go ahead and call her and see where she is," I suggested.

Todd picked his phone off the desk and made the call while I stood impatiently by the window, searching out into the night for nothing in particular. After an amount of time that was unreasonable for Serenity to not have answered her phone, I glanced at Todd, who responded with a confused shrug.

"That's odd," he said, running his hand over his buzzed hair.

I took a step and rested my hands on his desk, suddenly more anxious than ever to locate Serenity. It was probably ridiculous to be worrying about the feisty blond who I knew was packing, but still, the fact that she seemed to be missing at the moment bugged the hell out of me.

"Isn't there anyone else you can call to check on her—her sister maybe?"

"Yeah, that's an idea," Todd said before he spent a minute flipping through the directory and finally punching the number into his phone.

I stared at the Todd while he talked. By the one sided part of the conversation I was getting, I already knew that Serenity wasn't with her family. Damn.

"No, Laura hasn't heard from Serenity since this morning when she texted her about the paternity test," Todd said. He rose from his seat and pulled his jacket off the chair.

"What are we going to do?" I wanted to make sure I got the *we* part in. Because there was no way I was going home without knowing Serenity's whereabouts.

"Let me call Heather and see what she says. Maybe she can enlighten us about what she was talking to Serenity about earlier."

A minute later as he shoved the phone into his pocket, he said, "She isn't answering—probably has the phone charging. Our place is only a few blocks away. We can drive on over there and ask her in person."

I followed Todd out to his patrol car, leaving my jeep behind. The blood pumped hard through my veins and my movements were overly quick. I felt the pressure to hurry. Hopefully, I was dead wrong, but I couldn't shake the suspicion that Serenity had gotten herself into a bigger mess than she could handle.

33

SERENITY

November 18th

The going wasn't too bad since the path had obviously been stepped on recently, but still, the darkness under the trees was unsettling. Will must have thought so also, the way he stayed so close on my heels that anytime I slowed to stumble over an exposed root, he'd bump right into me.

The path meandered through woods, along hedgerows and out into small open meadows where the grass was so high, we had to push it aside with our hands. Somehow, we managed to stay with the unfamiliar trail, and after what was probably twenty minutes, I decided to pull out my cell and call Todd. I hadn't spoken to him all day and even though it was officially my day off, I got the urge to check in and see how the town had been fairing without me.

"Dammit," I cussed, slipping the phone back into my pocket.

"What's up?" Will asked, moving quickly to position himself alongside of me.

"Can you believe that I don't have reception here? I could have sworn that my phone worked in the entire Amish community," I said in a grumbly sort of way, thinking how it was always when you needed the damn phone the most, you couldn't use it.

Will laughed, "Are you going to have a melt down because you're out of contact with the rest of the world, Aunt Rennie?"

"Naw, I'm just going to complain to you about it until I feel better."

A few more silent steps and we cut through a gap in a fence row, and the sight of a huge old barn silhouetted against the night sky came into view. The building looked ancient, but its boards were still snugly nailed on as far as I could see from the distance. It was hard to tell with the way the vegetation was growing up the sides of the walls though.

The wind gusted and I zipped my jacket all the way up, for the first time feeling the bite of the autumn night. When the wind calmed, the breeze brought the sound of the trees scratching against the side of the barn. The noise drifted through the air like an eerie song.

"It looks as if the trail heads right into that barn."

"Yeah, maybe," I said distractedly. Finally, after a minute more of studying the barn, I came to the conclusion that it was the same one that I'd passed earlier, and the one that the bishop turned into.

A high pitched whinny pierced the air and Will jumped beside me. We weren't alone. I grabbed Will's arm and pulled him into the bushes beside the path, not stopping until we were completely hidden.

"What's going on?" Will breathed in to my ear with a brave voice. Good boy. I needed my nephew to keep his wits about him.

"I think that the Amish might actually be in that barn," I whispered, trying to peer out of the branches the best I could to survey the barnyard area.

"But there's no light. Why would they do such a thing?"

I looked up into Will's shadowed face and couldn't see much, but I imagined the confused look that he probably held.

"They're Amish. Who the hell knows what they're doing or why they're doing it. But obviously they are being secretive about it."

"Can you see any buggies?"

"Nope, they must be parked on the other side of the barn." After thinking another few seconds, I turned to Will and touched his arm. "Look, Will, I want you to follow the path back to your truck and get to a place where you have cell service. Call Todd and have him meet you."

"What are you going to do?" Will's voice shook and I smiled into the darkness.

"I'm going to sneak around the barn and see what I can find out." I knew he was getting ready to cut me off, so I shushed him and said, "Don't worry about me. I'll be as quiet as a church mouse. They'll never even know I'm there. Once I've figured out what's going on, I'll head back to my car and meet up with you there."

Will stalled, and I grew impatient with him that he wouldn't just do what I told him. When had he become so difficult?

"Why don't we just go together, and then you and Todd can come back as a team. That sounds like a better idea to me." His voice was coaxing, but I wasn't buying.

"Because, who knows how long they'll be in there, Will? And they might say something that will help me with Naomi's investigation. You don't want to miss an opportunity of learning the truth, do you?"

Will hesitated. "No...but I don't want anything to happen to you either. You're the only aunt I got."

"Really, you're being ridiculous. I'm the sheriff, remember? I can handle this. Besides, what do you think is going to happen? These are Amish people we're talking about."

Will shook his head and said, "It's just really freaking me out. That barn looks like a place where people are murdered and cut up into tiny pieces. Aren't you at all afraid to go over there, knowing there's probably a bunch of crazy men in the building?"

"You watch too many horror movies. No, I'm not afraid at all. Actually, I'm excited at the prospect of learning something. I've come to the realization that the only way I might actually get any answers from the Amish is to spy on them. Now, get going, so I can get to work."

Reluctantly, Will walked back the way we had come, looking over his shoulder several times before he skipped into a jog. He was probably hoping to get to his truck quickly, but I knew that even at a jog, he was probably at least twenty minutes from using his phone.

Once he was out of sight, I pushed the branches aside and slipped back out into the open. Luckily, I was wearing my black jacket and dark jeans so I blended into the night well enough. As I approached the barn, I moved silently and used trees and clumps of weeds as cover. Without a thought, my hand kept straying inside my jacket which I'd unzipped enough to touch the steel of my .38 revolver. The hell with the cold, I wanted freedom to reach my gun more than I wanted warmth.

I had lied to Will. My heart was beating fast and adrenaline pumped madly through my veins. The whole scene was bizarre to say the least. I wasn't convinced that it was dangerous, especially when I pictured the smiling faces of the Amish children, and the stoic looks of the mothers. But, even I had to admit, the men were another story altogether. They were definitely intimidating in their strangeness, and little visions of some crazy cult ceremony were swirling around in my head as I approached the barn.

As I closed in, I could hear the snorts and stomping of the horses. It sounded as if there were a herd of them on the other side of the building. I paused beside a rise in the ground where the weeds were tall. Hearing the human voices was not unexpected, but the sounds still sent a shiver through me as I strained to listen.

"Ah, shit," I mumbled to myself, hearing that the words were all foreign to me. What good would it do to spy on these people when I wouldn't understand a thing they were saying? It took only another second to make the decision that at least I might be able to see something through the narrow gaps in the aged wood. That was better than nothing at all.

Crouching low and moving swiftly, I crossed the ground to the barn in a few blinks. Once I was pressed against the coarse wood, I breathed a little easier and peeked into the gap that was only as wide as my eye. The clouds spread at that moment. The spray of light made me feel exposed, but I held my ground, searching between the boards.

There must have been a dozen men inside. I could barely make out their bodies in the pitch darkness, but I counted the outlines and the movements to come up with a solid estimation of thirteen, total. There were no lights at all, not even a small lamp in the interior. I strained my eye, glad that the moon had made its arrival at that moment. The little streaks of light through the barn walls was enough to see that the bishop stood close to the center of the building, with his congregation of dark clad, bearded men before him. They were lined up orderly in rows of about four men each.

Bishop Esch was the one doing most of the talking. Even in German I could tell his voice easily. Strangely, there was a sprinkling of English words here and there, and when my ears caught them, they pricked up. I heard the words redemption, obedience, fellowship, English and *sheriff.* I could only surmise that these words didn't have an easy translation into their language. Or perhaps, because these people spoke both languages, they mixed up the two languages sometimes.

Occasionally, another man would rattle off something, and the bishop would answer. The men were anxious and I pushed against the old barn boards tightly to see and hear better. Some of the men were becoming irate, their voices rising.

Then I saw the smaller one—a boy or maybe a young teen shoved into the moonlight shard by one of the men, and right in front of the bishop. My heart stuttered to a stop as my mouth began to open.

My fingers were almost to the revolver at my side when the cold hands went around my sides, griping my arms tightly. I was pulled back against a hard chest while I struggled against the superior strength. All too quickly my hands were pinned behind me.

"God damned, but you're a persistent little bitch."

I knew the voice well—and the smell of peppermints.

34

DANIEL

November 18th

"Whoa. Wait a minute. You're saying that the woman who brought the boy in with the leg injury was Esther Lapp?" I said, trying to remember something that was tickling at the back of my memory—a conversation that I'd only caught a slice of, not thinking it held any significance when I'd heard it.

"Yes, I won't forget her or her name. Most of the Amish women that I'd met at the hospital in the past have been friendly and fairly talkative, but not this woman. She was in a nervous state, her eyes darting around as if she thought the boogey man was going to get her at any second," Heather said.

Her face was animated in the light of the kitchen. A kitchen that was perfectly clean and organized—the same as the rest of the house she shared with Todd. I don't know exactly what I'd been expecting when Todd told me we were heading to his house to talk to his girlfriend, but the immaculate arts and crafts home with its intricate woodwork was definitely not it.

"And what did she tell you had happened to her son?" I asked in a rushed voice. For no real reason, I was becoming increasingly more worried about Serenity. The desire to get back out on the road with a destination was pressing on me. From a glance at Todd, who hadn't touched his cup of coffee, instead rubbing his chin with his fingers and staring at Heather, I gathered that he wanted to get moving too.

Heather took a breath, probably feeding off our tension, and said, "She told me that he'd fallen from a tree. And his injury was consistent with that kind of trauma." She paused and looked between me and Todd, before saying, "Why, do you think he was abused in some way?"

That idea hadn't even entered my mind, but as I gazed at the calendar beside the fridge, a sudden clarity came to me. I stood up, pushing the high backed chair away from me in a sudden movement that made Todd and Heather look up with wide eyes.

"She lied," I said.

"About what?" Todd asked, standing with resolve.

I met his gaze. "We saw her at the school house benefit dinner—me and Serenity. Serenity noticed Mervin limping and asked Esther what had happened to him. Esther said that he'd fallen from a horse…a few days before."

Todd shook his head slightly, "But, maybe he had fallen from a horse, after he fell from a tree. He's an Amish kid, after all. They're always having accidents. I can't count how many calls I've had—"

I interrupted him. "Don't you see—the timing is all wrong. Heather said that Esther brought Mervin in around the third week of October. The benefit dinner was just a week ago."

I turned to Heather and leaned over the table. "How bad was his injury? Do you think he would have still been limping from it a month later?"

"Not only would he still have been limping, the doctor told his mother that he shouldn't be riding horses or playing any sports for a couple of months or he'd have a real risk of needing surgical intervention on the knee."

"Why the hell would the woman lie to Heather about her son falling from a horse?" Todd questioned me.

I shook my head. "I don't think she lied to Heather—she lied to Serenity. And Serenity caught on to it at the Diner when you all were talking."

Todd picked up his jacket and headed for the door with me close on his heels. He didn't even turn around when he asked, "Do you know where this Lapp family lives?"

"Yeah, I sure do."

"So what do you think is going on here?" Todd growled as he cut through the last bit of traffic before leaving the town's bustle and heading into the darkness of the countryside.

I exhaled, not really sure that I wanted to share all my thoughts on the subject with Todd. But, glancing over at his anxious face, I caved.

"The Amish are secretive about everything—even things that they have no business being tight lipped or even lying about. For some reason, Esther didn't want the outside world knowing the particulars of Mervin's injury, which isn't totally surprising. What I can't get my head around is why Serenity is so interested in the kid."

Without hesitation, Todd said, "Serenity's smart. I've been impressed with her from day one. Even though Tony was a lot more experienced, working for Serenity has been a hell of a lot more enjoyable."

"Why's that?" I asked in a low voice.

Todd laughed at me, and the sound of it made the heat rise on my face.

The amusement in his voice came through clearly, when he said, "Hey now, you don't need to worry about me and Serenity. We've known each other since before puberty. Even though she's gorgeous and all, her personality is way too over-powering. It would take a very strong guy to put up with all that, but I'd imagine there'd be a pleasant reward in the end."

"You didn't tell me why you like working for her so much though," I said, not entirely believing Todd's words. I'd bet five hundred bucks right then that if Serenity showed her side-kick the time of day, he'd pee himself.

"Well, for one thing, she actually talks to me and the other guys in the department, and asks our opinion on matters. Tony never did that. He was a scary tough dude to work for. You just nodded your head and said, 'Yes, Sir,' whenever he told you to do something. I think Serenity's collaborative approach is nice."

I digested Todd's words as we sped down Route 27, heading toward the Amish community. The full moon was huge against the night sky, but the fluffy clouds kept blocking it from vision, causing the passing fields to darken and lighten intermittently. My heart still raced and I couldn't seem to shake the feeling that Serenity was in some kind of danger. I didn't even know the woman that well and already she'd gotten under my skin enough that I knew if something happened to her I'd be devastated. Dammit, I didn't like that kind of feeling at all.

The dispatcher came over the radio notifying Todd of a house fire at the same time his cell went off.

"No fucking way," Todd said angrily into the phone as he hit the brakes, nearly throwing me into the windshield, the seatbelt slicing across my chest and stomach. He made an abrupt U-turn while he grunted a few more words into the phone.

When he tossed the phone down onto the console, he looked at me with a wide frown on his lips.

"We need to go back to town, man. There's a house fire," he said.

"Dammit—let the fire department handle it. What we need to do is go to the Lapps and see if Serenity was there today."

Todd sighed irritably before saying, "Its Serenity's house that's on fire."

35

SERENITY

November 18th

There was no use in struggling further. Tony had me in a tight hold and I decided that conserving my energy was my best bet at the moment. There was a dreamlike feeling to the whole scene; the puffy dark clouds in the sky framing the moon's giant orb, the sight of a dozen black horses and buggies lined up in the tall grass, each hitched to a long length of wooden pole running down the side of the barn. And, of course the fact that I was being half dragged, half carried by the ex-sheriff of Blood Rock into a remotely located barn filled with riled up Amish men, added to the surreal feel of the night.

I was so pissed at myself that I couldn't completely let the fear that probably should have been gripping my insides take hold. I'd been such a fool to approach the barn by myself. I guess, somewhere in the sleepy part of my brain, I'd really believed that dealing with the Amish wasn't something to be feared. Unfortunately, I'd learned differently, the hard way.

My eyes were accustomed to the darkness, but I was still surprised when Tony hauled me into the inky interior of the building and I was able to make out the silhouettes of the men's frames. Our scuffling caused them to turn our way. The sight of the bearded men, with their black coats blending into the shadows around them, and staring their accusing eyes staring silently at me, made my heart skip. I swallowed a gulp when Bishop Esch came to us with long, purposeful strides.

"What is the meaning of this, Tony?" the bishop hissed, the whites of his eyes meeting mine for a second before he raised them to Tony's face.

I felt a little better that the Amish leader sounded bothered that Tony had a hold of me, but not much.

"Look what I found peeking in between the boards on the far side, Aaron—a little blond spy." Tony chuckled.

I began struggling again with more vigor and Tony gripped me harder.

"Let her go, Tony," Bishop Esch ordered.

When Tony didn't immediately comply, I said, "Yeah, Tony, listen to your boss like a good doggie." I probably shouldn't have goaded him, but I couldn't help it, feeling that the bishop might be swayed to my side. Again, the fact that these were Amish people kept invading my brain, telling me that, surely, they wouldn't hurt me.

"Tony, release her!" Moses Bachman called out from the group. The sound of his voice was music to my ears, and seeing him stride from the crowd made me go limp in Tony's arms.

"God dammit," Tony growled near my ear before he shoved me toward the group. The hard push sent me sprawling onto the ground and into the musty dirt that smelled as old as the barn looked.

The thirteen Amish men, plus Tony, folded in around me, making an impassable circular wall. No one came forward to offer me a hand up from the ground. Instead, they all stood silently watching me, waiting. What they were waiting for, I didn't know, but I'd been quietly observing the nonsense long enough.

I pushed myself up off the ground in as fluid a movement as I could muster. After wiping the dust from my hands to my jeans, I turned to face the bishop. I noted that Moses was beside the leader, but I ignored him, directing my question to the Amish preacher.

"Could you please explain to me, Bishop Esch, what the hell is going on here? And why your goon, Tony Manning, attacked me, forcing me into this building? Hell, if you're going to be answering questions, I'd like for you to explain to me why this shithead," I jabbed my thumb towards Tony, "is your bull dog anyway?"

"You're not in the position to be demanding answers, girlie," Tony said, all anger gone from his voice, to be replaced with an amused drawl.

I turned, walking the few steps to reach him. I pointed my finger in his face and said, "You are in such deep shit over this one, Tony. I'll see to it that charges are brought against you for assault and kidnapping. Being that I'm a police officer *and* the sheriff, you won't be wiggling your way out of it."

Tony lifted his head and laughed heartily, sounding like a mad Santa Clause. I noticed from the sides of my vision that several of the men were shaking their heads at Tony's display.

The bishop and Moses were statues though. From my quick survey of the circle and the men's closer proximity, I took in something else about my captors. Most of them were the older men of the community.

"I'm just shaking in my boots." Tony held out his hand. "Can't you just see how I'm shaking?"

"Hush, now, Tony. That won't help matters at all," Bishop Esch said. His voice forced my gaze back on him, and I reluctantly left my arch nemesis to stand before the Amish leader again.

"Are you going to answer my questions, Bishop? Or do I have to haul all your asses into town?" I made a sweep with my head of the group, before I settled back on the bishop, who, to my amazement and chagrin, held a placid expression on a face that hinted of no worry at my authority over him.

"Really, Serenity, Tony is right. You are in no position to be ordering me around. You are in our territory now—private property owned mutually by each and every Amish man in this building. *You* are the one trespassing and thus, breaking the law," the bishop said smugly.

I could barely believe my ears. Was he for real? Since I was investigating a murder I had some rights that the bishop was obviously not aware of. But the numerous posted NO TRESPASSING signs I had ignored on my way to the barn plagued my mind a bit. A good defense lawyer would have a field day with that.

"Regardless of the trespassing issue, Mr. Esch, it is a crime to hold me here against my will," I thundered the words to the room, hoping that at least a few of them would be willing to stand up to the others in my defense. My eyes met Mo's again, and I thought—of all the Amish, he owed me one.

With a sweep of his hand and a sudden opening of the circle, the bishop said, "By all means, Sheriff Adams, you are welcome to leave us. We do not keep you here against your will. So be gone from us with your meddling mind. We have nothing more to say to you."

Aaron Esch's voice held the determination of a serious man, and my heart suddenly plummeted realizing that I would get no evidence about Naomi's death, and besides the assault charges I could press against Tony, I had nothing on the Amish. I wasn't really confident that District Attorney Riley, a good old buddy of Tony's, would be all that helpful either.

Still, as embarrassing as it would be to walk away from the old barn and the laughing eyes of the Amish men, it would also be a huge relief. For a minute there, I really thought I might end up like the women in Will's horror movies—in several pieces.

Shaking my head in disgust, I turned and headed for the opening in the man-made wall. I didn't get the chance to cross out of the circle though, before there was a rushing sound up behind me, joined with the frantic words, "I know who done it, Sheriff. I saw who shot Naomi Beiler."

Just as I was turning to see who'd spoken, the force of a hard object hit the side of my head. What it was, I can't say, but immediately, a thousand sparks peppered my vision.

Then I hit the hard, dry dirt of the barn.

36

DANIEL

Early Morning, November 19th

The sight of Serenity's home completely engulfed in flames stopped my heart. Even with the two fire trucks and their hoses spraying water at the towering streaks of red and yellow, there was no doubt that the house would be a complete loss. But, much more important than the house, was Serenity, and the unthinkable—that she might be in there.

I was being kept back by a volunteer fireman who'd grabbed hold of me when I ran with Todd towards the flames. Todd had shouted to the man to restrain me. I felt pretty sure that if I fought a little harder I could have broken free from the burly, bearded fellow who held me, but the sight of the skeleton of the house collapsing made me stop struggling. No one could have survived that. If Serenity was in there, she was a goner.

The cries of a nearby woman pulled my shocked gaze sideways until she came into view. The woman had dark blond hair and a slender body. She was clutching a man, and a teen-age girl in a tight embrace. Recognition dawned on me—Serenity's family.

The fireman, who must have sensed that I'd given up try-ing to reach the house, released me. He jogged over to the nearest fire truck, but I barely noticed, my focus on watching Todd as he stood huddled with the woman, who could only be Serenity's sister.

Serenity couldn't have been in the house, my mind rea-soned. She would have had the emergency training to get out of a burning building. That is, unless, she wasn't able to. I started to think dark, sinister thoughts as I approached the little group, taking in the tear streaked face of the teenager as she stared, open mouthed at the remnants of her aunt's home.

"Are you absolutely sure, Laura, that you don't have any ideas where Serenity could be?" Todd asked, his one hand resting on Laura's shoulder.

She sniffed and wiped her face roughly with her hand. Shaking her head, she said, "No. She didn't say a thing to me about leaving town, or going anywhere, even for a day. Like I told you, the last time I heard from her was when she texted me about the baby's paternity. I texted her back, inviting her to dinner, but she never responded."

As activity swirled around us, voices boomed out, and the heat from the fire touched my skin with an awful caress. The whole fiasco had gotten so damn out of control. Did Tony Manning—or the Amish, have something to do with the burning of Serenity's house, and her disappearance? I could hardly believe that the Plain people would be involved in any of this, but then suspicions still nagged at me about the men I grew up respecting and fearing. I remembered with a cold chill, even with the flames at my back, how the older men, father included, would disappear some nights. There had been talk among the young people of secret meetings in the dark, where our community's business was decided and manipulated. Would Aaron and my father be so intent on protecting the community that they would hurt an outsider? I didn't want to believe it, but I couldn't completely deny the possibility any longer.

The fact that Todd stopped talking to Serenity's family to answer his phone attracted my attention and I stepped in closer to hear what he said.

"Damn, that's a fucking relief—let me talk to her," Todd said into the phone. Everyone in the little group stood up straighter and breathed out in relief at once, while Todd continued to hold the phone close to his ear, his free fingers pressed tightly into his other ear to block out the loud noises around him.

"Shit, you've got to be kidding me." Todd shook his head and gave us all an agitated frown before he said, "All right. We'll be there as quick as we can. Just hang tight for now—and don't go playing the hero, Will. Leave that to the professionals."

At the same time he slipped the phone into his pocket, Bobby slid into the gathering wearing a worried frown beneath his mustache. The coroner didn't get a chance to say anything. Todd held his hand up to silence the questions that were about to erupt from Serenity's sister.

"That was Will. He's been with Serenity part of the evening, but now he's on his own. She took it upon herself to investigate some secret Amish business and ended up out of cell range—that's why she didn't call me," Todd was telling me the last part, but then he turned to Laura, and said, "I'm going out to the Amish community where I'll meet up with Will, and then we'll get with Serenity. Under the circumstances, Laura," Todd nodded towards the burning boards that were once Serenity's home, "you should head back to your house and prepare the guest room. Serenity's going to need a place to stay for a while."

Laura nodded, and moved away slowly with her husband and daughter to the Yukon parked along the curb. Once they were out of ear shot, I faced Todd, who was talking quietly to Bobby. The old man nodded and turned back to the firemen who finally seemed to have the flames under control.

The smell of wet smoke fanned out in the air as Todd motioned for me to follow him, saying, "Don't worry, Daniel. I definitely want you along for this ride. Who the hell knows what kind of shit your kin have stirred up this time."

37

SERENITY

Early Morning, November 19th

Before I opened my eyes, I listened to the muffled voices. The words were indistinct at first, but after some time, the sounds became clear. Yes, Tony was still there. His voice boomed compared to the others, and he spoke in English. The Amish were using their own language, except to speak with him, making the conversation still jumbled, but I did get the main gist. They were trying to figure out what to do with me.

I continued to play dead, so to speak, the hard pounding on the side of my head making me feel closer to the word than I wanted to be. My face was pressed against the dirt, so not only could I smell the rankness, I could also taste it. Even with the discomfort, I barely moved a muscle, only opening one eye to take a peek.

Most of the men were standing to the side quietly observing the scene, while the bishop, Mo, James Hooley and Tony stood separately, talking in raised voices. Never before had I wished so deeply that I could understand another language as I did at that moment.

The fact that I'd actually been struck by something told me in no uncertain terms that these people were in fact dangerous. They would go to any length to protect their own from a perceived threat. Like I'd been told several times, the Amish take care of their own.

I closed my eyes again, feeling very tired. This was one of those times when I wished I had a different job. The last incident that had made me feel the same way flooded back to me. For a change, I didn't block the memory, instead embracing the vision of the darkened street.

Swallowing a gulp of dry air in my throat, I pushed the hood aside. The ability to breathe seemed to leave my body as I stared at the girl lying on the wet pavement. Now that the hood was pushed back, her brightly dyed red hair spilled around her. Catching my attention was the shiny stud on the side of her nose glinting from its own light. Finally, I settled my gaze onto the brown eyes that stared at a place above my head.

Everything had happened in less than a minute, but the memory always dragged on, taking an eternity for the sound of Ryan's voice behind me to radio in the ambulance, and for the girl to die.

I carefully took the 9 mm from her fingers with my gloved hand. The bullet from my own gun had hit her in the chest, and the blood was soaking through the t-shirt she wore, beginning to obscure the image of an angel with spread wings.

The sudden cough and gurgle brought me closer to her face. Her eyes focused on me and I saw fear in them.

"Shhh, don't try to speak now. The ambulance is on its way. You're going to be fine..."

I'd lied easily. What else could I have done? I knew that within minutes the girl would be dead, and there was nothing I or anyone else could do about it.

Later I found out that her name was Emily, and she was only sixteen years old. She'd entered the elderly couple's home with her jacked-up, twenty-something year old boyfriend, to steal whatever they could get their hands on to pay for their next fix. She probably hadn't wanted the old man to die, but it happened just the same. The forensics proved that Emily's gun hadn't fired the killing shot, but the fact that she'd had the revolver in her hand when Ryan and I'd confronted her, sealed her death sentence.

Yep, the choices a person made could drastically alter their future, or even end it.

I could still feel the heaviness of the mother's arms around me as she told me that she forgave me for killing her daughter. She'd understood why I did it, as did everyone else. I'd only missed an afternoon of work for the mandatory counseling session with the shrink.

In my mind, absolution didn't come easily though. The girl's frantic eyes still haunted me to this day. Emily knew she was about to die and she wasn't ready for it. All the regret shined brightly from the brown depths before her eyelids closed.

As my head pressed against the hard dirt, I wondered if poor Naomi knew that she was dying. Did she regret her decisions? Somehow, I felt that she'd left the world not regretting a damn thing.

I realized that I must be suffering from, at the very least, a major concussion, when a wave of nausea gripped me. I had no choice but to raise my head to vomit onto the ground. I hated drawing attention to myself, and dammit, I really hated throwing up under any circumstance, but it was completely unavoidable. Now, as I wiped my mouth with the back of my dirty hand, I watched in double vision as Tony stomped towards me, his boot catching my thigh with a hard thump.

"That's enough, Tony," the bishop said. His voice boomed in the moonlit darkness of the barn.

"I already told you all—there won't be any negotiating with a by-the-book paper pusher, like her." Tony's finger was pointed at me and I wished that his two fluttering bodies would fuse together. The wave of sickness rolled through me again. I swallowed it down and struggled into a sitting position. Once I was upright, my stomach quieted and although, far from clear, my vision improved.

Mo walked toward me. He bent down inches from my face and searched my eyes. "She needs medical assistance, Aaron. If we do not make a decision soon, one might be forced upon us—one that we will regret later."

I licked my lips, and forced the words out. "Mo, please help me. I only wanted to find out what happened to Naomi— bring her justice. That's all."

Mo smiled weakly, and said, "My child, even after all of this," He motioned with a small gesture of his hands, "you still don't understand, do you?"

I shook my head, feeling a shimmer of hope as my hand brushed the inside of my jacket, and my holster. I can't say that I was surprised to find it empty—a glance at Tony's smirking face told me he had my gun. When he pulled it out from its snug location at his belt and waved it in the air, I closed my eyes, reassessing my chance of survival.

There was still Will. He should have been able to make the call to Todd by now. If I could just stall the lunatics a little while longer, I might see the light of day. Glancing at Tony's sadistic face, I knew that he was the one that put the biggest kink in that plan. The man wanted nothing more than to kill me. And the really shitty thing about that fact was that he'd probably get away with it too.

"There's no need to taunt her. Please stand aside while I talk to the sheriff," Bishop Esch said in a ridiculously reasonable voice considering the situation.

He stood above me, not bothering to kneel the way Mo had done. I pushed myself onto wobbly legs. Mo's hand did shoot out, I'll give him credit, but I ignored it, using the little strength I could summon from my weak body to stand.

The bishop was a tall man, so I still had to look up, but at least I didn't have to crane my neck like an idiot. And, I was hoping, from a psychological view point, that the healthier I looked, the more difficult it would be for the Amish men to order me finished off. Again, I couldn't help but wonder, how in the hell Tony Manning went from ex-sheriff of Blood Rock to hired assassin for the supposed pacifist Amish.

"As you've already seen, Ms. Adams, our people choose to live a much different existence than the rest of the world. We have lived by a strict set of customs and traditions for hundreds of years. Amazing everyone who has witnessed our culture, we have not only survived, but prospered.

"Occasionally though, we are put into situations where outside forces try to press their authority onto our people. Naomi Beiler is a prime example of what I mean." He took an agitated breath before continuing. "She was one of our own. Her predicament caused no pain or trouble for anyone outside of our community—therefore, the matter should have been left for us to deal with."

"Oh, that's where you're dead wrong, Bishop. Will Johnson is my nephew." Seeing his eyes widen in surprise was priceless, but I only savored it for a second before I plunged on. "And he loved Naomi Beiler. Her death devastated him—and he mourned for her a hell of a lot more than her own family or her *people* did."

Bishop Esch recovered quickly and said, "It was nothing but a teenage infatuation that would have crumbled within months, if not weeks, of that girl living in the cold, hard world outside of her birth community."

I stared at the bishop in disbelief, realizing that nothing I said would penetrate his thick skull. Coming to that frustrating conclusion, I said, "If you don't mind me asking then, what would you and your people have done about figuring out who shot Naomi, and bringing them to justice?"

The bishop laughed, the sound filling the stale air in the large, open space of the old barn like a bugle blast. Others in the crowd chuckled in the background.

"Some of us, those gathered here tonight, have known who shot the girl from nearly the beginning...and tonight we were exacting the punishment," Bishop Esch said as his eyes locked on mine, daring me to judge him.

"So you lied to me then?" My voice trembled as the pieces of the puzzle came together. Sure, there were still some questions that needed answering, but I was beginning to understand.

"The heavenly Father is the only authority that holds sway over me. Any information that I kept from you or your people was none of your concern," he said with the surety of a mad man.

I looked around at the other men gathered. Their backs were straight and their eyes stared with unflinching agreement with their leader. Mo had the expression of a man that would never change his mind. Even if the truth slapped him in the face, he wouldn't accept it.

The heavy feeling of disgust rolled over me and made me fearless. Thoughts of the beautiful Naomi having to put up with this shit for eighteen years settled over me for a long minute while I again searched the faces of the people living within the boundaries of my county. People who were more alien to me than any foreigner living on the other side of the world.

The most tragic part of all was that Naomi almost escaped—*almost.*

I took a deep breath, and said, "As long as your ass is settled in my jurisdiction, everything that goes on in the Amish community is my business."

The kick at my legs sent my feet out from beneath me, and once again I was lying in the dirt. Now, joining the throbbing of the side of my head was an ache in the back of my calf.

I glared up at Tony, who roared, "Shut the fuck up. Can't you see that you're on the losing end?"

The sound of a pump action shot gun being chambered brought all our heads shooting towards the dark shadows of the corner of the barn. The *shick, shick* sent an automatic shiver through me, and all the men tensed at once. Well, except for Tony. He pulled his own Colt .45 handgun and pointed it towards the inky blackness.

Funny thing was that whoever had pumped the gun could see us, but we couldn't see him. If my head wasn't hurting so damn bad, I would have been giddy with joy.

"Who's there, hiding as a coward—show us who you are!" demanded the bishop.

The laughing that emitted from the gloomy corner revved my heart to full tilt. *I knew that voice.*

"I don't' think so. At least, not until your body guard drops his weapon."

"Fuck you," Tony said before he let several rounds fly from his gun, the blasts echoing through the barn like mini explosions.

Everyone hit the ground just as I was curling into a fetal position. Everyone except for the bishop—he stood resolutely, either thinking he was too damned good for the dusty floor or believing that God would protect him.

I wasn't sure whether Tony attempted to dive for cover or not, because the shot gun blasts met their mark perfectly, and he crumpled to the floor like a rag doll. He lay only a few feet from me, his eyes glazing over.

And, not surprisingly, his lips were twisted in a sick smirk.

38

DANIEL

November 19th

The sight of Serenity on the ground left my heart colder than seeing the man I'd shot. Rushing over the packed dirt of the barn floor, I dropped beside her and pressed my hands to her face. Todd's voice behind me seemed distant, even though I knew he was right on my heels.

"Dammit, you weren't supposed to shoot him," he said, kneeling beside me. "Serenity can you hear me?" Todd asked, not looking at her at all, instead leveling his full attention on the group of Amish men who had moved in closer. The fact that the crowd hadn't run for their buggies during the chaos seemed to be really freaking the deputy sheriff out, if the way he was aiming his revolver in turns at the Amish was any indication.

Serenity's murmur made me look down. I put my hands under her arms and helped her into a sitting position. She shook her head once and said with a stronger voice than I was expecting, "Good shot, Daniel. Don't go letting Todd make you feel guilty. The prick deserved it."

I pulled her softly against my chest as the warmth of relief began to spread within me. Pressing my face into her hair, I breathed in the lovely vanilla scent, almost forgetting that we were in an abandoned barn surrounded by a group of unstable Amish men—and that I'd just shot a man.

The groan coming from Tony's body got Todd moving to his side. He said, "Damn, he's still alive."

"I was aiming for his legs," I said, still holding Serenity snugly against me, although now, she was attempting to free herself and see Tony for herself.

"Maybe you should get into law enforcement, Daniel. Good thinking," Todd said, before the static sound hit the air from his radio that he was beginning to make a call from.

"Wait! Stop, Todd." Serenity pushed away from me and stood up.

"What the hell are you talking about? We need to call this in pronto. This jerk needs an ambulance..." He lowered his voice, "and we could use some backup here."

"Apply first aid. That's an order, Todd. These people have a few answers to give me before we bring the outside world in." She limped over to Tony's groaning body and using her boot, pushed him enough to reach down and free the gun from his pants.

To my amazement, she pointed the gun at the Amish men, singling out Aaron as she approached them. It was then that I caught my father's eyes, and what I saw there puzzled me. He looked at me with concern, reminding me of the time when I was twelve and I'd fallen from the hay wagon after one of the older boys had thrown a bale forcefully at me. I was knocked unconscious for a moment or two, and when I opened my eyes, father was there, staring at me with the same expression he held now. The look surprised me way more than the fact that my father was here in the first place.

"Is Tony Manning your friend, bishop?" Serenity asked bluntly with the revolver poised at Aaron's face.

The whole scene was unreal. I had difficulty absorbing it all. Glancing at Todd, I saw that he was doing what Serenity had instructed, creating a tourniquet from the sleeve of Tony's shirt. The injured man knew that Todd was attempting to help him and he was more than willing to be respectful now that his life was in jeopardy.

Aaron's voice brought me back to him and Serenity and their showdown in the center of the barn. The area was dimly lit by the moonlight shining through the gaps in the boards, but her blond hair and his white beard stood out clearly in the darkness.

As Aaron glanced at Tony, he said, "Yes, he is a friend—one of the few English men that I would give the name to."

"Well, I can tell you that if your friend doesn't get medical attention soon, he's going to bleed out. But we're not taking him anywhere until you explain a few things to me."

"What do you want to know, Sheriff?" Aaron asked quietly enough that I had to strain to hear him.

"First of all, why is that man there on the ground your friend anyway? He represents everything that's horrible about the outside world."

Aaron raised his chin for several seconds as if considering when Tony's cracked voice, spoke up, "Go ahead an' tell her, Aaron. It can't do any harm now. I believe the bitch would enjoy watching me bleed to death."

I was as interested as Serenity was to finally learn the truth about the disturbing event in my childhood and I rose silently to stand beside her. She looked up at me for an instant, her mouth set in a grim line. But, her eyes softened, and that was enough to calm my nerves. I turned to Aaron who regarded me briefly before he faced Serenity.

"A long time ago, a few of us passed judgment on Tony and exacted our own sense of punishment. Later, we learned that we were wrong about him, and we grieved the act of violence we did upon him."

"Act of violence?" Tony laughed for a couple of breaths before the pain must have been too much and he stopped. "Damn near killed me, you did."

"Yes. That is the truth of it, although at the time, we felt guided by the Lord in our deeds." Aaron ignored Tony's snort, and said, "After discovering the truth, we went to Tony and asked his forgiveness."

Aaron took a breath, gathering himself, but before he spoke again, Father stepped up beside him and said, "We were not expecting an English man, known for his vile language and behavior to know a thing about forgiveness. We certainly weren't expecting anything but contempt from him."

James Hooley joined the other two men, his body taller and rounder than his friends, but his voice gentler. He said, "For several years, that's exactly what we received from him— hatred. Until the day his family's farm was being publicly auctioned by the bank in foreclosure."

When James took a breath, Aaron took over, saying, "You see, the lot of us who did the violence upon Tony, pooled our resources and bought the farm from the bank that day. We then handed the deed over to Tony. It was our way of making amends for our actions.

"Tony was more than surprised. He was genuinely touched that we'd do such a thing for him and his parents. His kin had worked the earth on that very farm for nearly two hundred years. Nearly losing the property, only to have it handed back to him, softened his heart toward us. He was finally able to forgive us. On that day, we swore a blood oath that we'd be friends; always loyal to one another—and forever silent about the incident, until now."

An eerie quiet spread throughout the barn. It was difficult to feel the dozen or so other inhabitants within its walls. I couldn't help speaking up, and asked, "Blood oath? What do you mean?

Father looked at me and the others let him provide the answer. "The night that we fell upon Anthony, we spilled blood. It is not something we Amish do, but there have been times over the years, in differing communities in other places, that our people have done just that. In the name of protecting our church, our people—our ways, we've done what we've had to do. Our oath to each other and to Anthony, a young English man, was an oath taken from spilled blood, and therefore we call it a blood oath."

I swallowed, picturing the dried brown stuff on Father's shirt. Yeah, I guess it was an appropriate phrase.

Serenity's voice sounded out of place when she said, "What the hell does any of this have to do with Naomi Beiler and her death?"

Before Aaron could speak, Todd said, "Really, Serenity, we need to get Tony to the hospital. I'm feeling pretty damned uncomfortable with this whole business. Can't you interrogate these men in town?"

"No, I can't. Keep applying pressure to the wound," she said coldly.

"Wounds," Todd mumbled, under his breath.

"Whatever," Serenity said. Her lack of compassion bothered me. Even though I didn't really care whether Tony Manning lived or died, it made me uncomfortable for some reason to think that the woman I was falling for felt the same way.

Serenity stared at Aaron, flicking her gun to make her point.

"You are like no other woman I've met, Ms. Adams. I am so relieved that our women aren't born with such violent tendencies.

I held my breath, worried what Serenity would do with the comment. To my amazement, she stood still, breathing a little harder maybe, but for the most part not showing that his words affected her.

"You see, Tony was attempting to assist us with our own handling of the situation. At our request, he contacted you, trying to dissuade your investigation."

"Threatened is more like it," Serenity grunted.

"Well, unfortunately, Tony is still the same vile creature he's always been. Entering a blood oath with us didn't change his inner character. But that is beside the point."

"Thanks a lot, Aaron," Tony said weakly. I couldn't help looking over at him and feeling a pang of sympathy.

Serenity however, wasn't moved, and said, "Who was it that came running up behind me before jerk-face over there knocked me out?"

Aaron became stubborn and looking at his face and the stoic expression on Father's and James' own faces, I figured that they'd let Tony Manning die to keep their secret. Especially, since it was to protect one of their own.

I sighed, and said, "It was Mervin Lapp who shot Naomi."

All faces moved to me at once. I could feel the collective holding of everyone's breaths. "From what I found out tonight talking to Todd's girlfriend, young Mervin was probably on that stand at the edge of the cornfield, too tired or lazy to be out walking the way he should have been while turkey hunting. He was probably startled when he shot off into the corn. Of course, he never would have expected an Amish girl to be there in the stalks. An ill fate of timing for Naomi, I'd say."

Serenity turned her head to me for a second before looking again at the Amish men, never lowering her gun in the process. "Why cover it up if it was just an accident? Did the kid actually have the forethought to take Naomi's pack and place it a half a mile away in a dried up creek bed?"

I didn't know the answer to that, but movement from the shadows caught my attention, and I stepped in between Serenity and the newcomer, aiming the borrowed shotgun from Todd at the man.

"There's no need to shoot me, Daniel. I am unarmed. I only want to tell the truth—to be rid of the unclean feeling that has been upon me for weeks."

I knew the voice and I lowered the gun. Damn, I was hoping that my old friend wasn't mixed up in an accidental death cover up.

Serenity didn't lower her gun, and I couldn't blame her for it. She said, "Who are you?"

"I'm Lester Lapp. We met at the school house." Lester turned to me and said, "I almost told you that night, my friend, but Esther wouldn't have it. She was so worried that the outsiders would put David into an English jail, where he'd be attacked by other men."

Hearing the name, my mind jumped and I interrupted, saying it again, *"David?"*

Lester took a deep breath, "Yes, David. It was my eldest, David, who shot Naomi in the field that night—not Mervin. Mervin was nearby though—on his way to the place he went to be alone, when he heard the shot ring out. He ran to the noise, wondering what had been bagged, and by whom. When he came to the corn, he saw Naomi lying on the ground. He was beside himself with anguish when he realized she was dying."

His words settled into the thick air of the barn for some seconds, before Serenity said, "So, it was David who accidentally shot Naomi?"

The question hung in the air, but as Lester began to speak a shadow separated from the other men and came to us. He was taller than his father by an inch, but when he stepped into the dull light, I saw Lester's face from eighteen years ago, minus the beard.

David's eyes squinted in contempt when he looked at Serenity and that's when his face changed, to resemble his mother's. The boy might have been blessed with his father's good looks, but he'd inherited his personality from Esther, God help him.

David's voice was solid, with no hint of fear or sadness, when he said, "I came here tonight to confess my sins before the church. I don't need to tell you a thing." He directed the last bit at Serenity.

"I could care less about your damn idea of forgiveness, but you will eventually tell me what happened that night. I can swear that to you," Serenity said with a deadly calm, causing a chill to sweep over me.

I turned to Lester with pleading eyes, and he answered. "You see, it was Esther who learned the truth first. Mervin had limped the distance back to our farm after he'd seen what David had done. The boys argued about what to do, and when Mervin tried to leave, to bring word to us, David used the stalk of his gun to hit Mervin's legs out from under him. They grappled, but the Lord was with Mervin and he some-how got the better of his older brother. Mervin managed to strike David with a rock, taking him to the ground. David laid there in the corn, not far from Naomi's body, while Mervin came home." Lester paused, catching his breath, before con-tinuing. I couldn't believe what I was hearing from my child-hood friend. It was as if the world had turned upside down.

"Esther went with the boy all the way back to the place where Naomi and David were, hoping that perhaps he was mistaken, that maybe Mervin had dreamed the whole thing.

"But, no—what Esther found after trudging back through the fields were Naomi's dead body and David's unconscious one. She told me that she was terrified for our son and that's why she took the pack and hid it. Esther hoped to erase Naomi's identity, believing that if any Englisher found the body months later, they'd not know who she was and therefore have no one to question. It was foolish, I know, but my wife was not thinking clearly."

When he stopped talking, a heavy silence fell in the barn. Naomi's shooter had been revealed and I'd finally learned what happened that night, long ago when I was a small child. I should be feeling happy, but I can't say that I was. Instead, a strong dose of melancholy washed over me thinking about Naomi and Rachel, and how knowing the truth couldn't bring either one of them back to the living.

When I looked at Serenity, she was staring at David, her face scrunched up in concentration. She stepped closer to the young man, and whispered, "Why'd you kill her, David? Why would you do such a thing?"

David's cruel laugh wiped the depression from my soul, replacing it with a fire that burned brightly for justice to be done on the young man, who clearly had no regret whatsoever for the girl he had killed.

"She deserved what she got, she did. The way she always ignored me, like I wasn't good enough for her, even though I tried real hard to receive her favor. No, she picked Eli, 'cause he was confident and full of himself—the young man with the most prospects. When it didn't work out between them, hope came alive within me, that she'd have me then. But no—she picked an Englisher instead."

"How did you find yourself at the edge of the field waiting for her? How could you possibly have known that she was running away and going in that direction?" I asked. My mind raced, still shocked that David had purposely killed Naomi, and trying to put the last puzzle piece into place.

David turned to me, as if noticing my presence for the first time. His eyes widened and a grin touched his mouth that told me clearly that the young man had serious mental issues.

"Why, Sandra told me. She told me everything." He looked between me and Serenity, before his eyes landed on his bishop. By the look on Aaron's face, I knew that this was the first time he was hearing this part of the story as well. It hit me with sudden force that the Amish in the barn, including my father, had believed that Mervin had accidently killed Naomi—something they were all willing to cover up for the salvation of one of their own. But now, surveying the looks of shock, disgust, and down-right anger, I breathed in relief that they weren't in on a murder cover up. The implications would have been far reaching into the entire community of course, but even more so, I didn't want to believe that any of these people would condone such abhorrent behavior.

David went on, everyone waiting anxiously to hear each and every word he said. "You see, I'd been flirting with Sandra, getting her to trust me. She'd tell me things about Naomi. When she learned that Naomi was running away, she came to me, hoping that I could stop Naomi, make her see reason. But what Sandra hadn't counted on was that I'd decided a while ago that Naomi didn't deserve to live. She was a sinner, rolling in the grass with Eli and then throwing herself at the English driver." David ignored my father's sharp intake of breath, and plowed on. "I took up my position on the stand, and waited for her."

David's eyes went somewhere else and his voice became distant, when he said, "I've killed many animals, but I always wondered whether a person would die the same way." His eyes cleared and met mine briefly, before settling on Serenity. "They do."

Serenity raised her gun, aiming at David. She said, "Make the call, Todd."

Before Todd even got the radio turned on, the Amish men had surrounded David, the smooth flow of their movements silently pushing us to the side. Lester backed up, away from the group, his head bowed. The pity I felt for the man, my friend, was almost too much to hold in, but I didn't go to him. Instead, I stayed with Serenity, glancing down into her wide eyes. I could see the indecision there, but it was her decision, not mine. She'd been right all along about Naomi. The poor girl had been murdered. And, the Amish had concealed the truth, although, even they didn't know the extent of it.

Serenity's head whipped back toward the Amish group that had tightened even more around David, and then landed on Lester when she said, "I need to talk to your other son. Where is he?"

I knew it was her way of distracting the Amish from their business, while not having to arrest them all either.

Heads within the crowd began moving around sluggishly, as Mervin's name was called out repeatedly. After a minute, Father came to stand beside me, quietly saying, "He was here to tell us what happened that dreadful night—but he is gone now."

"You've got to be kidding." Serenity's words echoed my thoughts exactly.

39

SERENITY

November 19th

The bright, early morning sun shone through the car windows making the world feel warm and fresh again. I glanced at Daniel and wondered what was going on in his head. We hadn't spoken but a few words since we'd left the old barn. He was staring out the window at the passing Amish homesteads and my eyes couldn't help being drawn to them also, with all their quaintness. But, now, I knew better. The Blood Rock Amish community was anything but picturesque under its pretty facade.

It still boggled my mind what had gone down the night before. When I had snuck up to the barn, I'd honestly believed that the most excitement I'd have was perhaps overhearing some information that would crack the Naomi Beiler case open. I certainly hadn't anticipated being attacked by Tony Manning and subsequently held hostage while the old Amish coots worked out their problems and attempted to justify their actions.

Deep down, the fact that Tony would probably survive grated my nerves. He'd forever be a thorn in my backside as long as I was sheriff in this town. The part of it all that I still couldn't understand was why so many people, including the uppity Amish, would call him friend. And the craziness of the whole incident was going to be brutal when Todd and I began filling out the paper work. Lucky for me, this was small town America, and I'd already learned that fudging the truth for the better good of the local people was well enough accepted. It still would be a pain in the butt though.

I glanced again at Daniel's still frame, only to look away quickly when the fluttering of butterflies spread in my belly. When I saw the man, it was as if I was a hormonal teenager all over again. I really hated the feeling. Falling for an unattainable object really sucked—and Daniel fell into that category. He was too good looking and cocky for his own good. And, even more importantly, he was a known womanizer. The last thing I needed was that kind of heartache.

"Hey, slow down. You're going to miss the turn," Daniel said loudly.

I pressed the brakes and turned into the Lapp's winding driveway, glad that the man sitting beside me had no clue about what I was thinking.

"You must be relieved to finally know the truth about what happened to Naomi," Daniel said frankly. After I parked and shut off the ignition, I sighed and faced him.

"Yeah, I guess so. Somehow, it doesn't feel like I expected it to though."

Daniel nodded. He smiled sadly and met my gaze. "I know exactly what you mean."

Since he was turned toward me and was seemingly in no hurry to exit the car, I relaxed for the first time in hours, and said, "It's just so sad everything that Naomi had to go through, and then when she was almost away, she's shot dead by a jealous Amish teen. Who could have blamed her for ignoring him, the kid's a mental case. Life really did her a bad turn."

"It would seem so. But, in a way, when she made up her mind about leaving, she experienced the freedom that so many young Amish people never do. Even if it was only for a few minutes, it would have been worth it," Daniel said quietly, staring at my hand that was resting on the seat between us. I thought he wanted to reach out and touch me, but he was holding back. I turned away, knowing that I didn't have the nerve to make the first move.

"It sounds as if you talk from experience."

"It was the most difficult decision I ever made. And sometimes I wonder what my life would have been like if I'd stayed Amish. But then, I wouldn't trade my freedom for anything now."

"Oh, I can tell you what your life would have been like—an obedient wife at your side, ten kids running around, a huge farm to tend...and the occasional creepy meeting in a dark barn."

I wasn't joking, but Daniel laughed. The sound was contagious, and even though I felt it was the most inappropriate time to be laughing, I couldn't help but smile genuinely at him.

"Really, you've seen the worst side of the Amish imaginable. The community is full of hard working, decent folks who wouldn't hesitate to help you in your time of need. Murder, manipulation and mayhem are not the usual way of things."

"Sorry, Daniel, but it's going to take me some time to change my perception of the culture," I said with a snort.

"What about your house. You've been awfully quiet about it burning down. Are you all right?" Daniel's voice was not only kind—it was way too concerned. I looked out the window at the pristine white shed we were parked beside and the colorful hens pecking the dirt in front of it. How different this little building was from the ominous barn from the previous night.

"I have insurance. And my laptop was at the office and my cell phone with all my contacts in the world was in my pocket. All my important documents are in the safe deposit box at the bank. All in all, it's mostly just a huge inconvenience."

Daniel's voice showed his disbelief. "Seriously, you're not freaking out inside that your house and all your belongings burned up?"

I hoped that the chuckle that escaped my lips didn't sound too evil, but Daniel's raised brow told me that it had. "In this town it will be near impossible to implicate Tony for the arson, but I'd bet all my teeth that he had a hand in it. The desire for revenge seems to be keeping all pity-party thoughts out of my head at the moment. Well, except for my pictures. It will take a while to get a new set of my favorite destinations together."

"Now I know what to get you for Christmas," Daniel said with the smug expression of a man who thought he was so smart.

"Ha, as if you'll be around come Christmas."

"I'm not going anywhere," Daniel said in a whisper. His body slid closer to me unexpectedly, and I couldn't help leaning into him. It'd been a rough night. Ever since he stepped out of the darkness, holding the shotgun with his bulging biceps, I'd wanted his arms around me—needed to feel his skin against mine.

His mouth touched mine carefully, his tongue slipping in between my lips gingerly. I was impatient though, opening my mouth wider and meeting his tongue with force. His deep growl told me he liked it and his arms dropped to my lower back pulling me tightly into his chest. At that instant, I didn't care about the prognosis for the relationship. All I knew was that the man fit perfectly against me. I would enjoy it while it lasted.

The rap on the window separated us in a heartbeat. I wiped the wetness from my mouth with the back of my hand, while Daniel cleared his throat, opening his door. The little Amish girl's eyes were wide, her cracked lips round.

Oh, good grief, I could only imagine the gossip that this little scene would create.

Once the door was open, I heard the *clip clops* coming up the drive. I swiveled in my seat to see Lester and Esther's faces in the small window of the buggy as their horse hurried toward us. My heart sped up, instinctively knowing something was very wrong. Daniel must have sensed it too. He made it out of the car as fast as I did.

The horse came to a stop beside us. The sudden movement caused the buggy to push into its black body, sending the horse forward another step. A spray of saliva from the animal reached me and while I was wiping the goo from my shirt, Daniel surged into an animated conversation in the Amish language with the couple.

Gazing up at the frantic woman's face, I felt little pity. I could have already hauled her ass in, but Bobby had stalled me, assuring me that she wouldn't be going anywhere and that she certainly wasn't a danger to society. She was just protecting her child, he said. *Yeah, right.* Covering up a murder and lying to police about it was way overboard from what most parents would do. Hell, just a few years ago, Laura had told the police that she'd been driving when in actuality it had been Will who'd bumped into the shiny BMW at the local grocery while parking. Since he was only days away from getting his full license, Laura was willing to take the fall, but this was way different than that. A girl had died, and the total disregard Esther showed for Naomi was completely unacceptable. I didn't plan to take it lightly on her—regardless of what Bobby believed was best for the already strained relations with the Amish community.

Goosebumps pricked my arms when Daniel turned around and I looked up into his face. He was afraid.

"Mervin is still missing. No one has seen or heard from him either," he rushed the words out.

"Yeah, I'm sure the kid was pretty messed up himself after he was pushed in front of the bishop last night by his father to finally tell the truth about what his brother did to Naomi," I said, shooting a look of disapproval the Lapp's way.

Daniel stepped forward and took my hands between his large, warm ones. I almost pulled away wondering what the hell had come over him, when a glint in his eye caught my attention.

"Remember, what Rachel Yoder did about her guilt, Serenity." His words were soft, almost as if they were dandelion seeds on the wind. But the words hit me with the force of a baseball bat.

Damn.

"If he were thinking about something like that, where would he go?" I directed the question to Esther, thawing a bit.

She began to cry shaking her head until Lester put his arm around her and said a few soothing words that I couldn't understand.

"They don't know. They've checked everywhere. The entire community is out searching," Daniel said with some resignation, a sound that I didn't want to hear.

Dammit—another young person was not going to die needlessly. Not if I had anything to do about it. The pounding of hooves on the road from both directions told me that what Daniel said was true. There was an unbelievable amount of activity on the pavement, and even now several buggies were making their way up the driveway with speed.

The bishop was in one of the buggies, along with a couple of men I didn't recognize by name, but whom I'd seen before. He parked and stepped from the buggy. Mo hopped out of a buggy pulled by a tall bay horse, and joined the others just as they stood before us. Seeing them now, in the cool autumn daylight, with the bright hues of orange and reds behind them, it was difficult to imagine what I'd gone through the night before, and how all of these men had scared the shit out of me. Now, with their concerned faces and bodies ready for action, I nearly forgot how intimidating they were only a few hours earlier. But I made sure not to completely forget. No, those memories were seared into my mind. Especially with the reminder of the dull ache on the side of my head and the pain in my calf that had me limping. I knew what these Amish men were capable of—just about anything, like everyone else.

The men began talking and Daniel was in the heat of the conversation. I only half paid attention to the waving hands

KAREN ANN HOPKINS

pointing in different directions, instead, letting the foreign voices fade away.

If I was Mervin, and I wanted to do myself in because I'd witnessed a close friend die by the hand of my older brother, where would I go to do it? It would have to be a place that I felt safe that I wouldn't be disturbed. Maybe a place of significant memory...

Suddenly, I knew and I grabbed Daniel's arm, pulling him to the car.

"I think I know where he is," I whispered, opening the passenger door for him.

When the Amish men pushed in, ready to enter my vehicle, I held out my hand. "Sorry, guys. You're not going with us."

They didn't argue, but as I dropped into the driver's side and started the engine, I caught their annoyed looks. Daniel took it in stride, and said, "Where are we heading?"

"To the cornfield."

40

DANIEL

November 19th

Serenity pulled into the field as far as she could go before her little Honda was rim deep in the mud and unable to go an inch further. We both jumped from the vehicle and ran along the mowed corn. Serenity knew where she was going, so I followed her, amazed with each step that I took that she was able glide over the corn stumps like a gazelle, while I had nearly fallen twice already.

The day had turned out to be one of the prettiest ones we'd had in weeks, with barely a cloud in the sky—only bright blue above us and a cool breeze in the air. Ironic that this was the type of day that young Mervin might choose to leave the world. Somehow, the kid had managed to keep it all together for weeks following the shooting, but now, when the news was out in the open for everyone in the community and outside of it to hear, he couldn't deal with it any longer.

Serenity slowed, and I nearly slammed into her back. Our breathing was labored and we both stood for a few seconds catching our breaths. I questioned her with my eyes, unable to break the silence surrounding us. She brought her finger to her lips, and then she pointed up into a tree.

I saw Mervin then. He was sitting in the barely noticeable tree stand, his black coated back to us. He wore a matching ski cap and his head was bent down. Was he already dead?

Meeting Serenity's gaze, I saw her practical nature shining through. Either he was dead or alive—running forward wouldn't help either situation. So we proceeded carefully though the tall, dry grass that was between the last crop row and the hedgerow where Mervin was.

When we reached the spot almost below the old wooden boards, Serenity nudged me and pointed up to Mervin, who still hadn't moved. I was full of doubt now, knowing that the kid would definitely have heard our approach.

"Mervin?" I called, shielding my eyes from the sunlight.

There was a few seconds of unbearable quiet, and my heart felt the strain, pounding hard in my chest.

Just when I was about to give up hope, Mervin's voice broke the silence, and I finally breathed.

"I don't want to go back. And you can't make me," he said at the same time he lifted the shot gun, maybe the same one that had killed Naomi, into the air.

I wasn't worried about my safety or even Serenity's. What was making my heart race uncontrollably was the knowing that if he turned the gun on himself, we couldn't reach him in time.

"No one is going to make you go back, Mervin. I can guarantee you that," Serenity spoke and then motioned for me to climb the ladder to the platform. If she could keep the boy occupied, I might just make it in time.

"I'm only fifteen. I have no choice in the matter," Mervin said, anger peppering his words. I took a rung and stalled while Serenity spoke again.

"I'm the sheriff. I can make things happen." She glanced at me with a strange calmness and continued, "Why do you want to leave? Don't you like being Amish?"

"Are you kidding me? After what I seen last night, I want no part of it. It would be better to put a bullet in me and die the same as Naomi rather than to live here."

I took another rung, holding my breath.

"Yeah, I hear you. Everything I've seen so far about your Amish culture really sucks. I'd say most of you kids want out," Serenity said casually, but I could hear the slight elevation of her voice. She was doing a good job though, I was almost there.

Mervin set the gun down on the board with a thud. He leaned out over the side and peering at Serenity he said, "It ain't all bad—a lot of the others don't seem to mind. Naomi was different though. We had that in common. That's probably why I loved her."

It was enough time. I hurried up the last rung and through the opening, grabbing the gun. Once I had it securely in my possession, I called down, "I've got it."

Serenity sighed loudly and sat down on the ground. After a minute of her remaining there in the grass as quiet as a doe, I suddenly realized that she expected me to finish the talk with Mervin, who didn't seem at all surprised at my appearance. The boy obviously didn't want to use the gun on himself, but who knows what he might have done if we hadn't shown up. The ghost of Naomi lying dead some feet away might have pushed him to it.

Mervin was looking at his hands in his lap, moving his fingers in and out from each other. I reached back into my own childhood and tried to remember how I'd felt. It wasn't too difficult. The feelings had never completely abandoned me, even after all these years.

"Do you come out here to be alone a lot, Mervin?" I asked.

"Yep, it's the one place where I don't feel like I'm Amish. I'm just me. I never even hunted much. I just like to sit up here and watch the animals come and go once they've forgotten me."

"Is that why you were out here the night that Naomi was shot?"

Mervin raised his face, which was still heavily freckled, his green eyes intelligent. "I was so tired that day. We'd been bringing in the corn with the horses and I was helping Dat in the evenings put up the new fence. He'd told me that I could head to the house early to get cleaned up for the ball game, but I didn't want to go. I'm smaller than the others my age, and they don't talk to me much anyway. I came here instead. I figured David was already playing ball with the rest of 'em, when I spotted him on the stand. Couldn't hardly believe my eyes, I was so confused, but he had the gun raised and pointed. I stopped and stood stock still waiting. If only I'd called up to him at that moment—Naomi would probably still be alive. But I was afraid of David—certainly didn't want to do a thing to rile him. If I'd disturbed his hunt, it would have done just that. When the shot blasted and after the smell of the gun powder was in the air, I finally moved and shouted to him."

Mervin paused, looking toward the place where Naomi had died with glazed eyes. The poor kid was seeing it again.

"What did you say to your brother?" I pressed, hoping he'd follow through and tell the whole story.

He didn't look at me when he said, "I asked him what he got. That's when he turned to me and I saw something horrible in his eyes. The look made me go cold all over. I'd seen it once before—after he'd killed a small stray dog that was hanging around the farm. It was just a starved, scrawny thing, and Dat believed that it had caught one of the hens. Dat himself had told us that if we saw the mutt we were supposed to do it in. But, David didn't do it with the gun, the way he should have. When the little thing came up to us, all shy and whimpering, he hit her with a board, over and over again.

Mervin shook his head, trying to wipe the image from his mind. Then he looked at me, his eyes glistening. "I told Ma and Dat about what David did to the little mutt, but they didn't say a thing to him. Instead, they told me to leave it be—that what needed being done had been done. I didn't agree with 'em...and I still don't. All the dog wanted was some food and to be taken care of—that's all."

I sighed, glancing down at Serenity. Seeing the tightness of her lips, I knew that Mervin's words had disturbed her greatly. I certainly loved dogs too, and like Mervin, would never have had the heart to follow Lester's orders. But I also knew how life in the country went—a stray killing the chickens or livestock wouldn't be tolerated. Of course, there were other ways to handle the situation—like taking the dog to the animal shelter, though it was a bigger deal for an Amish man to go that route than an English one. Lester would have needed to hire a driver to take him into town with the animal, which was more cost and trouble than any Amish man would place on the stray dog's life—just one more reason why I was better off not remaining in the Church.

As I gazed at Mervin, whose face was tight with thought, I felt even more pity for the boy. Serenity was wrong. She might be able to pull some strings and get Mervin removed from his family and placed in a foster home—but that wouldn't be much better for him. Not now. It would be more beneficial for him to make the move when he was old enough to do it on his own. He needed to wait a few more years—but could he survive it?

Mervin began speaking without my prompting. "David didn't answer me. He just stood up and stared at where he'd shot. I was already scared when I started running into the corn. I felt...like something really bad was happening. Somehow, I just knew."

"Was Naomi alive when you found her?"

He nodded. "She was blinking, and when I tried to talk to her, she didn't seem to see me. She coughed a little and that's when I saw the blood spreading on her belly. Her coat was open, and even against the navy of her dress I saw the wetness and knew what it was. When she stopped moving all together, it was about nightfall. The moon was huge that night and I could see her perfectly." He stopped and took another deep breath before he said, "I remember how pretty Naomi was while she laid there, the moon light shining on her face."

I hated to put the kid through it, but the fear of him clamming up, pushed the next question out of me. "What did David do when he saw Naomi dying on the ground?"

Mervin looked me square in the eyes, and I believed at that instant he'd tell the same thing to a judge in a courtroom. "He done laughed. And the sound chilled me to the bone. He started saying all kinds of awful things about her and how she'd deserved it. He told me that we'd tell Dat and Ma that it was just an accident—that he wouldn't even get in trouble for it." Mervin shook his head angrily. "I wouldn't lie to protect him—and I told him that. That's when he went crazy like, and took his gun and hit my legs with it. I was on the ground and hurting and all, but I was so mad, I forced my body up and crashed into him. He wasn't expecting it. Even though he's bigger than me, I managed to get him down. We fought and rolled for a while—don't right know how long, but at some point, when I thought David would kill me too, my hand touched the rock. I was almost afraid to use it, knowing it might do him in, then I'd be a murderer too, but I had no choice. I hit him in the head with it."

We sat quietly for a couple of minutes as the birds called to each other in the bright sunshine of midafternoon. The breeze was gentle and smelled of decaying leaves making me feel nostalgic for simpler days.

Mervin didn't need to finish the story. I already knew the rest. Lester was an honest man and what he'd already told matched with his son's account.

When Mervin's eyes met mine again, the tears began falling. He sniffed, trying desperately to hold it in. I wouldn't let him though. Pulling him against me, I hugged him tightly until the tears flowed freely, his soft sobs vibrating against my chest. I wasn't sure if any amount of counseling would help the kid get over this kind of trauma.

But that was for later. Right now, all he needed was a friend.

41

SERENITY

December 22nd

I pushed the papers out of the way, gazing out the window at the white, fluffy world. Large flakes were still falling heavily, proving that the weather forecasters had gotten it right for a change—we really were going to have a white Christmas.

The gruff throat clearing brought me back from the winter wonderland. Bobby stared at me in shear annoyance.

"Really, Serenity, you're as bad as a toddler, losing complete focus since the snow began falling."

"Don't you remember the excitement of rushing outside after school to make a snowman or toss a hard packed snowball at one of your buddies?" I asked, leaning back in the chair and noticing that Todd had been doing the same thing as I had been doing—only I'm sure he was dreaming about the ski slopes.

"Trust me, when you get to be my age, snow loses its appeal entirely. The cold is not good for arthritis my girl. Now, I might be distracted if there was a warm beach with palm trees beyond the glass."

The thought of Bobby in swimming trunks made me grin and I hid my mouth with my hand.

"Have you heard that's where Tony is right now—recovering at some damn retreat in sunny, Florida." Todd snorted.

"Just shows that there's very little justice to be had in Blood Rock, Indiana, or the world for that matter," I said sourly. I still hadn't been able to prove that the ex-sheriff had a hand in my house burning down. To rub salt in the wound further, the local judge had only slapped his good old buddy on the wrist for assaulting me—something about how the two of us had been squabbling for a while now and there was no need to drain the tax payers' dollars about it in today's economic conditions. It made me sick just thinking about it.

"If you spend as much time in this town as Tony has, you'll have the friends to get you out of a fix too," Bobby said matter-of-factly. I shook my head. The statement just didn't deserve a response in my book.

"Getting back to what I was trying to tell you, Serenity. My friend from Ohio listened to the interrogation room audio tape and was able to give me a pretty good gist about what Daniel Bachman said to Eli."

Bobby's words pulled me from any remnants of my daydreaming with startling force.

"What did he say?" I rushed out, hardly believing that the old coroner had come through with the information. The man really did have connections.

"Daniel wasn't being the traitor you thought. He was actually helping us out."

"How so?" I asked, wanting to go around my desk and shake the information out of him so that I could hear it quicker.

"He told Eli that the unborn child was his, but that that was not evidence that could be used against the boy."

"And how was that helpful?" I immediately felt a blanket of gloom go over me.

"Hold your horses, and let me tell you everything. You're so impatient all of the time. I'm surprised that you can sit still for even a minute."

I motioned him to get on with it, and he said, "He also advised the young man to tell you whatever he knew about the incident—that it would serve him no good at all lying or keeping secrets for the benefit of the community. Daniel basically told Eli to not be the fall guy."

I thought back to that day and how betrayed I'd felt. I hadn't been able to bring myself to talk to Daniel about it in the weeks following the incident. I was still that worked up about the subject and I figured any discussion would turn ugly.

"I could hardly believe that Daniel would do such a thing when he was so hot for you, Serenity. It made no sense to me," Todd interjected into the conversation, but I ignored him.

Lifting my eyes to Bobby, I said, "Thanks for finding that out for me. It's a very good thing to know."

Bobby winked at me and then continued to shuffle through the small stack of papers in his lap. The knock at the door brought all our heads in its direction.

"What kind of fool would be out in this kind of weather?" Todd said stiffly.

It was true. We were operating on a skeleton crew because of the snowstorm. And the few people in the building wouldn't have knocked.

"Come in," I said loudly, anticipating some person as flaky as the white stuff falling outside.

"Hope I'm not interrupting an important pow-wow," Daniel said.

My stupid heart did the jumpy thing at the sight of him. His hair was dark with wetness from the snow, but his heavy Carhartt jacket made him look all comfy and cozy.

"Guess I'll get myself out of here before I'm asked," Todd said, winking at me. My eyes probably bulged at him the way he laughed and left in a hurry.

To my chagrin, Bobby was up and making his exit before I had time to stop him too.

"If I don't see you again before the holidays, Daniel, have a Merry Christmas," Bobby said cheerfully, reaching out to grasp the other man's hand. *What the hell?* When had they become friends?

When we were alone, Daniel went back out into the hallway for a second before returning with a large, wrapped object.

"What's that for?" I asked him, kind of kicking myself for my rudeness when Daniel's look immediately made tingly warmth spread in my belly.

Daniel sighed with controlled patience before leaning the gift up against my desk and seating himself in the chair that Todd had vacated. He stretched his legs out in front of himself, crossing them at his ankles. He then folded his hands on his lap and looked at me with just the touch of a grin on his handsome face.

"I don't know what your problem is—but you definitely have one," he said, surprising me.

"What are you talking about? I'm perfectly fine, thank you very much."

"No, you're not. Any woman that would kiss me with such passion one minute, only to completely ignore my calls and text messages the next, definitely has a problem." Seeing that I was about to let him have it, he swatted the air between us with his hand to silence me and continued, "That's why I'm here today. I put the jeep in four wheel drive and drove through a near blizzard to get this thing figured out. And, I'm not leaving here until I know the answer."

I looked at the determined set to his jaw and his sparking eyes. He meant it. Thinking back over the past month, I couldn't really say when I began shying away from Daniel's attention. We'd spent several days working together with the Amish people, getting their statements and clarifying some of the details. I agreed with Daniel that counseling for Esther was the most reasonable outcome for her, especially with the seven kids that still depended on her. What was I going to do—put the Amish woman in a jail cell with women who were jacked up on heroin and had real violent tendencies? I didn't like her, but I didn't hate her either.

Things had gone smoother than I'd imagined with David. He'd confessed completely, and after a couple of weeks of evaluations by the professionals, he'd been deemed unable to stand trial due to his mental health. He'd be spending the rest of his life in an institution, and unable to hurt anyone again. I had mixed feelings on that one. Part of me really would have liked to see him hang for killing Naomi, but after everything I'd witnessed first-hand in the Amish community, it wasn't surprising that occasionally one of them would go off the deep end. After some of my own research, I discovered that violent crimes rarely happened among the Amish—at least that were reported, anyway.

Daniel was thrilled with my handling of his former people and we'd gotten along fabulously during the days following the barn incident. But, when the dust began to settle, and Daniel was pestering me about going out to dinner or seeing a movie, I began to worry. I just couldn't believe that this gorgeous guy wanted me. And, I was fairly certain that when he realized what a difficult girlfriend I was, he'd dump me quicker than I could draw my gun. I just wasn't girlfriend material, even though I felt the pull to make an exception for this particular man.

"How's Mervin doing?" I asked him, hoping to deflect any more personal talk.

"Don't go trying to change the subject. This is important," Daniel's voice boomed and I glanced at the door wondering if anyone would come to rescue me. As sadistic as my fellow co-workers were, I wouldn't bet any money on it.

"It's important to me. So why don't you just go along with the conversation like a normal person," I said sweetly.

Daniel snorted a laugh. "Sure—okay. If that's what you want to talk about...for now. I'll humor you." He breathed deep and said, "Mervin is all right. Lester has allowed me to spend some time with the boy, and we went hiking last weekend. Yesterday, I took him to the Diner for lunch. I think he'll always be touched with a deep sadness, but he's learning to cope. He seems all right with staying with his family and the Amish, for the time being anyway. When he's of age, I'll help him get out if that's what he wants."

I nodded, happy to hear that Daniel had taken the poor kid under his wing. Mervin was too young to leave his Amish roots without some difficult obstacles, but maybe just having a non-Amish friend would help him.

"So, how are your family—and Bishop Esch? How's he doing?" There were quite a few things to get caught up on. I figured that I might be able to stall him to the point of such boredom that he'd forget his original intention for the visit.

He shook his head, and answered me with a rushed voice. "My father and mother are both fine. I've seen them a couple of times over the past month, and although I'll never be considered a normal member of the family, it's nice to at least have a relationship with them again. The rest of the family is about the same—friendly enough, but not doing back flips to have me around.

"As far as Aaron goes, he's the same as always—meddling into everyone's business and keeping the law and order of the community. And, before you ask, business has been slow, because of the weather and I have my winter survival kit packed and in the jeep."

My confused look made him laugh and suddenly he rose, moving around the desk in a blur. I didn't have time to escape, but even if I had, I probably would have stayed rooted in my seat anyway.

"Stop it, Serenity. Stop it right now." He breathed near my face kneeling before me. "Stop what?" I whispered, knowing full well what he was talking about.

"Avoiding me like I have the plague. Either you have feelings for me and would like to get to know me better—or you don't. Just give me a damn answer. You at least owe me that much."

His dark eyes held me captive and I couldn't look away. Why was I being so stupid? I began to lower my face to his, but he stopped me by putting two of his fingers to my lips and softly pushing me away.

"As much as I want to kiss you, I'm not doing it until you give me an answer. Hell, I'm willing to give this thing a go, even though you're the most pig-headed woman I've ever known in my life. I can't seem to shake you from my thoughts, to the point that I'm having difficulties getting my work done properly. Just tell me what you want. I need to know if there's a chance for us."

Daniel had been so much a part of my own thoughts, that late at night, if I closed my eyes, I could almost feel his skin brushing mine, his tongue sliding over my lips. Physically, we both wanted each other—mentally, I was into him. The only thing holding me back was the fear of being hurt.

Would he be true to me?

"Daniel, I think we should take it real slow. You know, be friends for a while first," I said.

He laughed bitterly and stood up. Leaning against the window sill, he looked out, ignoring me for a few long seconds before he said, "Sure thing—if that's how you want to handle it."

"I think it's best for right now," I said, not being able to keep my eyes from straying to the large wrapped object leaning up against my desk. He must have seen the path of my gaze. He closed the distance to the present and picked it up, laying it on the desk before me.

"It would be rude of you not to accept the gift. I don't have any use for it." Daniel pushed it forward and took up his position at the window again.

I didn't want to owe him a present in return. But he was right. Refusing to take the gift would be rude. Decided, I grasped the object and began unceremoniously tearing the paper.

I wasn't surprised. The shape of the object had tipped me off, but the picture itself touched me. When I freed it completely of the wrapping, I held it up and gazed at the image of a cornfield flowing up to a flowered yard with a plain white house. There was a black buggy in the drive behind an equally black horse. The sky was blue and the foliage was thick and green from the summer heat.

I couldn't help sniffing in all the emotions that began to bubble within me. The frame was of an old wood that felt rough against my hands, reminding me of the night in the barn that seemed like a dreamed up event now. The house made me think of Daniel's sister, Rebecca, and her pretty little homestead on the outskirts of the Amish community.

The corn...the tall green plants all crowded together in the bright sunshine, of course, made me remember Naomi. Staring at the leaves, I imagined her running through the stalks on a hot summer evening to meet Eli for a little bit of love making. In a way, Naomi was blessed. She'd found love two times. Some of us went an entire lifetime without experiencing it once.

I quickly wiped away the tear that threatened to run down my face. "Thank you. It's lovely. Hopefully, within a few months you'll have a house built for me to put it up in."

I met Daniel's shocked eyes when he said, "You want me to do the job?"

"Of course, you're the only builder I know in town that has the guts to put up with me, and that I'd trust with the contract." I was relieved that I'd finally asked him about the work.

Daniel smiled, "You know, that means we'll be spending a lot of time with each other for an extended period of time."

"Yep, I know."

Daniel nodded, the smile on his face growing larger. The soft rap at the door made me sigh in agitation. "What now?" I spoke to Daniel. Then I said louder, "Come in."

I was not ready for the two men who came through the doorway. Even Daniel straightened up to attention.

The dark clad figures looked out of place in my office, yet they didn't act like they were uncomfortable. Instead they stood still and calm, staring at me.

I rose somewhat apprehensively.

"What brings you into town on such a day, Bishop?" I asked, letting my eyes wander to the strange man who was at his side. The man was tall and exuded a sense of confidence that equaled Bishop Esch's, but this man was closer to my age, his brown beard shorter and more tailored than the other Amish men I'd been around. The jacket he wore was some-how different also—a little longer. His hat was larger too. I realized that the fact that I even noticed these subtleties was odd, but then I guess, after seeing the men and woman in my county dressed exactly the same, any variation stuck out.

The other thing that immediately made an impression on me was that this man didn't avoid my gaze the way the other Amish men did. Just like the bishop, he stared straight at me, as if he were attempting to read my soul. Although, it bugged me with Bishop Esch, it felt much more inappropriate with the younger man staring at me so intently. And the fact that he was good looking didn't help the feeling of awkwardness either.

"This is Rowan Schwartz. He resides in an Amish com-munity about a hundred miles north of here in the Poplar Springs settlement."

A feeling of dread began to surge through me, and not wanting to waste any more time finding out what was going on, I said, "Okay. So why are the two of you here in my office today?"

Rowan's eyes flicked over to Daniel and narrowed. I swiveled my head to see Daniel's response, which was tight lips and a steady look back at the newcomer.

The bishop, ever on top of things, spoke up, "This is Daniel Bachman. He's Mo Bachman's son. He left our way of life when he was quite young."

"Nineteen, actually," Daniel said.

Rowan ignored him completely, instead turning back to me.

"Aaron has informed me that you have experience investigating situations within Amish communities," Rowan said softly. His voice held more of a strained accent than I'd heard from my Amish people. With sudden clarity I recognized that I now considered the strange Plain people of the Blood Rock community to be *mine*. I guess it was definitely easier to deal with the craziness you had grown accustomed to, rather than totally new and unknown insanity.

I lifted my chin, and met his hard gaze. "I guess you could say that."

"Well, our community has need of the help of someone who understands the rules and laws of the outside world, but also respects and is willing to work with our culture's differences." He took a breath, and went on to say, "We will pay your travel expenses, and you'll find accommodations with one of our families if you choose to come."

My mind was whirling. Was this conversation really happening? I glanced at Daniel, but his eyes were guarded, not giving me any indication of what I should do. The idea of going to some far off Amish community and living in one of their homes in order to investigate, *something*, was insane.

Yet, it was also very intriguing.

"What kind of trouble are you having up there?" I asked apprehensively.

Rowan looked at the bishop, who nodded his head once solidly, before he turned back to me.

"There has been a rash of barn burnings. At first, we believed that they were random accidents, but when they continued, we realized that they were being purposely set."

"Have you talked to local law enforcement? The fire department has ways of establishing arson, you know," I said, totally perplexed as to why this man was in my office in a snowstorm.

"The authorities in our area have turned a blind eye on the problem. They will not help us," he said with some harshness.

I started to think about all the toes I'd be stepping on if I got involved. I knew firsthand how small rural areas did not welcome outsiders—English or Amish. The very thought that my mind had already begun to prepare for the turmoil ahead told me that I was truly losing it. But I had to admit that something about these secretive people fascinated me. And here I was, being given an invitation into their hidden world. I was up for two weeks of vacation after the holidays anyway. Maybe it would be a good idea to take a working vacation—but, not alone. Shit. I looked over at Daniel, and by something in the way his eyes softened, I knew that he'd go with me if I asked.

But I'd wait until the last minute to talk to him about it. I needed to make sure that I really wanted that kind of drama added into the mix before I impulsively invited him.

Shifting my focus back onto the Amish man, something about his posture and his eyes told me there was more that he wasn't telling me.

"Is there anything else I should know about this case, Rowan—I don't like surprises."

The man lifted his gaze to the ceiling and he shifted his weight before he settled and seemed resolved.

"There is one thing that would interest you. In the last barn that burned...there was a body found."

My heart slowed. Damn.

CPSIA information can be obtained at www.ICGtesting.com
Printed in the USA
LVOW10s2314190516

489138LV00033B/982/P

9 781506 157207